Freewheeling Summer

STEPHANIE J. SCOTT

Cover image and design: Melody Jeffries Design

Edits by MK Books Editing

ISBN ebook 978-1-954952-08-9

ISBN print 978-1-954952-09-6

Contents

Author's Note

❤

Each book in the Love on Summer Break series can be read on its own. Throughout the books, you'll find common characters and settings that take place during different summers.

For bonus content, book release news, and discounts, join my author newsletter at www.stephaniejscott.com

Chapter One

♥

The first day of the rest of my life, and I'd already screwed up everything.

Our class valedictorian, Holli Hayes, looked across the sea of faces from her position at the podium. "Our futures are wide open."

Yeah, that's the problem.

She went on about hope, change, achievement. Words meant to be inspiring, but they lulled me into a funk.

My life, my future felt as uncertain as ever.

Plus, listening to someone awarded a legit title for over-achieving only solidified my uncertainty. I'd never been an over-achiever. More like a medium-achiever.

Clapping filled the auditorium. I followed along—Holli was my friend, after all. I had nothing against her or her full-ride scholarship to University of Michigan. I just couldn't relate.

I fit nicely on the edges of a bell curve. I did average in my classes and liked every class about the same. I kicked butt as Townsperson #4 whose sole purpose was to stand to the side and let the star actors shine.

As the ceremony droned on, dread filled me at my future plans. Or lack of. I had my whole life in front of me, and I couldn't escape the thought I'd already been left behind.

An elbow pierced my side.

"Chelsea. That's *you*." Beside me, my friend, Elena DeWilde, nearly shoved me into the aisle. We happened to have last names sorting us next to each other for the commencement ceremony.

Looking to my left, sure enough, the seat was vacant. Tyler Decker had already crossed the stage, high school diploma in hand.

"Chelsea Devlin," West Ginsburg's principal announced with a tight smile. It was apparently her second time saying my name.

I scrambled forward, cringing at the synthetic swish my graduation robe made as I headed toward the stage. *Don't trip.*

I made it up the steps, crossed the stage, and shook hands with important people. Grabbing the diploma was the easy part. Every step after this? Uncharted territory.

Off stage, my classmates with last names earlier in the alphabet stood in clusters chatting and high-fiving.

"Took you a second, huh?" Tyler laughed and patted me on the back.

We weren't exactly friends, but we'd known each other since kindergarten and ended up in classes together ever since I could remember.

My responding laugh came a little too loud. "Just excited I guess, so I missed my name." Which made no sense, but Tyler wasn't exactly a sharpshooter.

"Where are you headed this fall?" he asked.

Fall. When everyone else would move into dorms or commute to classes. A select few would travel abroad or join a non-profit service organization. All great ideas for someone else.

"Oh, you know," I told Tyler. "Figuring things out. I'm taking a gap year."

His face scrunched. "Gap year?"

I inwardly sighed. Mom said the term was totally mainstream. She'd suggested it earlier this year after what we now referred to as *that time*.

That time when I maybe sort of told my parents I was applying for colleges but didn't. *That time* where I melted down in sobs because nothing felt right about moving out and rooming with a stranger. Or signing up for classes I had no interest in.

"Nice move, Devil." Elena, now beside me, clutched her own diploma to her chest.

The play off my last name Devlin had become a regular occurrence with Elena, but today it made me feel more like an outsider. Like I'd devilishly worked a scheme to stay exactly the same, only now everyone else would move on without me.

Elena steered me away from Tyler. "Chels, are you okay?"

I tugged at the collar of my robe. "I feel lame."

"The robe isn't doing you any favors." She slung an arm over my shoulders. "Kidding. You're not lame. Not everyone is Holli Hayes with straight As and colleges salivating over her. Don't sweat it. Besides, we've got the summer together."

True enough. Another summer at Midwest Wild Adventure theme park where we'd grown closer as friends. After I'd stupidly spent half of last summer being mad at her.

Her boyfriend, Jonah, slipped into the increasingly crowded backstage area as more graduates exited the stage.

Elena threw her arms around his large, tall frame. "How'd you get back here? It's forbidden."

"I guess we'll live on the edge," he said before leaning in to kiss her.

I tamped down a wave of jealousy. They were so stinking cute together. I doubted anyone really cared if someone from our rival school East Ginsburg lingered backstage. But seeing Jonah here reminded me Elena had more going on this summer than hanging out with me.

Teachers funneled us out from backstage into the lobby, shushing us to keep our voices down along the way.

Soon, the lobby filled with parents and the rest of West Ginsburg's current crop of graduates. My parents, along with my aunt and uncle and three cousins, found me immediately and descended with hugs. My grandparents weren't far behind.

The whole dang Devlin family showed up. They were great at showing up and providing support. I smiled despite today's frustration. They loved and cared about me which felt great.

"Our very own graduate," Mom gushed. "How do you feel?"

I edged out of her embrace, her wispy sheer scarf sticking to my robe from static. "I'm fine."

Dad leaned in. "I hope you're celebrating today. This is a big deal. You have plenty of time to figure the rest out."

"You'll be enrolling to college before we know it," Grandpa added, which he surely thought was encouraging.

"Dad," Mom said to Grandpa. "Young people are pushed into a capitalist working culture as soon as the diapers come off. It's ridiculous. Chelsea needs time to discover herself and her passions."

"Back in my day, passion didn't put food on the table," Grandpa grumbled.

Mom looked at me with a reassuring smile. "Maybe you'll become an *artist*."

Never mind I was terrible at anything artistic. She should have known by now with all the crummy art projects I'd brought home over the years. Though I enjoyed gel pens and doodling, I wouldn't get into art school with my spiral notebook as my portfolio.

Elena and her family joined us then, sparing me from another session of Mom's outlook on discovering life, love, and—cringe—*passion*. I shuddered just thinking about it.

"Did you say Chelsea is doing art?" Elena's mom asked. "I thought she hadn't enrolled anywhere."

"Chelsea *is* planning to take a couple classes," Elena pointed out.

Her mom, lean and toned from regular yoga, smiled brightly. "Oh, great. Which ones?"

"Um, pottery?"

It wasn't a question. I really had signed up for pottery like Mom suggested. Only it wasn't for-credit coursework, but one of those life education courses retirees signed up for. I knew that last part because my own grandma had taken the same class. She'd been the one to recommend it.

"Pottery sounds cool," Jonah said from beside Elena.

I nodded. I had zero opinions on pottery. Vases and earthenware bowls existed, but I didn't really care how they came to be.

"I've got an internship at my office if you're interested," Elena's stepdad chimed in. "It doesn't pay anything, but I promise it will be more than making copies."

Dad raised a gentle hand in the air. "It's a kind offer, but Chelsea needs a year to breathe. To find herself."

Never mind I had no idea what I'd be *doing* this year in order to find myself. I found it hard enough to put into words what I was feeling about my future, so to have it explained out loud by my parents made it even more awkward.

Sometimes I wondered if it would be easier if they'd insisted I go to college. Like if they'd given me an ultimatum. *Go to college or else!* But imagining my parents delivering on any *or else* was pure fantasy. With my parents, groundings were empty threats. They were extremely supportive but not the hovering type. They loved to tell me to explore and decide my own fate.

As corny as it sounded, I liked living with my parents. Sure, they were dorks, but I had my own social life. I had a lot of time to myself since their friends and social commitments often kept them busier than me.

My cousins, all boys and old enough to know better, laughed loudly and shoved each other. Capital-L Looks came our way from families better trained to behave in public.

More friends and families stopped by to offer congratulations, to remind us of upcoming open houses, to pass along their well wishes. I lost myself to distractions and tried my best to enjoy the moment and celebrate, like Dad said.

The thing was, I'd grown to like high school. I'd found a comfortable rhythm with friends and afterschool clubs. I'd even dealt with past hurts and jealousies, a sure sign of maturity.

But right when I'd felt like I could make sense of my life, everything shifted again. Everything I knew was about to end. I had to change now and fast.

I wanted Time to freeze, to let me catch up. For things to stop moving so quickly.

Elena's family and ours headed our separate ways. We had dinner plans at a restaurant with my grandparents who had already left to, as Grandpa was fond of saying, beat the crowds.

Elena snagged my slippery robe sleeve. "Hang in there. Remember. We have the whole summer."

I hugged her back. That was the part hitting so bittersweet.

We had all summer but all we had was this summer. Then everything would change all over again.

Four nights later, I discovered an envelope taped to my bedroom door.

An invitation, the looping script read.

Ooh! What was this?

Excitedly, I tore into the envelope. Inside, a note on plain cardstock.

Dinner: Casa Devlin, tonight

(It's lasagna.)

Love, Mom

Lasagna was great and all, but what was with the formal invitation?

I tossed the card and envelope onto my desk. Both spiraled to the carpet. Piles of worn clothes took up residence on the desk.

I'd been non-stop social the past few weeks. With school ending *(forever!)*, we'd planned my open house party, then I had graduation itself and a big school-sponsored grad night party. I'd barely been home the past week, especially with my summer job at Midwest Wild Adventure theme park starting again.

Mom probably wanted to check in whether we as a family were grounded, as she liked to say. Not grounded like punishment but grounded as in toes in the earth and feeling our roots or whatever. She was really into roots and the ground in a metaphorical way.

After dumping the clothes from my desk into a laundry bin, I made my way downstairs. Delicious Italian spices greeted me. As did our dog, eager for a good nuzzle to his muzzle. I bent to give Chucky B, a beagle mix, a rough rub along his chin and ears.

"There she is." Dad had on his *License to Grill* apron despite manning the oven inside. He hummed theme song music I didn't recognize and handed me a bowl. "Salad is in the big bowl. Fill her up over there."

Mom glided into the kitchen humming what Dad hummed and took plates from the cupboard. Instead of setting the plates on the table we always used positioned right off the kitchen, she carried them past me into the dining room.

I followed her with my still-empty salad bowl. "Is Aunt Kate coming over with the boys?" I was so out of the loop I must have forgotten we had a family thing tonight.

"No, it's just us." She had already poured water into glasses at three place settings. "It's a shame we don't use this dining table more often. It's a lovely piece."

Sure, whatever. I returned to the kitchen, dished salad into my bowl and two others, and took them back to the dining room table. Charles the dog, aka Chucky B, followed at my heels, apparently thrilled by the prospect of dinner scraps in a new venue.

Before long, Dad brought in the lasagna and side of whole grain rolls. Mom sat across from me and drained half her water. Dad dug into his salad and gestured for me to start eating.

I grabbed a roll, applied light butter, and ate most of it before I noticed something distinctly un-parental about my parents.

They weren't talking.

My parents tended to have a constant commentary going about any and all things, both interesting and dull. They weren't the type to eat in silence. In fact, I got a little grossed out sometimes when they talked with food in their mouths, though I was guilty of the same, so what could I say?

Obviously, I could say more than they were saying right now. Mom and Dad exchanged glances and gestured at each other with their eyes. Like a whole conversation happening with their silent faces.

"What? Why are you two so quiet?"

"We're not quiet," Mom said at the same time Dad answered, "Can't we enjoy a meal without talking every second?"

I leaned back, unconvinced. "Go ahead. Spill."

Now their glances became excited. Mom waved a shooing hand at Dad. He nodded at her. "You go."

"No, you tell her."

Oh my goodness. "Tell me what?"

They each reached a hand to each other. My parents were typically pretty affectionate. A thing I rolled with so long as they weren't being *nauseatingly* affectionate. Especially in public.

Giving me her full attention, Mom spoke. "We're moving."

I waited for the rest. "Moving what?"

"We, us," Dad said. "We're moving. To Traverse City."

I blinked. "I don't understand."

"Your father applied for the job he's been wanting. It's the transfer he's been waiting for. Isn't it great?"

Transfer…job transfer…Traverse City. My vision narrowed to the plate in front of me. "Why Traverse City?" That was like, way upstate.

"It's where the job is, honey," Mom said.

A dull roar sounded in my ears. "But we live here."

Their glances reverted to nervous blinks. "Yes, well, that's the rub now, isn't it?" Dad laughed a soft, uncomfortable rumble. "We'll need to put the house up for sale."

Little splotches dotted my vision. Sweat prickled at my neck. This was not happening. No...it *couldn't*.

"We'd like to downsize anyhow," Mom went on despite my heartbeat thundering around us. Couldn't they hear it? "Don't look so worried, Chels. We're moving as a family."

I fumbled for anything halfway normal to say in this very abnormal conversation. Our family didn't move. We'd never moved. I'd lived in this house since I came into existence.

Besides, I didn't want to move. If I moved at all, in my own time when I was ready, I wanted it to be temporary, like to a dorm. Then I'd have my bedroom to come back to. My little room had always been my safe place. Our family room, our backyard where Chucky B barked competitively at the neighbors' dogs.

"You're done with high school now," Dad was saying, as if everything else in my life wasn't already shouting this my general direction. "I waited to apply until you finished. We didn't dream of taking you out of school."

They wouldn't have to take me out of anything now. My seasonal water park job wasn't exactly a career. I had absolutely nothing lined up adding up to a conflict with moving.

Yet, everything inside me signaled alarm. My head buzzed. "What about Aunt Kate and Uncle James? Won't you miss them?"

Mom nodded. "Of course. But your cousins are nearly out of the house themselves. We'll get together for holidays. Even for a weekend."

From what I remembered, it took three or four hours to drive to Traverse City. Not exactly a quick there-and-back day trip.

My breathing came quick and my thoughts blurred. Everything felt fast all over again. Too fast, and too many things to consider for my brain to keep up.

"I don't understand—" No that wasn't it. "I mean, I understand the job thing, but why now?"

"I know it's a lot, Chels," Mom said in a calming tone. "We knew you might not take it well."

The lasagna. My favorite meal. To smooth things over for me. A nerve deep inside me pinched. I was nearly a verified adult and my parents needed to soothe me.

My emotions warred. I hated this new development and felt guilty for hating it at the same time.

Dad pushed food around his plate. "These openings only come up every so often. It could be years until the next one."

"An opportunity came up last summer," Mom said. "But your father refused to disrupt your senior year. The company even offered him an apartment to live in during the week, but he turned it down."

I hadn't known any of this. "Why didn't you tell me?"

"I didn't want to be a part-time dad." He rubbed at his light beard scruff. "I know it's not a fair thing to say. Plenty of people have challenging commutes and jobs. I didn't want to make life complicated for you. We didn't want you to worry."

Worry wasn't quite the right word, but I sensed what he meant. They had protected me. Coddled me. Made my life easy.

Which, I couldn't say I wasn't grateful for. It would have been weird to have Dad working so far from home all week. And how annoying would to drive back and forth every weekend? Not to mention hugely disruptive if they'd wanted all of us to move before senior year and I'd had to transfer schools.

They'd put me first and hadn't told me so I wouldn't worry or obsess.

Dad watched me with obvious concern.

Concern over *me*.

"This is the job you've always wanted, isn't it," I said more as a statement than a question.

As busy as I'd been the last couple of years with school, I couldn't brush aside how Dad had seemed a bit restless. He'd complained about work more often. I hadn't put much thought into it.

He breathed as if he'd been holding it in. "It is. When the company downsized a few years back, I hung onto what I had. Each year, what I do gets further from my skills. This is what I've wanted to do but couldn't do here in Ginsburg. Better hours, more pay. Your mom can go part-time, or not work at all if she wants."

She waved him off. "I'm too young to retire." She worked as legal assistant in an attorney's office, and honestly, looked kind of geeked about the possibility of retiring.

"Your mom and I, we'd talked about heading up north one day, and this placement felt like a sign. There's all those artists' galleries and access to coastal towns—it's really beautiful up there."

Beautiful for vacation, but to live there? The job would be great for Dad, but what about me? "What would I even do there?" I blurted.

Mom moved her hand to mine. "Whatever you'd like. It's up to you."

I pushed back from the table. I wanted to dive into the safety of my bedroom. Curl up and stay there until the world stopped changing. Only my stomach growled and food existed here in front of me. I contemplated taking my plate and stomping off, but my body rooted itself in place.

I had no idea what to do. Before today, I'd had no idea, but at least I was dealing with familiar surroundings. Now we were talking about uprooting to a tourist town far from everything I knew.

"You're at a crossroads in your life," Dad said. "The doors are literally wide open."

I stared at the lasagna, usually so comforting. "How long?"

They looked at each other again with their silent communication. Mom drew the short straw and spoke. "A real estate agent is coming by in the morning. We'd like to list as early as next week."

A rock formed in my gut.

"They'll put me up in company housing for the transition," Dad said. "I start in three weeks."

Three weeks and he'd be off to the next new opportunity. Three weeks and we could be packing too.

"We'll have time to look for the right place for the three of us," Mom continued. "We don't have to rush."

The three of us. As we'd been for my whole life.

Looking at their eager, excited faces, I wanted to share their joy, but I only felt dread. They'd outgrown their life, our life, and were ready to shed our current existence for the next thing.

The fact they were moving on when I couldn't was, well, really hard to digest. I was supposed to be the person moving out and moving on, only I couldn't. I was stunted, stalled, static.

The one constant in all this was me. I wasn't ready to move on at all.

Chapter Two

❤

Now that my parents were moving up north, I needed a plan and fast.

No matter how hard I tried to envision it, I couldn't imagine myself moving with them to Traverse City. What would I do there? Pick cherries? Learn to operate a sailboat? I'd probably end up selling T-shirts in a tourist gift shop. Away from all my friends and everything I knew.

It sounded miserable.

Sure, most of my friends would be away at college. Almost of all of them had enrolled somewhere down-state or nearby in Ohio or Indiana. Elena would attend a small liberal arts college not far from Ginsburg. The farther I moved, how would I ever see her or any of my friends again? I'd have to drive all the way back to Ginsburg during any of their school breaks to get together. Maybe stay with my aunt and uncle or something.

Which gave me an idea. I could move in with them. Sure, I'd have to bunk with one of my gross boy cousins, but at least one of them might take a bribe in exchange for their room. Or I could take up residence in their basement. Theirs wasn't insulated or carpeted like ours, but they had an old couch down there and a TV. I'd make do.

The realization hit me square the chest.

I wasn't going to move with my parents to Traverse City. This was the first thing I'd felt absolutely sure of in months.

I wasn't moving with them. Nope, not going.

But then what? Where would I go? What would I do?

I needed to figure it out. Only instead of a whole year serving as a gap between my life as a high schooler and my undefined adult future, I now had mere weeks. Maybe only the length of the summer, tops.

We had a lot to do to get sale-ready (cringe) as Mom repeated back from the real estate lady. She'd also called it a seller's market, and said our house was in a desirable neighborhood with good schools, which buyers looked for. A few home repairs and we'd be good to go.

They'd be good to go. Because I wasn't going anywhere.

Popcorn and pool water might be my favorite scent combination.

Maybe I was a weirdo for that, but I loved to catch salty popcorn air as it wafted through the wave pool on a hot afternoon. It was like an ocean deepfake. In Michigan, we had lakes, no oceans or bodies of salt water, so I took what I could get.

Opening day at Midwest Wild Adventure happened weeks ago, but this was my first weekend working now being fully out of school. Fully *graduated*. I still had to get used to my new reality.

Mom had helpfully suggested I hold off giving notice to quit Midwest Wild Adventure so I wouldn't make waves (then she'd laughed since I literally monitor a wave pool at the water park) until the house sold. Fine by me. I didn't plan on quitting Wild Adventure. I needed a job for my plan to work.

Of course, my parents didn't yet know I didn't intend to go with them. I only needed a little time to, you know, sort out my entire life and future.

No biggie.

"Chelsea." My shift leader, Marcus, a built guy who looked like he could bench press a freshman, found me poolside as I dragged abandoned foam noodles from the shallow end. "Being as I'm new, can you recommend someone to follow up on shift breaks? The last guy didn't leave a lot of notes."

"I can do it." I took the clipboard he offered with the schedule for the various zones at this end of the theme park. I scanned who worked where. I pointed to a shift block. "You've got Starla here and she needs to stay in this zone because she doesn't know Kids or Water Park. Have Jake cover Starla instead of Cody and move this break here." I penciled in my notes.

"Thanks, Chelsea. In my limited experience so far, you've shown real leadership ability."

I waved him off. "I picked up a lot working here last summer. You'll get the hang of it."

"Believe, me I know leadership when I see it."

"Thanks." It was actually nice to hear. I'd always been fairly organized and I was pretty darn good at telling people what to do. Whoever knew those things translated into leadership skills?

"You might have a real future here," he said.

People didn't tend to stick around at Wild Adventure. They cycled out after a couple of summers, except for a small group we called the Lifers. The Lifers all had a tie-in with Uncle Frankie who owned the park. His endless list of "cousins" and buddies stuck around year after year. As casual as my parents were about my life plans, I imagined they'd have an opinion if I joined the Lifers. This park wasn't exactly run in the most professional way. I'd had to beg my parents to let me work here to begin with.

But I couldn't dismiss the possibility of sticking around. I needed a job, and I'd need more than my paltry water park wages to prove to my family I had what it took to live on my own. That mattered whether I crashed in my aunt and uncle's basement or found a place to rent myself.

How much did apartments cost anyway? Did they come with electricity, or was it like our house where my parents paid separate utility bills?

No idea. I knew nothing.

I looked at Marcus, who grinned at me, showing off gleaming white teeth against his rich dark skin. I imagined doing his job the rest of the summer through early fall and—crud. Early fall. Midwest Wild Adventure *closed* for the year in the fall.

Even if I stayed on and even if I leveled up, I would need a new job once the park switched to only weekends in September and October. There would be nothing for the winter months.

Leveling up to Marcus wasn't going to cut it.

"You're the best, Chelsea," he said, breaking into my thoughts. "If you can relieve Patty and—well, I'll let you handle the rest." The walkie clipped to his belt squawked. Someone on the other end reported a biohazard incident at the Tilt-a-Spin.

Marcus looked puzzled.

"That's code for puke," I told him.

He winced. "I've got to go."

Yeah, I definitely did not want to level up to a Marcus. Which confirmed I needed a plan beyond Wild Adventure.

Clipboard in hand, I first checked in with Jake, who'd replaced KJ, a classmate of mine a year ahead of me who'd left for college last fall and decided not to return to the park. KJ was also the very basic and obnoxious reason Elena and I had been fighting last year. A hefty dose being my fault.

After ensuring Jake headed to his new assignment for coverage, I headed to the Lil' Adventurer Zone.

"Hey, Patty."

She monitored the play area, a part playground and part imagined petting zoo. Brightly painted low-to-the-ground animals allowed for smaller kids to climb on.

Patty spoke without taking her eyes from the play area. "We actually need you at the showplace. Can you skate?"

I rechecked the clipboard as if doing so would make sense of her request. "I'm sorry, what?"

"The stage crew needs an extra roller skater for the eleven o'clock."

I rubbed my forehead. Lil' Adventurer Zone featured the Wilderness Stage where several times a day a variety show entertained kids. Well, *entertained* might be generous.

There was live content. And it was free.

"I don't know, I—"

"Look." Patty moved closer into my personal space, now looking me in the eye. "I've got a slipped disc and a bum knee. You're young. Just go handle it."

Patty was a straight talker. She was older, wiser, and despite a bad back and knee, I didn't doubt for a second she could take me down.

"I'm on it." I passed through the water misters and rounded the corner until I found the stage. Permanent bleachers in two sections framed an open area of smooth concrete with the Midwest Wild Adventure logo painted on it. Beyond it, a small stage.

The usual fare at the Wilderness Stage included low-level circus stuff. Like, trained dogs, not lions. Sometimes dancing, sometimes a folk band doing kids' songs.

I wasn't exactly the performer type, having horribly bombed in my high school musical audition (thus the role of Townsperson #4, which kept me safely at the back of the stage production). You couldn't hate on a gal for trying, but you could hate on a gal for not taking a hint. I knew my place and that place was solidly back row. Back there, I wouldn't crush toes from bad dancing or split ear drums from off-tune singing. I was the warm body who smiled on cue.

A twenty-something looking woman approached. She wore stage makeup and her hair was dyed cotton candy pink on one side and a lavender purple on the other with each side pulled into pigtails. "You're our fill-in from the park?"

"I'm Chelsea. Yes, I work in the water park."

Annoyance instantly flashed on her face. "And you can skate?"

I scratched the back of my neck. "I used to roller skate around my cul-de-sac."

The woman looked past me, nodding. "Okay, I can work with that. We need someone who can spin in a circle and then skate backward through our formation."

"Um, formation?"

She seemed to steady herself with a breath. "We do roller dance. The others are in back getting ready. Well, the others who bothered to show up. We had someone bail on us."

I used to love roller skating, but I'd never heard of dancing in skates, and I sure wasn't a star-of-the-stage performer. "I'm more of a, *I'll put on skates and stand where you need me* type of fill-in."

Miss Pink and Purple pressed her fingers against her forehead, rubbing in small circles. "Okay. Change of plan. You can be our prop dummy. Watch for our cues and we'll hand off the props. Think you can handle that?"

I tried not to be completely offended at *handling being a dummy*.

Before any witty comebacks sprang to mind, she stomped over to a bin set on a bleacher seat. She pulled out a pair of skates decorated in rainbow colors. "Size nine?"

"Seven and a half."

She dug back in the box. "There's only nine and nine and half. We can stuff socks in the toes."

Well, this spelled certain disaster. I hadn't skated since middle school and those were with my own skates that fit.

Two women emerged from behind the stage and skated past me to circle the middle showcase area in lazy figure eights. They wore shiny outfits with sequin details, kind of like what figure skaters on ice wore, but two-pieces not one, and not as fancy. One had a skirt with wispy strips of fabric grazing her knees, and the other wore a hot pink tutu.

Pink and Purple clapped her hands twice. "We've got fifteen minutes until show time." She looked me over. "Red or yellow?"

"Red or yellow what?"

Clearly annoyed, she disappeared backstage.

The skaters swept past me, turning to skate backward, then forward again, and doing little spin tricks. They were definitely talented. And coordinated.

Neither of those descriptions fit me.

Then again, I used to be able to skate backward. I'd even practiced jumping off the curb onto the street in front of my house. It'd been several years, but I could probably pick up where I'd left off.

If anything, I was optimistic when I needed to be.

Pink and Purple returned with a neon yellow thing held in her outstretched hands. "Here."

"Uh..."

She shook it at me. "Take. It's your costume. And here's the wig."

The costume unfolded into a shapeless, definitely polyester, neon yellow jumpsuit. This *thing* looked nothing like the form-fitting outfits the other skaters wore. This suit was dumpier and felt weirdly heavy in my arms. Running my fingers across the fabric gave me the same sensation as nails against a chalkboard. At least it smelled clean.

A snarl of synthetic rainbow chunks must be what she viewed as the wig. One section clumped together as if fused by gum or glue. Another section had shorter chunks for several inches. Bangs? Unless this was the back of the wig.

"Ten minutes," Pink and Purple said.

Ten minutes, ten minutes. I grabbed the too-big skates and rushed to the backstage area through the door marked Employees Only. I switched out my Midwest Wild Adventure staff T-shirt and shorts for the yellow...thing.

The pants flared at the bottom and reached just above my ankles. A high-water banana look no one would be wearing this fall.

Big, fat yellow snaps enclosed the bodysuit up the middle, leading to a collar with rainbow zig-zag trim. I avoided looking in the mirror.

Next, I pulled on the skates. The socks stuffed inside made my toes hurt. I tried removing the socks, but my foot moved around too much. If I tried to cut the sock in half, maybe?

I searched for scissors in the few open lockers and around the vanity area by the light-up mirror. Shoot, nothing. I wouldn't root around in the skaters' personal belongings. It was stuffed skates or nothing.

Could I choose nothing?

I shoved on the wig and moved the sticky part to the back. On the way out, I caught myself in the mirror.

Mistake. Big mistake.

Back outside, I rolled slowly, fighting to keep my balance.

The other skaters gathered behind a false wall a few feet away. I peeked around them to see a Wild Adventure staff person funneling guests into seats. Someone from the dry rides, a Lifer. At least none of my friends would see me in this getup.

A guy skated toward us wearing a similar shiny outfit to the other skaters. His in bold blue wasn't quite as tight-fitting, but sequins glittered along the pant leg. He looked closer to my age than the women, and was tall, lean, and angular. He glided effortlessly to stop in front of us. Despite the ease in which he skated, he scowled.

Couldn't blame him—I didn't want to be here either.

"Who are you?" A note of confusion and surprise surfaced in his question. Caramel brown eyes softened from the hard stare he'd had a moment ago.

Oh. Oh wow. He was cute. Really cute.

And I was dressed as a polyester banana.

I willed myself to respond despite the hot, hot humiliation steaming beneath my collar. "Last minute fill-in. I work at the park."

His eyes did a quick once-over of the banana jumpsuit before he turned away. He said nothing, but even his silence couldn't squelch the obvious pity he felt for me wearing this thing.

"Any tips?" Instantly, I regretted asking.

Mainly because I'd lost balance and rolled forward, sending my wheel angling into a crack. I flailed my arms. Remembering the stoppers on the front of the skates, I dragged one toe down and my body pitched forward.

The guy spun and caught me before I collapsed into the other skaters. His steady grip on my arms only added to my embarrassment. He appeared to cringe at the texture of my sleeves. The corner of his mouth twitched up, like he wanted to laugh, but his scowl returned. He let go of me. "You alright?"

Nope. "Fine. I'm fine."

An honest-to-goodness tip into the arms of the best-looking guy I'd seen in ages would have been welcome had it happened over in the water park.

Given the wig, maybe he wouldn't recognize me if I met him again by the water slides. A girl could dream.

"What's going on back there?" the tutu-ed woman whisper-shouted our direction. "We're about to start."

A low grumble came from the guy. "Let's just get this over with."

Same here, buddy. "I'm ready. No sweat."

Lie. I was already sweating. And we were fully shaded back here.

Pink and Purple picked up a megaphone. "Roller Dreams is here to entertain you with wild tricks and thrilling moves!"

A blast of techno-dance music sounded and the hot pink tutu skater sprung forward into the performance area.

The next skater and the next went out, following music cues and Pink and Purple's introductions.

"Now for Sunshine. Come on, Sunshine!"

Drenched in yellow, that must be me. Sunshine.

As I emerged into the arena, the music switched from cool, crisp techno to squeaky tuba sounds over a jolly circus tune. A smattering of laughter carried over from the crowd.

"That's right, folks," Pink and Purple shouted through the megaphone. "Roller Dreams has our very own clown on wheels!"

Chapter Three

♥

A clown on wheels. I had not envisioned this for my day.

I found my footing with the skates. Pink and Purple dashed by and returned with a plastic bin filled with colorful objects.

"Sunshine—catch!"

On command, I held my hands out. The colorful item hit me in the chest with a weighty *thwack*. And then exploded. A water balloon.

The kids in the crowd went nuts.

A group of heckling tweens liked that too. A little too much given their eager grins recording with their phones.

More water balloons pelted me. The yellow suit proved surprisingly water repellent. Too bad since I was sweltering out here in the direct sun.

The roller dancers moved on to their next performance piece and criss-crossed the space in spins and turns.

As their prop dummy, as Pink and Purple so gently described my role, I caught and tossed back their various props. Their hoops flung over and across me.

Colorful scarves were tossed my direction, then caught among the skaters and used to pull each other along or whip forward with added momentum.

Then the water squirters. Those they aimed at me.

The guy and Pink Tutu did a move where they held hands at arm's length and spun in a circle. After letting go, the skaters parted, gliding backward to perform complicated footwork.

As the two other skaters spun each other, I steered clear. Only their move was different. Pink and Purple wound off into a jump, kind of like in figure skating. She landed gracefully, which looked awesome.

But after landing, she tumbled into the guy. "What are you doing?" she hissed at him.

He managed to stay upright. "You did the wrong move. Never mind—doesn't matter."

The guy did his own spin jump, then barreled ahead, straight at me.

I couldn't move quickly enough, so I braced myself. Sucked in my breath, core tight, threw my arms up in defense, and took the hit.

"Oof!"

The impact jolted me, but I remained upright. I moved with him, using his momentum to get me turned the other direction and skated away.

But not before my wheel snagged on a bunched-up scarf on the outer perimeter. I tripped and flung my arms out for balance. Pitching forward, I fought with everything I had not to go down.

Guffaws erupted from the movie producer tweens who aimed their camera phones at me.

I made a mental note to murder them once I caught my balance.

The guy grabbed my hand. "Got you." He arced in a half moon around me, as if we were spinning like the other skaters. Only he did all the work and I...well, I slipped on a water-soaked patch of concrete and stumbled around some more. The music switched to my tuba soundtrack. Giggles erupted from the kids on the bleachers.

The Hot Guy Who'd Now Caught Me Twice used his momentum to gently push me forward. The transition, let's just say, was rough. A slide whistle sound effect narrated my bumbling. Whoever ran the sound booth, I made a mental note to murder them too.

The other skaters wove around me, showing off their cool tricks.

The guy looped around to me again. "Can you skate backward?" he asked low enough the crowd wouldn't hear.

"Yeah." *Sure, sure, easy.* I steadied myself as I rolled backward, but my steady went sideways. Again, I scrambled to stay upright. Hot Guy skated behind me, apparently ready to catch me a third time.

The kids' laughter came louder now. Laughter from the really little kids, but I'd take it.

Right. *This is the point.*

Yukking it up was exactly the sort of thing kids laughed at. Wasn't that the point of clowns? I'd have to think it through later—the point of clowns.

Right now, I needed to be funny and not die.

I pinwheeled my arms, though I'd regained my balance. More giggles from the kids.

Hot Guy caught my gaze and winked. "Nice."

The song switched over and Pink and Purple slowed as she circled us. "Nice *improvising*." She glared at the guy. Looking to me, her expression softened. "You can sit this one out." She nodded toward the backstage area.

She didn't have to ask me twice.

The skaters performed more complicated choreography to a mix of pop music. Impressive. I'd always avoided the stage productions here because, honestly, they were terrible. These skaters weren't terrible.

Modest applause sounded after the song ended.

Pink and Purple picked up her megaphone and thanked the audience and announced a short intermission.

I hoped I could escape since my arms itched. This fabric and my skin were not friends.

Pink and Purple glided to a stop in front of me. "Sorry you got stuck as the clown, but it's easiest to work with last minute."

I resisted the urge to say "that's okay," because none of this was okay. I was pondering the purpose of clowns and had a list of people to murder.

We hydrated, wiped off our sweat, and returned to the performance for another fifteen minutes of hilarity.

After the show finally ended, I tugged off the wig, not even caring if the tween kids caught it on film.

Pink and Purple and Hot Guy argued on the sidelines.

"Good thing this is our last gig," the guy said and skated off.

Rough day for all of us, it seemed.

I made my way backstage. Some of my toes were numb while the others formed new and exciting blisters. My shins hurt, my back ached, and I felt wet in weird places.

Pink and Purple and the tutu woman stayed behind to change.

"Hey, I'm sorry you got stuck doing this," Pink and Purple said again. Her creamy white skin was flushed from the sun and performing as she toweled off. "I'm Lyah."

She pronounced it Lie-yuh. "Pretty name. I've done some strange things working here, but I can't say I've ever been a roller clown."

The tutu woman, now tutu-less, beamed a smile at me. "Now you can." Her bronze arms looked sculpted beneath a clean short-sleeved top. "I'm Nina. Nice to meet you."

"Would you like to—" Lyah started.

"Give her a minute," Nina warned. "She's still in the jumpsuit."

I looked between the women. "You think I want to steal this or something?" I yanked the top down, not caring if they saw me in my sweat-soaked sports bra. "I'm pretty sure this banana nightmare gave me a rash." Sure enough, little red dots flecked my arms up to my shoulders.

"We should burn that thing," Nina said.

I peeled the jumpsuit from the rest of my body and wiped myself down with wet paper towels.

Lyah handed me a real towel. "I have an extra."

I gladly took the small towel and patted down before slipping my work clothes back on.

"We're looking for someone to join us," Lyah said.

Nina huffed out her frustration. "I told you, *ease in.*"

I held my hands up. "We all know now I'm not cut out for roller dance. The clown thing I could fake for a little bit, but..." I couldn't believe we were having this conversation. Clowning wasn't simply a matter of bumbling around on skates. It took skill and a skill I was not interested in gaining. *Hey, Mom and Dad, I'm going to clown school!*

At least it would be school. They'd be proud, especially if clowning became my passion.

My mind flashed back to the hot outdoor stage I'd escaped only minutes ago. Nope. No passion there.

Lyah packed her skates and costume into a duffel bag. "You did great considering what we threw at you. Literally. Staying upright on skates isn't easy with performers throwing props at your body."

I was positive she just felt bad about the suit and wig. "Thanks."

"And when Rob ran into you, you took it like a linebacker." Nina laughed at her own comment, but Lyah's expression turned sour.

A nervous laugh fell out of my mouth. "I played backyard football with my cousins for years. My oldest cousin says it's to toughen me up because I don't have siblings."

I winced, remembering the bruises from all those tumbles into the grass. But my cousin was right. Playing not-quite-tackle-but-not-quite-not football with them *had* toughened me up. Besides, playing in the yard got me out of boring kitchen chores. I'd take knee scrapes and bruises over dish duty any day.

"We really appreciate you filling in last minute," Nina said. "Somebody ditched on us. This is our last roller dance gig and well, it was barely above a disaster, so thanks for sticking with us."

Lyah huffed out a loud breath. "Nina, you're taking too long. We don't want you for Roller Dreams, Chelsea. We want you for derby."

"Derby? Like, with horses?"

"Roller derby, not the thing in Kentucky. You can take a body blow on skates."

My speech, it was none.

"That's a compliment," Lyah clarified. "We'd love to have you check out our team."

She handed me a paper flyer that looked like it'd been folded in half seven different ways. A photo of a group of women posing in skates and matching tank tops was centered beneath large, jagged text:

The Ginsburg Tornadoes

A whirlwind experience of roller derby fun for the whole family

All Ages at Pines Point Roller Rink

I tried to hand the paper back, but Lyah motioned for me to keep it. "You should come see us. In fact, we're skating tonight."

I hadn't planned on attending a second roller-themed event today, but here I was, parking in front of a one-story building with an ancient sign reading *roller*

rink. The *k* at the end hung on half-heartedly with a bird's nest wedged on top of it.

Couldn't blame a girl for being curious.

I needed a real plan for my life by the end of summer, but as soon as I'd mentioned my day to Elena, she'd insisted we follow up on the roller skating invitation. As if coming here would get me any closer to a shiny new adult existence.

Thankfully, Elena offered herself as my second for this journey to the outer limits. The rink wasn't even in Ginsburg, but in the next town over in a mostly rural area best known for a corn festival. Every August, my family hauled ourselves to Cobb Farm— you know, like corn cobs— because my parents couldn't resist the siren call of any local festival within an hour's drive.

"Will you put that away?" I swatted at Elena's phone which played video footage of me as roller clown earlier today.

Yeah, the video had made the rounds with staff. Apparently, the star tween director was related to somebody working the dry rides on the other end of the park. So basically, everybody I worked with had seen it by now.

Elena held the phone out of my reach. "What, you're funny. And now some fierce ladies want you for their roller derby team. You can be their little devil skater."

As if I had any real menace to me. I hit the auto-locks right when Elena made a move to get out. Then I snatched her phone. "Ha. And I'm not joining. I'm only here to be nice."

Elena quickly retrieved her phone and tried the door handle repeatedly until I hit unlock again.

We both got out to heavy, sticky summer air. Elena took my hand and led me forward. "At least it will be air conditioned."

Inside, the rink looked like it had seen glossier days—in the nineteen eighties. This place looked like a time capsule.

Yesteryear arcade games lined a short walled-off area beyond the entrance. A knock-off PAC-MAN chomped dots across the wall above the games. At the opposite corner, faded pine tree imagery bordered the counter of a refreshment stand. Ahead of us, the skating rink.

"Well, I feel right at home." Elena grinned at me.

Her end of Wild Adventure in the Go Zone was the oldest section of the theme park. Their staff area looked a lot like the rink, in hues of orange, brown, and olive green.

"Ooh, T-shirts!" Elena strode ahead of me toward a folding table angled off the rink.

A banner hung from the table with *Ginsburg Tornadoes* hand-painted on a plain white bed sheet. A black sharpie scribble was probably meant to be a tornado. Bonus points for the glitter lightning bolts.

"Hi." A woman with short hair formed into spikes dyed red, white, and blue greeted us from behind the table. A kid in a Girl Scouts uniform sat beside her. "Is this your first time at derby?"

"Yes," Elena announced with near glee. "This is so cool." She picked up a shirt. "How much?"

"Fifteen."

Elena handed the woman cash.

I peered over her shoulder. "You haven't even watched a..." Match? Meet? What did they call these events, anyway?

"Support local," Elena said to me through her teeth. "The Mid-fits are going to be so jealous I'm here."

Her go-kart buddies at Wild Adventure probably *would* be into this. Being misfits and all.

Elena being Elena immediately slid the new T-shirt over her tank top and tugged it down. The graphics looked better on the shirt than on the sheet, but still looked pretty homemade.

I told her as much.

She scowled and steered me toward the seats. "First of all, you're being judgey and this is *your* thing. Second, the look is supposed to be DIY. Have you ever heard of 'zines? This is like, 'zine culture."

Okay, she had a point. I was being judgey. I wasn't sure why other than leftover embarrassment from roller-clowning earlier. I mean come on. *Roller clowning.*

"Fine," I conceded. "Sorry I'm being a butt."

She nodded at me approvingly. "You *are* being a butt. Way to properly identify your issues."

Oh, I had issues. I hadn't told Elena yet about my parents moving. I didn't like keeping secrets, but if I told her the news, then I'd have to tell her I wasn't moving with them, and *then* I'd face a long list of questions I didn't have answers to. Just for one more day I wanted to not think about any of it.

People filled in around us. Not exactly a crowd, but all of the tables in the area were occupied and the benches bordering the rink were taken. A waist-high wall lined the rink on our side with higher walls on the far end.

A banner across from us noted this event was affiliated with a flat-track roller derby association.

"You want food?" Elena asked.

I twisted to locate the refreshment stand, wondering how much worse or better fare we were in for compared to Wild Adventure. I considered myself an expert at junky food options. At the park, I knew what to eat and what to avoid. This place? Total wild card.

Elena's phone buzzed. "I've got to take this. Hold on."

"I'll get us food." I got up, signaling for her to keep her money. I headed for the eighties-tastic refreshment stand.

Apparently, I was really killing it today because I ran directly into someone for no reason at all.

And the guy was carrying a drink. Which spilled down his shirt.

"I'm so sorry!" I fumbled for what to do. *Pick up scattered ice cubes? Run away screaming?*

The guy tugged at his wet shirt. "Ah, no biggie. I hated this shirt anyway."

He looked familiar. Incredibly familiar. Oh no. I offered up a quick prayer he wouldn't recognize me—

"Hey, it's you." He pointed at me with a delighted grin on his face. "From today at Wild Adventure." He looked completely different without his scowl of frustration from hours earlier.

There was no sense denying it. We'd been up close and personal more than once today. A blush stormed in on my face. Thankfully, the low lights in the skating rink hid my blush better than earlier out in the blazing sun. "I hope my hair looks better now."

A laugh burst from him and it sounded downright musical. Each note chipped away at my husk of humiliation.

He was tall but not too tall with light brown hair, possibly lighter from the sun since he looked pretty tan. He had a boyishly cute look about him, making me think he was probably older than I thought but maybe still a teenager.

Shoot, I was nearly eighteen myself. The age range described *me*. I didn't feel any different than when I'd turned fifteen. I was almost two years to twenty!

"I really am sorry," I told him. "I can buy you a team shirt to replace yours." I turned, pointing toward the merch table.

His expression shifted. I wouldn't call it horrified, but absolutely a twinge of disgust. Then again, their merch was a touch on the janky side.

"Sorry, probably a dumb idea," I started at the same time he said, "No, it's just, I—"

I stopped and waited for him to finish, but he was waiting on me.

"I—"

"It's—"

We both stopped again and laughed. He made a hand motion for me to continue.

"I feel bad I made your shirt wet. I can't even blame it on bad skating."

His peach-toned cheeks deepened into his own blush. "It's okay. I can't believe the theme park had you show up to our gig fifteen minutes before show time. I would have played the clown had I known."

"Oh, really?" Not playing the clown would have been so much better. Though, I didn't know how to do the spins and choreography their skate dancing required, so what other choice had there been? Other than bailing entirely, and their dance team had already been bailed on by somebody. "You're Rob, right? I'm Chelsea."

"Yeah, hi. You skated great, by the way. I'm seriously impressed how fast you got the comedy piece of it. Besides the technical aspect of the routines, the clown is the hardest role to perform. You shouldn't have had to—" He stopped himself. "I owe you a thanks. We all do."

He was being overly complimentary, but I didn't detect sarcasm. Come to think of it, he'd altered the skating routine to make sure I wouldn't fall on my face. Or on my tailpipe—*yeowch*. Maybe he and Lyah had been arguing about his spur-of-the-moment changes. "I heard today was your last performance."

"Yeah. A lot has changed the past few weeks." His attention darted past me and then returned. He smiled again, softer now, but with something else going on. "Is it your first derby?"

"That obvious, huh?" I tugged at my necklace with its sparkly butterfly charm. Nervous habit.

He nodded, taking this in. "I love derby. Even if you're not into sports, there's a lot to love about derby. The community. The nicknames." He cleared his throat. "Anyway, I hope you enjoy it."

"Thanks." I thought back to how he'd caught me and how nice his arms felt around me.

He scanned the rink beyond me. "It was good to see you again, but I should get going."

"But the match thingy hasn't started yet."

He leaned toward me, close enough to be heard as he lowered his voice, but not in a creepy space-invading sort of way. "I'm not supposed to be here. I thought I could blend but…" He pulled at his shirt again. "Cover blown."

"I blew your cover?" I whisper-shouted. "Here I am, a total derby newb, and I blew your undercover roller scheme?"

He turned so his back faced the rink and stood almost side-by-side to me. "I came to pick something up from Nina, but I really shouldn't be here." He pressed a finger to his lips. "Shh. Don't tell."

Okay, this guy was definitely trying to make light of the whole drenching him in his own fountain drink. That he paid for. "At least let me replace your drink. You can take it on the road."

"Don't feel bad about dousing me. We'll refer to this as Operation Agent Orange Soda."

His face shifted through more expressions. I couldn't help being drawn to him as I tried to figure out what was happening. The guy looked truly conflicted.

"I should go," he said finally. He flashed an apologetic look and took off, leaving me next at the order window.

I returned to Elena with nacho chips and cheese, licorice straws, and fountain drinks in a cardboard carrying tray. I skipped telling her about dumping pop on the very guy who'd seen me at peak humiliation, but

I did mention I met someone cute in line who had to leave.

Elena dug into the chips. "Bummer. We need to find you a summer fling. The new guy at the Log Jam is cute."

"I refuse to be known as a serial Log Jam groupie."

Elena covered her mouth as she laughed. "No one would think that."

"Craig would hear about it. The Wild Adventure network is strong."

My ex from last summer had moved on from running the Log Jam ride—and had moved on from Wild Adventure itself—like so many others. Craig was a year ahead of me in school, so now going into his sophomore year of college. Our break-up had been the least drama I'd experienced last year. About a month into fall semester, after he'd left for a university in Ohio, he'd returned for a weekend visit. We just knew. Both of us. We were in different places with different goals.

Elena elbowed me. "Sorry about the summer fling thing. You don't need to date anybody to have a rad summer."

"Rad?"

"I'm going with the eighties theme."

Loud guitar rock pumped out of the overhead sound system. A stream of skaters entered and circled the rink. The energy shifted.

Women of varying ages and body types swept past. I felt the sound of their skates in my gut, a loud and low thrum as they circled with increasing speed.

Elena stared, a half-bitten chip hanging in the air on the way to her mouth.

A thrill ran through me. Each skater wore a black top with the Tornadoes logo and team name written in bright pink. Their accessories ranged in a colorful mishmash individual to the skater. Ripped black tights, animal print biker shorts, a pink tutu.

"That's Nina." I pointed her out to Elena. "The tutu must be her thing."

"Baller-Nina," Elena said.

"Huh?"

"The back of her shirt says Baller-Nina. It's like their skater names."

"Like a basket baller?" Weird. "Oh. The tutu. Like a ballerina. But baller-*Nina*." I laughed. "Cute."

Elena leaned across the table and squinted. "That one says Becky Bruiser. And...Mary Kiss Kill."

I watched the shirt backs myself. "Bonecrusher." Yikes. The woman was short and sturdy with tattoos decorating her arms and her legs.

A guy in a striped referee shirt and green athletic pants skated to the middle of the rink and blew a whistle. Overhead, a man's voice boomed from the sound system. "Welcome one and all. This is a good old fashioned roller derby bout we're having here tonight featuring the Ginsburg Tooor-nadoooooes!"

Shouts and cheers surrounded us from the fans and the merch table. Distant whoops sounded from the refreshment stand.

"The Tornadoes would like to let you know they are *actively* recruiting."

Elena elbowed me again.

I kicked her under the table. *"Stop it."*

The announcer went on. "This is not an official competition, but a chance to see the team in action before the new season begins. There's a storm a-formin' with a bout against Detroit in three weeks. And another with the Capitol Rollers. Add us to your calendar and don't miss the derby *actionnnn.*"

Elena handed me a leaflet. "Here. You'll need this."

"Doubt it." I took the brochure anyway. It detailed the derby schedule, practices and competition dates against other teams.

It was one thing to stand in skates as a roller dummy, and another to do whatever it was these skaters did.

"Who here is a first timer at derby?" the announcer asked. "Raise your hands."

Elena threw both hands up and wiggled her fingers. She grabbed my arm and yanked it up.

Several others around us raised their hands too.

A song about celebrating good times came on. "Let's get this derby starteeeed!"

The music switched to a rap song I'd heard earlier today at the water park. The skaters flooded the rink again, some bopping to the music. Others cracked knuckles and flexed their arms.

"Blue versus Red," the announcer called out. "Check out the armbands." The teams each wore a blue or red bandanna along her bicep.

"And find your jammer with the panties on the helmet."

Elena made a choking sound.

Someone behind us whistled loudly.

Elena's eyes narrowed as she looked across the rink. "It doesn't look like they're actual panties." She sounded disappointed. "It's like, a helmet cover with a star on it."

Weird sport.

And then they were off. I found my attention totally captured watching the skaters zip by. They aimed to pass each other, while others pushed and blocked.

"That's Blocker Barbaric Barb," the announcer stated. "Great job, Barb!"

Barb looked close to Patty's age from Wild Adventure. The woman was certainly in good shape and kicking serious butt. Her blond curls were big and bouncy, kind of like—

"Barbie," Elena said. "I get it. All her accessories are pink, too."

In front of us, Nina wiped out and went down. I gasped and rose to my feet to see over the barrier wall. Nina found her footing and scrambled to catch up to the other skaters.

The event ended after an hour. The skaters stayed in the rink and invited fans to learn more about derby. One of the skaters dragged a bucket of roller skates into the rink. Two girls younger than us dashed to the skates and slipped off their shoes.

Baller-Nina in her tutu skated our direction. "What'ja think?"

"It was amazing," Elena burst out. "Hi, I'm Elena."

Nina assessed her, then turned to me. "And?"

"This was fun. Thanks for inviting us."

She cocked her head toward the rink. "Try on some skates. We've got more sizes here."

Going for the sales pitch. "No thanks. Looks like you've already got some new recruits."

She followed my gaze to the young girls now chasing each other around the rink.

"Those are Barb's girls. They aren't old enough yet." She made a clicking sound through her teeth. "Come on."

Elena hauled me up. "I'll put on skates too. Let's go."

I wanted to remind her I'd already had my skating time today. A thought struck. "You said they weren't old enough to join. What age do you have to be?"

"Eighteen," Nina answered.

Yes. Home free. "Too bad," I added with what I hoped sounded like genuine remorse. "I'm only seventeen."

Elena snorted. "Yeah, for like, two more weeks."

Why had I brought her again?

Nina handed me skates from the bucket. "Sounds like enough time to train before Detroit."

Behind Nina, Lyah skated over, doing a slow spin before she stopped. I caught the back of her shirt—-*Pretty Little Lyahs*.

"Nice to see you, Chelsea." She looked between me and Elena. "You both interested in derby?"

"Just Chelsea," Elena responded for me.

I shot her my deadliest glare.

"I've got freshman orientation and a camping trip in the next month," she said without sounding defensive in the slightest. "My parents would kill me if I joined another thing only to immediately quit."

Same. Only I couldn't say that to her. I should have told Elena about my parents moving and my advanced timeline toward adulthood, but this was not the time or place.

Nina shrugged, looking at Lyah. "She doesn't have the build for it." She turned to me. "You on the other hand. You could be our own secret linebacker."

I'd been told before I had an athletic build, but the joke was on them. I was uncoordinated and not very flexible. I didn't add anything to team sports other than moral support from the bench. Backyard football didn't count—the rules always changed and all I did was run and shove...

Which was what they wanted me to do, only on skates.

"Ooh—I bet we could do a fun name with linebacker," Nina was saying. "Liner...eyeliner...Eyelinebacker. Eh?"

"We already call her Devil," Elena offered.

"*You* call me Devil. I'm not even evil."

Nina's eyes grew wide. "Devil. That's *amazing*. Devil on Wheels. Devil's Disguise. Cruella Dev-*il*. You were born for this team."

Too bad roller derby wouldn't fast track me toward post-high school purpose.

Elena put skates on and used my shoulders to steady herself. She gently pushed off and rolled a few inches. "Look—I'm skating!"

Good thing these weren't inline skates or she might have had worse trouble finding her balance. Four wheels were sturdier.

I found myself putting on the skates—at least they fit. They were nice ladies. I was showing a kindness, humoring them. Then I'd leave and do something else with the rest of my life that didn't involve getting all bruised up.

I allowed myself to get comfortable on the skates. This felt so much easier in my own clothes and out of the hot sun. Also, no sticky clown wig.

"I need you or I'll fall," Elena shouted from a few feet away. She barely moved, but somehow became off-balance.

I took two strides toward her and arced around to face her, skating backward. I grabbed both her hands. "Let's do a few laps around the rink and then we'll be done."

A few other skaters came up beside us. Becky Bruiser and a woman with the name Queen Bacon on her shirt.

"I joined two years ago," Becky Bruiser said, ironically, bruise-free from what I could tell. "I do customer service during the day. I need a place in my off-hours where I can legally punch people."

Ah, so *she* did the bruising.

Queen Bacon shoved her lightly. "Stop, you'll scare her off. We aren't allowed to punch anybody. There *are* rules."

The conversation turned to training schedules, where to find knee pads for cheap, and signing waivers. They were trying to be helpful. Trying to persuade me.

Ending by Nina, we rolled to a stop.

"Did they give you the hard sell?" Nina asked, looking at the others.

At least she didn't deny it. "Sorry to disappoint you, but I don't think this is for me."

Nina sighed. "Well, thanks for coming out."

I untied my skates and slid my shoes on.

Lyah skated over. "You're letting her go? We can't do Detroit without another skater."

"I *know*." Irritation was clear in Nina's tone. "We can't force her."

"We can train you," Lyah said to me. "Look, I love this derby team and we've been through a lot. *A lot*." She gave a pointed look at Nina with fully-loaded subtext.

Nina rolled closer to me. "Here's the thing. Derby changed my life. It made me stronger, not only with my body, but inside. I love this team just as much as Lyah and I love competing. We need another person or we can't compete. We're short and we really want to get this team going again so we don't fold."

Elena and I exchanged looks. This was where Elena had grown since I'd known her. She knew when to lay off and give someone the space they needed. Even if she'd had the most recent update on my life, she'd give me that space to decide on my own.

"I wish I could but..." It was too much to spill here. My thoughts, too complicated.

Lyah put a light hand at my shoulder. "It's okay. Please don't feel bad if you say no. We saw promise with you and hoped you'd be interested."

Elena and I placed our skates in the bin, said our goodbyes and thank yous, and left the rink.

Chapter Four

♥

I crossed the roller rink parking lot with Elena at my side and headed toward my car. Everything instantly felt wrong. My life, walking away, everything.

I turned to my best friend, who'd weathered so many things with me the past year. "My parents are moving to Traverse City." There, it was out.

Elena stopped and leaned a hand on a dusty Dodge truck. "You're kidding."

"I didn't feel like talking about it, so I didn't tell you. That's why I can't join derby."

"How soon?"

I gave her the details.

"Wow."

"And...I'm not moving with them. I...I can't. I know it's not where I'm supposed to be."

"Oh, okay. If you're staying here, why can't you do roller derby?"

"Because I have to find a real job. I need to pay for an apartment and electricity and probably Wifi—definitely Wifi. If I can't get myself together and I live in my aunt and uncle's basement, if they'll even have me, they'll want to see I have a plan. To take classes somewhere, and not pottery with the grannies. I don't even know where to start. The last thing I need is to add some distraction like competitive roller skating."

For once, Elena didn't have an instant comeback. She leaned against the stranger's truck, in thought. "You gave yourself a year to figure things out, right? You're not on the books anywhere, which leaves you the option to *be* anywhere. Chelsea, you can do anything. No limits."

"What if that's the problem?" My throat tightened as the words escaped. "I think I need limits. I don't know what to do with a blank page."

"I hear ya. Independent study was a bad idea for me. I had no focus. I actually got a B in studying independently. Can you believe?"

A woman and her two kids walked up to us. "This here's my truck."

Elena sprung forward. "Sorry. Just leaning for a second." She pulled me toward my car parked another row over. "Hear me out. I got my roommate assignment and we've been texting. She's cool. You could stay with us for a while this fall. Drop in on a few classes, try college out pro bono."

"Live with you in your *dorm*?"

"It's small, sure, but we're planning bunk beds and the couch I'm bringing is a futon. We'll make room."

"I can't just drop in on your classes. People pay thousands of dollars for each class."

"I was reading online you can auditor a class. Auditor? No...*audit*. Anyway, you sit in a class you don't pay for and check it out."

"That doesn't sound right."

"Would the internet lie to me?" She paused to consider her own question. "Okay, new idea. Find a roommate and stay in Ginsburg. Isn't Joanie Spense staying local? She was always nice. I can't see her wanting to live at home. Remember when she dated that YouTuber who was arrested at Wild Adventure's Freaky Fest?"

"I can't call up Joanie Spense and ask her to be my roommate. I barely know her."

"I don't know the person I'm planning to live with in a twelve-by-twelve cellblock, and as you pointed out, I'm paying thousands of dollars for the luxury."

"College is weird and that's exactly why I didn't apply."

"Point taken." She tapped her nails against the roof of my car. "Jonah's got some friends who rent a house. I'll ask them how they found it. Maybe they need a roommate. Would you mind living with dudes?"

"My parents would disapprove." I might disapprove. Who were these guys?

"What did they say when you told them you weren't moving with them?"

My face gave her the answer.

"Right, okay. That tracks. How about one of these derby ladies hooks you up with a room to rent? Perfect timing."

"I met them *tonight*. And I'm not even on their team."

She crossed her arms. "Well, it sounds like you've made up your mind to not try anything and just freak out."

I grunted my frustration. "I *am* freaking out. When I let my parents think I applied to colleges when I hadn't, they got mad, but really, they were *concerned*. You saw them this past year. They showed up to everything. They were extremely present in my life because they thought I needed it." And maybe I had. And it was nice, having them around. Not going to lie. But something shifted knowing Dad put his dream job on hold. "My parents told me Dad passed on a job offer so I wouldn't be disrupted senior year." I rubbed my forehead where a dull ache formed. "They deserve to do what they want without being worried over me."

Another truth I felt as sure of as the other thing. "I really don't want to move. I feel it down to my bones."

Elena looked past me to the roller rink. "You need a reason to stay. Some kind of commitment extending past the summer. Some kind of, oh, let's say a team thing, where they are definitely short one member and definitely see promise in your skating skills."

Roller derby. Maybe tonight was a sign I had a reason to stay after all. Right when I'd felt overwhelmed, this new opportunity came along.

What was I so afraid of? Falling and hurting myself?

Yes. Yes exactly. With scrapes and broken bones.

But it was more than that. I was afraid of pretty much everything my future held, including the blank canvas staring me down in a few more turns of the calendar pages.

If not this, then what?

Nina and Lyah wanted me here. They saw potential in my sturdy stance on skates. If they simply needed another number for their ranks, I could fit the role and hang at the back. Nobody said I needed to be a star skater.

They just needed *somebody*. I was great at the warm body thing.

And Elena was right. I needed a reason to stay. I needed a reason to plan around. Maybe that reason happened to involve roller skates.

As if by divine sign, the rink doors opened and the Tornadoes team members scattered to their respective cars. Lyah headed toward us.

"Hey," I called over. "You still have an opening on your team?"

A hesitant smile formed on her lips. "We do."

Excitement rose in my chest at the sheer absurdity of my decision. "I'll do it."

I had two days until my first derby practice. I needed to get comfortable on skates again.

The street in front of my house only got me so far. Besides, my parents would definitely wonder what I was up to, and I wasn't exactly ready for that conversation.

"There's a skate park off Mill Road," Elena said to me at work when I stopped by the Go Zone on my break. I'd brought her a snow cone from the food vendor on the way here. Our favorite reliable shaved ice treat with neon-colored syrup.

I shot her a skeptical look. "Isn't the skate park for skateboarders?"

"I've skated there," her co-worker Nando offered. He wasn't much younger than us, and despite finishing his last round of braces, he hadn't hit his growth spurt yet.

His charm typically made up for any lack in height. "I went with my older cousin so he could find a girlfriend. Only he got his butt kicked instead."

Elena jabbed him. "Not helping. You can skate around the Wild Adventure back lot. Most of the potholes got filled in last summer. But watch out for the south corner. It's the raccoon gang's HQ."

Yikes. "I'll try the skate park. Thanks for the suggestion." I had my skates in the trunk, hoping to find a place to practice on the way home.

We didn't have much time to hang out since the park grew crowded in the afternoon and Elena needed to cover for her coworkers' breaks.

"Report back," she called after me.

When my shift ended later in the afternoon, I took off from Wild Adventure and drove into the heart of Ginsburg. With school out for the summer, the skate park was fully loaded.

I'd found knee pads and wrist guards at a local second-hand sports equipment place at Lyah's suggestion. I put on the padding, then the skates, and made my way to the concrete wonderland of Ginsburg's skate park.

Holy intimidation. A skateboarder glided up the half pipe and did a flip trick with his board, then effortlessly sailed down the ramp.

Smooth concrete surfaces offered low ramps, short sets of steps with railings, and mini-jumps. Most of the skaters rode skateboards, but a few wore in-line skates. Nobody wore skates like mine with two wheels in front and two in back.

"Move." A squeaky voice sounded behind me.

A kid half my height stomped past, threw down his skateboard, and jumped on.

Rude, much?

Then again, I should probably *do* something instead of standing here by the entrance.

I followed behind two rollerblading women who zigged in and out around the area. Ah, there was a pattern. The in-line skaters kept to one side of the park while the skateboarders had the other.

I aimed for a ramp and built up speed. The derby track was flat, but I'd be skating fast and I'd been too cautious on my skates practicing at home. I needed to take some risks and work on my balance.

I made it up the small ramp and felt the speed against my skin. A paved trail extended from the park in a few spots where I'd seen other rollerbladers go. They skated out from the concrete portion of the park, circled the skate park itself along the trail, and fed back in at the other entry point.

I did a few laps until sweat soaked the underside of my sports bra. This was hot, but it was *fun*.

Back in the skate park area, a rollerblader jumped a three-step flight of stairs.

I could do that, right?

Time to be fearless.

I kept an even pace, looking out for other skaters. Then, I made my move.

And chickened out.

At the last possible second, I veered left into a swath of grass. The lost momentum pitched me forward onto my knee pads. My hands flew in front of me and I ended up on all fours.

Well, that was dumb. Derby didn't even have jumps. What was I doing?

"Need a hand?"

I turned toward the voice behind me. Blaring sun forced me to squint, leaving only the silhouette of a guy holding an outstretched hand.

"I'm good." I declined the assist and hoisted myself up, only to wobble against the grass.

"I've got you." The stranger moved toward my back—not touching me, but there in case I went down.

My face flamed. "Thanks. I was being overly ambitious I guess."

"Inspired by the Tornadoes?"

I found my footing and blinked at the guy. "Hey." I pointed. "It's you." Rob, the former Roller Dreams skater turned roller spy.

He grinned. "Third time's the charm?"

Oh, he definitely had charm. Despite this being the third time he'd found me in an uncompromising position, he barely seemed fazed.

He wore in-line skates with knee pads and cargo shorts. His shirt, weirdly enough, was the same shirt he'd had on the other night.

He noticed where I looked. "I swear I own more shirts than this. It's clean. I put it in the wash that night. You know, since you dumped my drink on it."

I made a show of smacking my hand against my forehead. "I'll never live it down, huh? What are you doing out here?" I cringed at my own words. "Besides skating."

He didn't let on how my comment was more than obvious. "It relaxes me to skate out here." He skated backward, moving away from the stairs toward the grass bordering the concrete. I followed, steadying myself so I didn't wipe out again. Though I wouldn't mind if Rob had to help me up.

Get a grip, Chelsea. It was like Elena was channeling her commentary through my own inner monologue. "So, are you practicing for *spy* missions?"

He shook his head, laughing. "I'm such a dork. I can't believe I told you I was gathering intel. Anyway, it's cool you're here skating." He looked past me. "Here by yourself?"

I ran a hand through my ponytail, wet at the ends from sweat. "Yeah. I sort of maybe joined the derby team and need to figure out what I'm doing."

His grin froze on his face. "You...joined the Tornadoes?"

My hand flew to cover my face as I connected what he was thinking. I barely knew how to skate and I'd joined a friggin' roller derby team. "It's probably a really dumb idea."

"No, it's...it's not." He shook his head, appearing to think through something. "Derby is very cool. And fun. You'll love it."

"I wasn't going to join—kind of a long story. I decided I needed to start taking action this summer to figure out my life." Why was I telling him this? "Anyway, I went for it. No offense to the team, but they seem pretty desperate. They couldn't compete if they were short a skater. That's kind of my deal. I fill in and serve the warm body role."

His jaw hung slightly and his skin darkened at the cheeks.

"Warm body as in like, they need another breathing human." I stuck an awkward hand in the air and wiggled my fingers. "Breathing and at least ninety percent human, right here."

Rob laughed, a gentle laugh that should have sounded cautious or weirded out by my unnecessary declaration of being human and of breath. "What's the questionable ten percent?"

"Well, nine percent is strawberry snow cones."

"And the last one percent?"

"Hmm, probably more snow cones. I trust the snow cones at Wild Adventure, so I eat a lot of them. Definitely steer clear of the circus cheese."

"Ah. I'll avoid any cheese of the circus variety next time I go."

I started to say maybe next time I'd watch the roller dance from the stands, but the team was no more. Perhaps a sensitive topic and probably why he'd had a weird reaction to me joining the Tornadoes. He and Lyah didn't seem to get along.

"Anyway," I said for what felt like too many times. "I'm here on my own. If you don't mind a skating buddy, we could do some laps. Maybe ride the rails." I nodded toward a skateboarder sliding down a stair railing who wiped out on the concrete.

He audibly winced. "Ouch. Looks like she's okay." He turned to me. "Yeah, sure. We can noodle around."

I *loved* his use of noodle.

And I liked the idea of a skating buddy. A cute one, at that.

We moved through the park, testing different obstacles. He'd loosened up and showed off some tricks, relaxing into his moves. I watched him first and tried the move myself. I jumped a single step and spun into backward skating, testing out my balance and just having fun.

"Argh!" A tween boy fell in front of us after bungling his jump landing.

Rob hit the brakes and circled around. "Hey, buddy. Here's a hand."

The kid grabbed Rob's hand and pulled himself to standing. "Thanks." He took off again.

I couldn't help notice the strength in Rob's arms. He was a lean guy, but also kind of cut. Not that I was imagining anything further. Nope. Not a single thought whether those washboard-worthy abs could adequately scrub laundry.

We found ourselves slowing to check out other skaters. Rob cheered them on and his enthusiasm became infectious. Rob must have had cheerleader genes in his DNA.

After an hour, I was truly beat with every last drop of hydration drained from my water bottle. "I should probably head out."

"Skate you to your car?" Rob glided beside me.

"Hey, look." I pointed to a car with a sticker reading Derby Live above an image of roller skates. "Someone else here must do derby." I scanned the parking lot, wondering if one of the Tornadoes had shown up.

"That's my car. I'm a...fan." Rob slowed to a stop. "How much do you know about derby?"

"Remember the other night at the rink?"

"I believe I do."

"And how it was my first derby? That's what I know."

He nodded, in thought. "You're comfortable on skates. Now you need to learn the rules. Did you get a lesson yet?"

"I'm supposed to watch training videos before practice." I'd queued one up online and became so overwhelmed, I'd switched over to my favorite YouTube streamer and got lost in an hour of spoof music videos. "It's a little overwhelming. If you have any tips, we could meet up again."

Rob looked past me, then above me, basically anywhere but at me.

My stomach dropped. He must have thought I was asking him out for real, not for skating purposes. Maybe he had a girlfriend. Maybe he wasn't into girls. Maybe I'd read this all wrong. "Just a friend thing," I added. "For like, skating purposes."

His focused snapped to me. "Sorry, I spaced out for a second. Let's meet up again. I can help you with derby terms and rules—but only if you want. I'm sure you're totally capable of learning derby without a dude like me explaining it to you."

"I might be capable, but I'm a little overwhelmed," I admitted. "I'd love your help."

Never mind I had no business going after a guy when my own life needed all my focus. This would be a friends thing. An educational opportunity. I'd learn derby, make a new buddy who happened to have a stupidly contagious grin and startlingly chiseled forearms. Perhaps another distraction, but at least a cute one.

Perhaps another reason to stay.

I was beginning to like this game.

Chapter Five

♥

I planned to meet with Rob again the very next day. The day following would be my first roller derby practice. And I knew zilch about roller derby.

I'd taken a second stab at the training video, which was far more interesting than any of the training videos I'd been required to watch for Wild Adventure. But I was a learn-by-doing gal. I needed to be on skates to really absorb the derby mindset.

So here I stood, again at the skate park, with my new friend and tutor.

"See? Different shirt. Just for you." Rob winked at me as he walked over with skates in hand and wearing a well-worn shirt reading East Ginsburg High School.

"You're a Beastie Eastie?"

He clapped a hand across his chest. "I'm offended." He grinned. "Haven't heard that one in a couple years."

It struck me, I had no idea how old Rob was. "How long you've been out?"

"I graduated last year. You?"

"This year. West Ginsburg."

"Ah. Natural rivals." His grin wavered. "I never got into the whole East versus West stuff. Then again, the entirety of my high school sports career was going to the homecoming football game and my buddy's swim meets."

"What about Roller Dreams?"

He took a measured breath. "I was talked into Roller Dreams. Did you see the pants? With the sequins?" He threw up his hands in a what-can-you-do gesture. "I would have quit, but I prefer to follow through on things. At least it's done with now."

"I wasn't into sports either," I admitted. "I went to all of West's football games, but I didn't play team sports. Only football outside with my cousins."

"That's actually helpful to know." He nodded to the pads I carried. "A big part of derby as a blocker you can relate to defense in football. The blockers' goal is to prevent the jammer from breaking through to win points. Every skater they pass, they score."

I slid on my knee pads, elbow pads, and wrist guards. "The jammer is the one who wears the star thingy on their helmet. They're the ones who have to break through the pack."

"You got it." With his skates on, he slowly moved backward along the path circling the concrete skating area as I skated facing him. "As a blocker, which you'll probably be, you'll need to avoid illegal moves."

He jutted an elbow toward me, though we had plenty of distance between us. "No elbow jabs. And no tripping other skaters."

It'd looked kind of rough out there during the skating demo I'd watched, but perhaps it had been all elbowless defense and unintentional tripping. I hadn't recognized the difference.

"There's also a thing called back blocking. No hitting opponents in their back or bum. Then there's no passing out of the boundary line. There will be lines in the rink as a border."

Rob pivoted to skate forward and we picked up speed until we completed the path and ended up in the skating area by the in-line skaters.

"How is the blocking like football?" I asked.

"Remember how the skaters form a huddle at the starting line? That's what the jammer, who starts at a line behind you, has to skate past. Like your football running back or quarterback moving past the opposing team's defense."

"You said you weren't a sports guy."

"I played enough *Madden* with friends. Not my favorite game, but you can't always play *Skyrim*."

"Fair enough."

"And I've watched a lot of derby. Here. Let me show you what I mean about the defense."

Rob moved to a grassy patch—the same patch I'd fallen into yesterday where he'd found me. He held his arms up at right angles in front of him. He relaxed his knees.

"Now come in closer." He looked at me with intensity. "If I'm your teammate, we need to block anyone from coming past us. You can stand next to me, side-by-side, and the blockers form a chain, or a wall."

I turned so we faced the same direction with our shoulders touching.

He straightened and returned to a ready position. "So, actually, this requires holding hands." He lifted his arm.

I went for his hand, but instead of taking mine, he slid his hand up my arm to lock on. Right, not like, *holding hands* holding hands, but like, a grip on the arm.

"Lots of ways to do this," he continued. "The jammer will come from behind. You can have another blocker in front for more support."

"Like a Red Rover situation."

"Oh?"

"On the playground, as a kid. We played Red Rover. You linked arms and stopped the runner from breaking through."

"Ah, right. Only you're on wheels and a chick with tattoos and a mohawk under her helmet is your jammer."

He shifted to face me again, our arms still touching. He stuck his other arm in the air as if joined with an invisible figure. "You can do a tripod with three blockers where we'd face each other, moving as a unit to block the jammer. Do you remember seeing anything similar from the bout?"

I had, but it had been difficult to make sense of what was happening.

Our faces were mere inches from each other, which I should have considered a possibility when I'd suggested he teach me. Then again, I'd pictured us zooming around on skates, not bracing our bodies together in a stronghold.

Seeming to realize our sudden closeness, he straightened and stepped back. "You'll go over strategy with the team, but I think it helps to get a feel for these moves. The big thing to practice is stopping. Control over your wheels is key. Control over your body on wheels."

"Right. My body. On wheels." Right now, my body was all het up and I doubted the heat came from the overcast skies.

Cool it down, Chelsea.

"We can practice a plow stop. Let me show you."

He was surely oblivious to the heat crawling up my back. I'd barely done anything to require a sweat other than lock arms with him.

Rob skated off and returned, turning his foot perpendicular to me in a fluid motion, coming to a stop.

"Oh, like with skis."

He shrugged. "I've never gone skiing."

"I've downhill skied exactly three times in my life. Never got off the beginner hills, but I learned the stop. They teach you a V like this." I positioned my feet with toes pointed in and heels out. "Then you learn to slide the other foot over so your feet are side by side. Not as cool looking without the skis."

"I get what you mean. The plows will feel different depending on the surface. It might not work as well here as in the rink."

We practiced stopping. It was awkward and not easy. "I don't think I'm doing this right."

Rob talked about balance and shifting weight. He demonstrated again, more slowly to break down each motion.

"You're good at teaching."

"Nah, you're a natural. You're picking this up fast."

"Hardly."

"Hey, don't underestimate yourself. The skill will come in time."

His comment was probably to save my ego. I hadn't gotten the hang of the stop yet. I tried a few more times, still jerky with the movement.

We agreed the concrete surface might be the problem. Or at least, I agreed with him, because I had no idea.

"You want to build up strength while off your skates too," Rob said. "You want to avoid rolling an ankle."

He sure was all business. Then again, business was what I was not paying him for.

Did tutors require tips? I never carried cash on me. A Venmo request might do the trick—

"Ready for a quiz?" he asked, breaking my thoughts.

Oh crap. "A quiz?"

"Just kidding." He clapped a hand on my shoulder. Instantly, he removed his hand, probably grossed out by the dampness of my T-shirt. "Sorry, didn't mean—anyway, you're doing great. You'll be awesome. A great asset to the team."

I certainly was further along than I'd been before today. I'd go into practice as a newb, but not a totally ignorant newb.

"Thanks. This has been...awesome." *You're awesome.*

I held that back.

He smiled. I pictured him teaching this to kids or to other skaters. I could see him on the sidelines of his friend's swim meet, cheering him on, and actually learning about swimming terminology to talk to his friend about it in detail. He seemed like a guy who paid attention to detail.

"Will you be at the derby games?" I asked. "I mean, bouts? You seem like a super fan."

"Oh, uh, yeah. Maybe. Probably. Sure." He ran a hand through his hair. "You'll catch on quick. You won't need me around."

He said it with an air of lightness, but I sensed his nerves were on edge. Was it possible he'd felt some heat like I had? Possibly I wasn't alone in the crush I found myself forming.

I glanced at Rob as he peeled off his own padding. I wouldn't mind that so much after all.

The next day, I returned to the rinky dink country roller rink for my first practice. This time, without my gal pal sidekick, who had *definitely* been gloating via text she'd known all along I'd end up joining the Tornadoes.

My parents, now totally consumed by packing belongings and planning home repairs, barely noticed when I came or went. Or to where. I didn't intend to keep my plans from them forever, but I'd barely gotten started with the team and needed time.

"Devil!" Nina opened her arms wide as I crossed into the rink. "I really expected you to ghost. Ha—ghost, devil. It all works."

I gave her a weary smile.

I needed to woman-up. I'd decided to do this and if I was doing it, I needed to be all in. I'd already switched my evening Wild Adventure shift to practice with the team. No way I'd not show up after all my schedule shifting. "Sorry I was such a pain about joining."

She made a face. "Don't be. I totally guilted you. I'm surprised it worked."

"You are?"

"I throw a lot of spaghetti at the wall, so to speak. Sometimes I'm shocked anything I say makes an impact." Her face clouded a little at her own words. "Anyway, I'm glad you're here. Did you bring pads?"

I held up my gym bag. "Yeah. I even found my old skates. My feet apparently haven't grown."

I followed her into the locker room.

Bonecrusher rocked a fist in the air as I entered. "New blood!"

Hopefully, she didn't mean that literally.

Lyah emerged from the bathroom stalls, drying her hands on a paper towel. The team captain, I'd discovered. She smiled when she noticed me. "Did you bring the forms?"

My parents were supposed to sign a waiver so I could practice with the team since I wasn't eighteen yet. A small hitch in my plan. I hated to do it, I really did, but my dad's signature was pretty easy to copy.

I handed the papers to Lyah, the guilt practically steaming off me. "I'll be eighteen in two weeks. Less than two, now."

"Well, happy early birthday," she said, seemingly none the wiser she held forged documents.

I'd tell my parents soon. I had to. Holding back the truth too long wouldn't help me gain their trust when I unloaded how I wouldn't be joining them in Traverse City.

I put on my skates and the padding, then tied up my hair. My stomach fluttered in a nervous dance. Being the youngest here and so new to derby meant I had my work cut out for me.

Out on the rink, Lyah started with a round of introductions. "We've got two newbies to the Tornadoes. Welcome Chelsea" —she pointed at me, pausing for claps and cheers— "and Taylor." More clapping. "Taylor we picked up a few weeks ago, but she had to miss our demo bout. Welcome to you both. We'll do team initiation later. For now? Get ready to work."

The team didn't look as flashy and put together as during their match. Some wore T-shirts and shorts, others tank tops and stretchy long pants. No fun make-up or accessories.

Nina blew a whistle. "Laps. Go, go, go!"

The group took off around the rink. I fell in line, grateful for my few days of practice on my own and with Rob.

The downside? My still-sore legs screamed at me.

Lyah ran us through drills. We skated hard from one end of the rink to the other, circling around staggered cones, then back again.

Drill after drill went on for an hour. We practiced a move where one skater grabbed our hands and flung us forward. I'd already forgotten the term for it. I had so much to learn.

For now, I needed to keep up.

I glanced to Taylor, the other newbie, as we caught our breath on the sideline.

"You okay?" I asked her.

She pressed a hand at her side. "Just a cramp." She winced.

Taylor looked to be in her early twenties. She was paled-skinned and full-figured and barely broke a sweat, despite the pain in her side. Me? I'd never sweat so much in my life. And I worked outside all summer.

Cool wet rags waited for us in one of many plastic tubs bordering the rink. After wiping down, we gathered in the center again.

"Y'all are looking good," Lyah told us. "Newbs—you kept up. I'm proud."

"Nice work." Barbaric Barb with the blond Barbie curls held up her hand for a high-five. She motioned for the rest of the team to join in. "Let's show these gals some love."

High-fives and fist bumps all around as the compliments showered down.

Nina wiped down her neck with a rag. "Truth? Not everyone makes it through the first practice."

Taylor and I caught each other's gazes, grinning.

Lyah skated to us carrying a small plastic bin. "Some skaters just want to pick a fun derby name and wear cute tights but can't handle the cardio. It's why we wait on the fun stuff until we're done running drills."

She tossed a plastic Hawaiian lei at each of us, the cheap plastic type found at party planning stores. "We'll get you shirts, but we need your derby name."

"Taylor Fist." Taylor held her fists up in a ready-to-brawl stance.

The group voiced their approval, then swung their attention to me.

"The Devil rises!" Nina bellowed.

Barb winced. Queen Bacon's forehead scrunched in confusion. Taylor looked at the others and shrugged.

Only Bonecrusher pumped a fist in the air. "That's like a top-tier pick from a derby name starter pack. How about Devil's Spawn?"

"It's a play on my last name, Devlin," I explained. "I'm not actually evil."

"But you *could be* in the rink." Nina ground her fist into her open palm. "We need a touch of evil on our side."

Queen Bacon looked thoughtful. "What's your middle name, Chelsea?"

"Mae, spelled M-A-E, after my grandmother. She's Southern."

A smile lit up her face. "How about Devil Mae Care? It's playful and softens the devil, if it's a concern for you. Since you seem a caring type."

A warm glow filled me. "That's really sweet. I like it."

Lyah patted my back. "Road test it another practice and then we'll order your team shirt. Okay, up next is our derby oath. This is important, and it's good to renew for all of us. Huddle up. Yes, we're sweaty, but it's time to get close."

The group closed into a tighter circle where we faced each other. Barb's arm hovered over my shoulders. "This okay? You steady?"

I nodded and she let her arm rest down as I stretched my own arm toward her.

Lyah looked at each of us. "The Ginsburg Tornadoes value the team over the individual. We all support one another here. On the rink and off, if you need us. Team over me. Repeat."

"Team over me," we all shouted.

"Winning matters, but not more than our health," Lyah went on. "Physical and mental. Find at least one member of this team you trust to talk to if you need help. Our oath to each other is we won't let anyone on this team get knocked down without helping you up. We lift each other up. Repeat."

"We lift each other up!"

An energy ran through the circle as we each committed to the team.

"Lastly," she said. "No fraternizing with the other team. *Don't cross the derby line.*"

Everyone repeated Lyah's last words, except me. I flashed a look to Taylor, but she seemed in on whatever the last part was about.

I cleared my throat. "Excuse me, what's this about another team?"

The group fell into steely silence.

Nina spoke first. "Sorry, Chelsea, I didn't know you didn't know. It's Ginsburg's other derby team."

Okay. "Ginsburg has a second derby team?"

Murmurs ran through the group.

"The Great Lakes Brawlers," Lyah said. "You really didn't know?"

I shrugged beneath Barb's weighty arm. "I'd never heard of roller derby until you invited me."

I internally cringed. They probably thought I was a moron. A kid who didn't belong on a derby team at all.

"It's okay," Lyah said. "We moved you into this fast. How about we'll fill you in at Shiney's—that's the diner down the road. We're headed there now. This team is here for you. The Brawlers? They are not your friend.

It's a betrayal of this team and our oath to befriend any of them."

It was a lot to take in. I felt dumb for blurting out I didn't know roller derby existed until a few days ago. I wanted to explain I'd studied the video and practiced with a friend, but it seemed a very high school thing to say and I was no longer a high schooler.

I'd joined a team of adults and needed to act like one. It would help me learn to be the adult I was supposed to be to get my life straight.

Barb squeezed my shoulder. "You'll be fine. You've got us."

Chapter Six

♥

We hit Shiney's diner, a run-of-the-mill greasy spoon I'd been to a couple times with my grandparents for their Sunday afternoon early dinner special. The main draw was the free soft serve ice cream with any purchase over five bucks.

The fact Ginsburg had two different roller derby teams made my head spin. I supposed it was easy enough to stay away from the other team. It wasn't like I could handle *two* roller derby teams.

Taylor found a seat next to me as the group pushed tables together.

"Do you know what happened?" I asked her. "With the teams?"

As the others got situated, Mary Kiss Kill, whose actual name was Mary, caught my question. "The Brawlers are—were—the core team. Then there was the split."

The server passed around plastic laminated menus as we sat.

Taylor leaned in beside me. "Do you think one of them stole the other's boyfriend?"

Mary's eyes flashed to what I imagined as her *kill* setting. "This isn't *high school*." She blinked. "Sorry, Chelsea. I forgot you literally just graduated high school."

She looked down along the table, then leaned toward us, lowering her voice. "Lyah lost her mom—cancer, that *son-of-a-mother-grunting disease.* Mayhem missed the wake to go to some party and showed up hungover the next day at the funeral. And not because she was grieving. Mayhem—that's Mayhem Meg, the Brawlers' captain—is Lyah's best friend. *Was.*"

I drew in a breath. "Yikes."

"You better believe yikes. Then it was like every tiff they'd ever had with each other exploded. Total meltdown. Friends since third grade. You should have seen the church ladies at the funeral. Once the swearing started, they covered the casseroles. No food at a funeral? The crowd took a real turn. Almost worse than after our bout last year in Cheboygan."

Mary glanced toward Lyah, who gestured with her hands as she spoke to the server. "That's why for the rest of us, our oath to each other matters." She shrugged. "You getting eggs? They've got great eggs here."

I scanned the menu, absorbing what Mary shared. No wonder the team was all about loyalty. They'd been through a lot.

The group buzzed with conversation as we each ordered.

Lyah clinked a spoon against her water glass. "Attention: 'Nados. Let's go around the table and introduce ourselves. Name—real name—age if you want, job and or life status, plus one thing you're proud of about yourself. Chelsea and Taylor go last."

"You first," Nina said to Lyah.

Lyah swatted her, grinning. "I was going to already. You didn't let me start."

"Too slow—I'm Nina." Nina made her voice extra sweet as she held a hand in Lyah's face to block her reaction. "I'm twenty-five, single and not-so-ready to mingle, and I work as a lab tech at a medical clinic. I'm most proud of leaving my dead-weight boyfriend."

Whoops and cheers went up around the table. "Proud of you, Nina," Queen Bacon said. "I'll go next. I'm Kam, short for Kamara. I'm twenty-three and in a Master's program for financial management. This week I'm most proud of acing my statistics course. Summer semester is killing me."

We congratulated her achievement and continued on around the table.

Their accomplishments and backgrounds fascinated me. Everyone led such different lives, but each ended up here at this table after a sweaty session of roller skating. Becky Bruiser acted in community stage productions on the off-season from derby when she wasn't working customer service.

Mary Kiss Kill spent most of her time raising two young kids and joined derby for a physical outlet. "Besides my kids, I'm most proud of bench pressing one-seventy with my trainer."

"I'm Barb," Barb said. "I've been married for ages. If you need a mom in your life, I'm here. My own wild kids were obviously hatched—I no longer claim them. Age: no comment."

Taylor went next. "Taylor and I'm twenty. I'm in college and commute." She mentioned a nearby school. "I'm proud of succeeding at school despite having dyslexia."

Claps sounded around the table again.

My turn. "I'm Chelsea Mae Devlin, as you all heard earlier. I recently graduated from West Ginsburg—"

"Whoo-hoo! West Ginsburg!" Bonecrusher made dog woofing sounds as she fist-pumped. The table quieted. "What? I'm alumni."

"Moving on," Lyah said, now looking at me again.

I'd been grateful for the stall. All through the introductions, I'd been racking my brain to come up with what I was most proud of. My parents were more proud of my recent graduation than I was.

My mind drew a big, fat blank.

I thought back to last summer fighting and then making up with Elena. We'd done a little light crime by sleuthing in the main office at Wild Adventure looking for documents to clear her boyfriend's name after accusations by park staff.

"I think...I'm most proud of helping a friend when it was hard. At the time, I didn't think we were friends anymore, and a lot of that came down to me. Moving past our hurt feelings felt, I don't know, freeing. I guess I'm proud I got over my grudge."

The group fell silent. They were really good at that—sucking all the sound out of the room. A nearby diner coughed and a heavy pot clanged deep in the kitchen.

My stomach dropped. *Oh no.* I'd said I'd gotten over a friendship grudge after Mary told me the derby team divided *specifically* over a friendship grudge.

Heat saturated my cheeks. Barb started clapping. "I love to hear it, Chelsea. Isn't it great?" She looked pointedly at the rest of the table.

A smattering of claps followed. At the end of the table, Lyah's smile grew tight.

My first day, and already I'd poked the proverbial derby bear.

The server arrived with a giant tray filled with plates. "Food's here," Mary announced.

Barb leaned toward me. "The team is a little sensitive from the split. That's not on you. Don't feel like you can't speak your truth."

I swallowed. I didn't like knowing my enlightening experience might make someone else feel less than awesome.

If Elena were here, she'd say to get over it. She had a hard time letting things go too, but it came out differently for each of us.

The conversation moved on to what everyone was watching on TV or streaming. The mood lightened as if nothing amiss had happened at all.

"I've got yours—you and Taylor." Nina nodded toward the bill when it came. "We prefer to do cash and one bill when we go out. Otherwise, it's a nightmare of separate tabs and it makes us look bad, you know? We're kind of old school that way."

"Thanks. I'll pay you back."

Nina waved me off. "On the house. You survived. Way to go."

The group continued talking. I checked the time on my phone. My eyes grew heavy and my knees wobbled like poached eggs. A pretty weird combo I couldn't say I'd experienced before.

"Do you have a curfew, dear?" Barb asked me.

"Actually, I don't. But I'm beat." My parents thought I was working at the park.

I said my goodbyes, thanked Nina again for the meal, and ventured into the parking lot.

Halfway to my car, a familiar face appeared.

I smiled as Rob strode toward me spinning his car keys around a finger. "Hey, Rob. Hi."

His instant smile froze in place. He looked me over, hesitating before he spoke. "So, uh, here with friends?"

I nodded. "The derby team."

He ran a hand up the back of his neck into his short clipped hair. "Derby team. Right, that makes sense. At Shiney's, that makes sense."

Before I could make sense of his sense-making, he looked past me and his features hardened.

From behind me, a voice sharp as steel carried over. "What are you doing here?"

Lyah marched forward with the force of warring air pressures pushing her ahead.

Rob's hands flew up. "I'm here to meet friends."

Lyah stopped and looked between us. "Chelsea. You know him?"

"We met doing Roller Dreams." I purposefully did not mention the other two times.

She blinked. "Oh, right." She'd apparently forgotten the whole debacle already. She recommitted her glare at Rob. She moved in front of me, as if to protect. "Stay away from us. She's ours."

Rob took a deliberate step back. "I didn't know you all came here."

"Right," Lyah spat out. "Because *you all* have your fully functioning rink and a whole mess of nearby places to eat after practice. This is what we have out in the sticks."

You all. The other derby team. Rob was connected to the Brawlers, not just the roller dancers. He'd kept this from me. On purpose.

Rob shook his head. "I'm not trying to start trouble, I swear." He looked at me, a sympathetic tinge in his gaze mixed with something else.

Guilt.

The hurt at his omission hit me in a wave. "You're with the Brawlers?"

Lyah's hands went to her hips. "He's their coach. He also happens to be their captain's sister."

If Rob's sister was the captain, his sister was Mayhem Meg. Lyah's ex-best friend and the reason the derby split into two rival teams.

The reason we had an oath to not befriend the other team.

Rob was the enemy.

Chapter Seven

♥

"Hold up, you took an oath?" Elena looked at me, mouth gaping, after I'd filled her in on the latest. We stood beneath the shaded open shelter of Wild Adventure's Go Zone.

"It was more like a commitment to the team." Oath *did* sound pretty heavy. "There weren't like, robes and candles or anything."

She leaned against a worn counter. "I've watched documentaries about cults. Did you lay your hand on a sacred book?"

"Like, the derby rules binder?"

She glared. "It's a valid question."

"No. No sacred book." To be fair, I'd questioned myself how easily I'd agreed to taking an oath for a team I hadn't known about a week ago. I didn't know those women.

But the thought of giving up on derby when I'd just started sent a weird pang through me. A not good pang. The kind of pang that made me sit up and face what I was dealing with instead of shoving my feelings to the side.

I wanted to skate. I liked it, and the more I liked it, the more reason to stay put in Ginsburg.

"Promise me it's not a roller cult," Elena said. "I'll never forgive myself for forcing you into it."

"You should feel bad about that."

Elena gasped and I laughed. "It's not often I can get you to admit you strong-armed me into something."

"Well, as long as it's not a cult, then I think it's good for you."

Like taking vitamins. Making new friends and doing something completely different in my life was a good thing.

After work, I debated with myself all the way to the skate park.

The one obvious place Rob might be? The skate park. So, naturally, I should avoid going there. He was a Brawler and I'd taken a literal oath not to cross derby lines.

Which was completely frustrating since Rob's derby tutoring had been incredibly helpful. Plus, the whole him being cute thing didn't hurt. As my grandma would say, he was easy on the eyes. I deserved something easy, even if it only applied to my vision.

The skate park was the best place to practice other than the rink, and it was on my way home from Wild Adventure. Hopefully, Rob wouldn't be there. Then I could do my thing and not worry I'd cause any problems for the team.

After parking, I put on my skates and grabbed a hat and my sunglasses.

Adjusting my wrist guards as I glided forward, I skated across the parking lot.

And ran into a solid body. "Uf! So sorry— Oh. You've got to be kidding me."

Rob stopped, on foot, sweat-sheened and carrying his skates. "Were you looking for me?"

"I came here to skate. *Alone.*"

My defensiveness tasted bitter. I didn't like bitter.

His mouth opened, then closed. He shook his head. "I shouldn't have assumed."

We stood facing each other. I couldn't seem to pick up my feet to roll past him. "Were you really spying on the Tornadoes the night I met you?"

He set down his skates and shielded his eyes from the afternoon sun. "I never would have said that if I'd known you planned to join the team."

"So, you *were* spying?"

He sighed. "Not exactly. I really did need to see Nina to finish up Roller Dreams. The skating group was our side gig to make extra money and it fell apart after the teams split. We'd contracted with Midwest Wild Adventure for the summer. Nina negotiated to get out of it, except for that one performance. The park said we were on the hook to give them time to find another act. I considered sticking around to watch the bout, but the cold soda shower shocked me back to reality." He tugged at his shirt, a sky blue ringer tee. "Look, different shirt."

His attempt to make light of things made me sort of want to throw him a bone. "Meg and Lyah were close, right? What really happened?"

Rob's shoulders relaxed. "Meg and Lyah were like sisters. Like, going on our family vacations with us kind of close. Meg didn't handle things well when Lyah's mom died. She really messed up, and instead of apologizing, all this other stuff came out. Both of them tore into each other with the worst things they could think to say. It was as if they'd been storing up everything they'd ever been mad about and let it loose. *At the funeral.* They didn't understand the impact it would have on everyone else."

"So, the team split."

He nodded. "Lyah and Meg both, they made people choose sides. Some skaters refused and dropped out of derby altogether. When Lyah said she was starting her own team, I didn't believe her. But here you are."

I didn't love being connected to a team with a checkered history. I hadn't been there when all of this had gone down. I didn't have the same loyalties as the others.

He slipped out his phone. "How about we work out a schedule where we aren't at the skate park at the same time. I tend to come here Thursdays and Saturdays—"

"Stop." I actually laughed out loud. "This isn't a custody battle."

He grinned but more of a sad grin.

I looked up at the bright blue sky. "Maybe I'll quit."

"*No.*" Rob's reaction came instantly. "Please, don't let their problems affect you. Derby is really cool. It's why I'm stuck around to coach. Also, our old coach bailed."

Probably hard to find blame for that. "I didn't know derby would mean solemn oaths and fractured friendships."

"Oaths?"

I wasn't up for explaining the oaths again. "They warned me about crossing derby lines."

"Oh." He rocked back on his heels, wearing shoes popular with skateboarders. His were worn and tattered in a way that looked cooler than if they were new. "I'm sorry. I didn't say anything when you said you joined the Tornadoes because I didn't want to influence your opinion in any way. I wanted to stay out of it."

As Rob liked to say, that made sense. I wasn't sure what to do with the information.

I liked Rob. He'd been nothing but nice to me. Beyond nice. He'd spent the better part of two afternoons teaching me about derby and practicing our skating together. Standing here with him now, removed from the team, I could tell he was genuinely sorry. The rift with the team happened because of his sister and Lyah, not him.

The way he smiled at me sent hopeful vibes we could be friends. Maybe even more than friends if I'd been reading him right.

Or I'd read him totally wrong and his nervousness the other day had been about lies of omission, not a growing crush on me.

If I was honest with myself, I was supposed to be figuring out my life, not going after the one guy my new friends warned me away from.

Then again, I wasn't exactly being honest in several areas of my life.

All of it made my brain fuzzy. These decisions made me want to crawl in bed in my safe little bedroom in my familiar house on my same old street where nothing much changed.

Only my safe place had an expiration date. My safe place would be up for sale within days.

"I'm gonna take off," Rob said at the same time I said, "You should stay and we should skate."

"Huh?" His nose scrunched in a very cute way.

Dangit, something about him kept roping me in. This summer, I needed to let myself take chances. To decide things for myself. I liked Rob and it was up to me what to do with that. Not up to the derby team.

"I know you're headed out, but if you wanted to stay, we could hang out. For practice purposes, of course." I chewed at my lip. "The team doesn't have to know."

He appeared to consider this. "My sister would be steamed if knew I was hanging out with a Tornado recruit."

"Their history isn't my history."

He stroked his chin with exaggerated contemplation. "Compelling argument." He picked up his skates. "If you're here to skate, well then, so am I."

After warming up with a couple of laps along the paved trail circling the skate park, Rob and I regrouped.

Since we'd covered derby basics, Rob brought in a new tactic. "A crucial skill is how to take a fall. You've already got some practice."

"Way to remind me how you found me here. I totally bit it."

"But you bit it *well,*" he said. "I watched you. I mean, I wasn't like watch-watching you. I recognized you from the rink and by the time I skated over, you'd fallen."

"Lyah and Nina noticed I could take a hit at the roller dance thing." His expression remained neutral when I mentioned his former friends.

"Learning to fall and not hurt yourself is a big deal. Because you're going to fall."

For the next ten minutes, we practiced falling along the trail into the grass. The pads helped, but so did knowing where to throw my weight and how not to panic.

He helped me up for what seemed to be far too many times, only this time he held onto my hand. "Sometimes you'll need to be the aggressor. You have to do it in a way that doesn't violate the rules. Do you remember the big three?"

"No elbows, no tripping, no butt-blocking."

He snorted. "I'd ask you to demonstrate that last one, but I'm already embarrassed for you butchering the lingo."

I stuck my tongue out. "Thing is, I'm not exactly an aggressive person." It was one thing to skate on my own, another to move in a hoard blocking an aggressor. Or to be the aggressor.

"It's not uncommon to get time in the penalty box, but you'll want to make those violations as minimal as you can."

As if I'd brawl on the rink. Then again, the rival team were called the *Brawlers*. I would be the recipient of said brawls unless I counter-acted their moves.

As he explained further, his lips drew me in. The way they looked so soft when he threw out an easy grin sapped my focus. When it stretched wider into a smile, my stomach flipped.

"And go!"

I'd totally missed what he said. "Sorry—it's the heat." Or something. "Maybe I need a break."

"Sure. It's hot out here."

Was it ever.

We skated to a bench overlooking the skate park. "So, you're a coach for the Brawlers." We hadn't acknowledged that part of the conversation from the diner parking lot.

He finished the rest of his water bottle. "More like a co-coach with Meg. It sort of happened over time. Turns out, I like coaching skaters. It's fun. I feel useful."

"You're very useful!" I instantly regretted my bright tone. I could be neon, I shined so bright.

"Thanks for the enthusiasm. I miss it."

"Miss it? What do you mean?"

Rob stretched his legs in front of him. "Morale on the team has been pretty low. Lots of arguments. Disagreements. It's draining some days."

The dynamic with the Tornadoes seemed upbeat and positive. I'd only seen the darker side revealed at the diner, hearing how the teams split. "It sounds like the team dividing had a big impact on everybody."

"I have ideas, but Meg—she wants to be consulted about every single thing. I don't know if it's because I'm her little brother and she thinks she needs to boss me around or what. Sorry. I shouldn't be telling you this."

"I'm not going to report back or anything."

Rob's shoulders stiffened, as if he only now realized reporting back was a possibility all along. "I guess I should watch what I say."

"I'm not a spy."

He shook his head. "I know. Just be careful who you trust over there."

"What's that supposed to mean?"

"It means exactly that." He leaned forward with his elbows at his knees. "Lyah has a temper. Nina will do anything for Lyah. Their influence sways the whole team. If you cross them... I'm just saying, be careful. Skate and have fun."

Which was what I'd been trying to do before all this other baggage dumped out in front of me.

But the team's baggage wasn't Rob's fault. His warning was in my best interest. I didn't know the team well—barely at all. Maybe they needed to earn my loyalty.

"You're a good guy," I said to Rob. "A good friend." I added the last part to be sure we had our boundaries set. Doing anything more than practicing would land me in big trouble if I wanted to keep on with the Tornadoes.

He grinned, but it faded at the corners. "Yeah, I've heard that often."

Chapter Eight

♥

I walked into derby practice two days later better prepared than day one. My confidence soared after practicing with Rob at the skate park.

He clearly liked teaching, based on how excited he got showing me moves and detailing scoring strategies. He must have made a great coach.

I couldn't help wonder whether Lyah told the team about seeing Rob at the diner the other night. Did anyone else know I knew Rob?

I nearly eye-rolled at my own thoughts. How dumb was it to think skating with Rob threatened the Tornadoes? It couldn't really matter.

I dropped my bag at the side of the rink. Lyah had sent an email earlier about the locker room springing a water leak, so we were asked to pile our stuff in plain sight of the rink. I grabbed my skates and pads.

Only half the lights were turned on, which was apparently a way to save money when the rink wasn't open to the general public. I didn't mind. Fewer lights felt cooler when we worked up a sweat.

"Chelsea." Lyah appeared in front of me. "We need to talk."

My confidence vanished. She had her all-business face on and hadn't bothered with any "how are yous?" like usual.

I sat to put on my skates. "Sure."

She remained standing, facing away from the rink and the few skaters. "When I followed you out the other night at the diner, it was to apologize. I'm sorry I acted weird when you talked about working things out with your friend. Then I saw Rob and got so mad all over again."

A dozen responses popped up in my head. I decided to go for none of them. This seemed like a time to listen.

Lyah caught on that she had my attention. "I heard Mary filled you in on the team history, but you don't know the whole story. I'll save the details for another day so we don't lose rink time. And just so you know, I didn't tell the others you were talking with a Brawler. Let's just call it a grace period with the oath."

"Oh, sure." The less I said, the better.

"And seeing him reminded me what's most important." She clapped a hand on my shoulder and squeezed. "Thank you for reminding me."

I let out a slow breath. This was good. It was good I'd shared about making amends with Elena, even if it made Lyah frustrated in front of the team. The point was that friendships mattered and resolving grudges made life better. It was the right thing to do, even if it felt super difficult.

"I'm so glad to hear it," I said to Lyah.

"*You* matter," she went on. "The team matters. Not the Brawlers and not that traitor of a friend or her sidekick brother. He can't think on his own—none of them can. They followed her like little lemmings and cut us out from our own team. We don't even have *sponsors*."

This conversation definitely rolled off course. "It's just—"

"Lyah," somebody called over. "Did you know the bathroom's flooded?"

Her eyes fell shut. "Doesn't anybody read the team emails?" She looked back at me. "We'll catch up later. Did you watch the videos? We really need you up to speed. Figuratively and literally."

I cracked a forced smile. "I'm ready."

She didn't need to know how I'd prepared. Or who'd helped me.

Sore and bruised, I collapsed on the couch in our family room ready to veg out in front of the TV. I finally had a night with no practice or work.

Half-filled moving boxes lined one wall. The built-in bookshelf around the TV showed bare shelves absent of the usual framed family photos and our DVD collection. The old footstool I'd planned to prop my feet on had been relocated to the dining room, where miscellaneous furniture and boxes waited in Jenga formation along a wall beside the dining room table, now also piled with stuff.

Apparently, we needed a major purge before the house showings to prospective home buyers. The real estate agent explained to my parents how to "stage" the house for visitors. The sample pictures she'd laid out, now partially buried on the dining table, looked like a house from a magazine.

Like going to the zoo, our house would be an exhibit for strangers.

But for tonight, I didn't have to think about gawkers invading our space. I positioned ice packs on both legs and propped them up on the coffee table now that the footstool was out of commission. Chucky B laid his little snoot on the floor below me.

Dad sauntered in. "There she is." He made a show of pushing his reading glasses to the top of his head and blinking. "I thought maybe you'd run off with the circus."

"I already work at an amusement park. The circus kind of loses its appeal."

"Glad to see you, kid." He sat in the worn recliner Mom and I avoided. The cushions were sculpted to Dad's body, poky springs and all. The chair should probably be carted off to storage too. Or thrown in a dumpster.

"Where's Mom?"

"Historical society or the animal shelter. Or it's the thing where the historical society is teaming up with the animal shelter? Hard to say."

Her extra-curriculars made even the high-achievers at my high school look like kid's stuff. Well—they were kids and my mom was an adult, but not the point. She was a busy lady and loved spending time helping the community. Wouldn't she miss all those people when she left? I didn't understand how she could be so excited to move clear across the state when she had so much here already.

"So, tell me about this roller-skating league."

All my internal alarms activated. "Wh...what?"

How did he know? Other than I was very obviously icing my shins. I'd planned to tell him my legs were sunburned. Or I'd been standing too long at work.

Not that I'd pre-planned a lie, because lying would be bad and wrong. I generally tried to avoid bad and wrong. I wasn't ready to admit to my parents I joined derby until I had a more solid plan for my life. Now I'd run out of time and faced direct confrontation.

Dad swiped at his phone screen as he spoke. "You and Elena went to see those skaters. How was it?"

Right. I'd told them we were going to watch roller skaters, having no real idea what derby was at the time and definitely not having any intention of joining the team.

"The roller derby, yeah, it was fun. I didn't know roller derby was a thing until I met the skaters at work."

"Funny that roller girls are still popular."

"Dad, *roller girls* sounds super outdated. Call it derby. They're tough women."

He held up a defensive hand. "My bad. I'm surprised roller skating has had such a renaissance. I looked it up online after you told me you were going."

He probably knew more about the team's history than I did. My picture would eventually end up on the Tornadoes' website, so I'd have to tell my parents soon.

Mental note: check team website.

I repositioned the ice packs to beneath my calves. "The event I went to with Elena was at a rink in the corn festival town. Who even knew this area had more than one roller skating rink. This isn't the 1980s."

"Hey, the teen movies you have today wouldn't exist without what came first in the 1980s. And MTV. Those were golden years—music television on twenty-four seven."

Teen movies and MTV? "I use my phone to watch people lip sync to songs they film in their bathroom."

"Tragic. You know, you always liked roller skating," Dad mused. "You practiced for weeks and weeks a few summers ago."

More like five summers ago, but he was on Dad Time. His expression looked dangerously nostalgic. "You remember going to the rink in downtown Ginsburg, right? Heck, I skated there when I was around your age."

"Yeah. I've always liked roller skating. In fact, I dug out my old skates and gave 'em a whirl. In fact..." I took a breath. *Tell him you joined the team.*

"Well, hang onto them then. I bet Traverse City has some great waterfront paths you could skate on around the bay." He returned to his phone. "I'll check out the city's website now."

Low rumbling sounded outside. Chucky B opened one eye and chuffed.

"It's too early to be this dark." Dad craned his neck to see out the window into our backyard. "There a storm coming? I've been so busy prepping the move, I haven't checked the weather." He tapped again at his phone.

Like Chucky B eyeing a darting squirrel, Dad was up from the recliner and at the window, scanning. The actual dog followed him. "Those clouds are trouble. Flip to a local channel, Chels."

I hit the remote to a TV show about firefighters. A yellow banner ran across the bottom of the screen with a weather warning. "Tornado Watch. Includes our county."

I turned to see Dad's dust cloud. He was already at the sliding door off the kitchen. He slid the door open as another rumble carried over. Flashes formed in the sky.

Chucky B tore into the fenced yard barking at the clouds. The neighbor's dog joined in for a bark-off.

"Looks like a real storm." Dad moved into the yard after the dog.

My phone buzzed on the coffee table. Mom. Calling, not texting.

"Chelsea," she said when I hit the accept button. "I'm at the animal shelter. There's the cutest cat here—I must restrain myself, but she needs a home. Are you at the house?"

"Yeah. I saw the Tornado Watch. Dad's in the backyard."

"Of course he is. Listen, it's looking rough this side of town, so the volunteers are going into the storm shelter. We're working on moving the animals. Get to the basement in case, okay?"

The banner on the screen switched from yellow to red. The harsh digital tones of the tornado alert sounded from the TV.

Then from outside, the town's siren.

"Did you hear the sirens?" Mom asked. "Tell your father to get inside. Both of you go down—and get the cats. Love you."

More thunder boomed, louder this time. Chucky B ran circles around Dad in the yard, making noise like he was training for American Ninja Barker.

"Dad! Come on in. It's a warning now."

The sky shifted hues. A stark line of purple and blue storm clouds formed against a sickly green sky. More dogs distantly barked between the siren's blares.

Dad stood at the fence talking to our neighbor.

"DAD," I roared. "Tornado WARNING."

He turned and waved. "You should see this sky, Chels. I think a funnel is forming about ten miles out."

I focused on Chucky B instead. "Here, boy. Come on—time to come in!"

The dog had more sense than Dad and returned to the house. Our two elderly cats, Cloak and Digger, were surely holed up under a bed by now. Upstairs on the second floor, which was the worst place to be during a suspected tornado. Their mischievous days mostly behind them, I'd need to fetch the two cats.

Dad took the hint—only because the neighbor peaced out first for shelter—and finally joined me inside. He locked the sliding door and drew the blinds shut. He closed curtains in the family room and secured the front door.

"You take Chucky downstairs. I'll wrangle the cats." He looked energized and not at all panicked.

Dad watched the weather channel on purpose. Like, for entertainment programming about storms. He talked about pressure systems like I talked about friends at school. He truly must have been busy if he'd missed this incoming storm.

I shut off the TV. Picking up the dog, I set him in front of the open door to the downstairs where he lumbered down on his own after a loud thunder crack.

Dashing to the fridge for water bottles, I grabbed a banana and my cell phone. Then the cordless handset for the landline my parents insisted on keeping. I'd been asked to memorize our phone number as a kid. I wouldn't forget the number, even when this house was no longer ours.

Our finished basement had a carpeted area with a couch, beanbag chairs, and an older model TV. I flipped the TV to the same station as earlier, only now the firefighter show was interrupted by a live weather alert. Radar showed a menacing blurb of rainbow colors, with the red and orange center headed straight for Ginsburg.

Dad arrived holding a cat in each arm. They were old and gave up being chased pretty easily. Plus, they loved being held. I heard them purring from ten feet away.

Harsh wind seared past the house creating its own eerie sounds.

"Mom's safe—" I said at the same time Dad said, "Your mom texted, she's at the shelter—literally *in* the shelter."

Dad dug out flashlights from the closet by the furnace room. He eyed the water bottles and the lone banana. "You brought supplies. Smart."

Outside, tree branches thrashed. I folded my knees up and hugged them. Cloak and Digger tucked themselves on either side of me.

Dad paced as the TV absorbed his attention. "Look at that, Chels. They've spotted a funnel."

A storm tracker team from the news fed back live coverage of a gray swirling mass in the distance across flat land.

"Where is that?" I asked.

"West of here, but not far. It's really picking up, too." He pointed to the screen and described how the air pressures forced the shape, as if describing how it worked would calm my nerves.

The kids across the street usually left their bikes strewn in the yard. Hopefully, they'd brought them in. I imagined a *Wizard of Oz* style cyclone with colorful kids' bikes floating within it.

This wasn't my first tornado. I'd spent time downstairs with my parents riding out storms. We drilled at school, going to the lowest level to an interior hall with no windows. But this seemed so *close*.

Chucky made little yip sounds, pacing behind Dad. "You're scaring the dog—sit down."

Dad sat on the edge of the couch, his focus glued to the TV.

I grabbed my phone and texted Elena.

Me: *Are you OK? You're not working, are you?*

Elena: *No, I'm with Jonah. We're at his house with his mom in the basement. You OK?*

Me: *Yes. All animals accounted for.*

We chatted back and forth a few minutes. Another text popped up. Rob. Only I'd tagged him as Skater1 in my phone. Because I was a coward.

Skater1: *Hey, big storm out there. Are you in a safe place? Hopefully not outside skating.*

Skater1: *Maybe this seems very obvious. I was just worried. The sky is apocalyptic.*

Skater1: *Apocalyptic not in a metal way*

My skin warmed at his concern. I quickly sent a response.

Me: *Home safe in the basement. Thanks for asking.*

Skater1: *I had to drag my parents downstairs.*

Me: *Me too! Dad was out with the neighbors.*

Skater1: *It's all fun and funnel clouds until a microburst hits your tree farm*

Me: *Dare I even ask?*

Skater1: *My grandparents own a tree farm. I guess respect for mother nature skips a generation. My mom keeps going upstairs!*

Hard rain battered against the house. I set my phone aside to pet Cloak who purred immediately.

"Hey, kiddo." Dad focused on the TV in a storm trance. "We'll be alright."

For the next ten minutes the rain played games with our heads. It pelted for minutes at a time, then eased up, only to come down hard again. The thunder sounded more distant now, but flashes of lightning reached in through the high-positioned windows in the basement.

I curled onto my side, the cats and now the dog all adjusting to fit around me. My eyes came heavy with exhaustion from the past week of roller skating and working outside.

A gentle hand shook my shoulder. "I'm home," Mom said. "Come up to bed."

I must have crashed hard. "What time is it? Are you okay? How is the shelter and the animals?"

"Everyone's fine. I managed to come home without another animal so that's a win."

My brain still fuzzy, I got up and followed her upstairs. "Where's Dad?"

"Assessing damage. It's mostly downed branches, and of course the Winstons' kids left their bikes out. One of them was found across the cul-de-sac. The bike, not the kid."

A small part of me secretly wished for roof damage to delay putting the house up for sale. Only because we were all safe and no one was hurt.

The upstairs TV was turned to local news where the storm led the headlines.

A woman on the screen narrated from the newsroom. "Our storm tracker crew caught this footage of the tornado touching down outside Ginsburg's city limits. Here's a first look at resulting damage."

Wind blew trees nearly sideways as the funnel appeared on screen. Two houses on a country road were missing parts of their roofs. Okay, never mind. I wouldn't wish tornado damage on anybody, and especially not my parents.

On the TV, a gas station's sign bent at an odd angle. A familiar looking gas station.

"Hey, I stopped there the other day..." My words trailed off at the next scene.

"And a longtime family business in this rural community," the newscaster went on, "the roller rink. Sadly, the storm damage did its worst on the old building, nearly decimating it entirely."

I gaped at the screen.

The rink. *Our* rink.

The Tornadoes' practice space had literally been torn apart. By an actual tornado.

Chapter Nine

❤

By the time I made it upstairs to my bedroom, three new texts had arrived on my phone. Lyah and Barb, who sent messages at nearly the same time stamp.

Barb: *Bad news, girls. Our rink got hit.*

Lyah: *The rink! Emergency video chat for anybody available.*

A third text appeared with a chat link. I tapped to accept. Lyah, Nina, Barb, and Bonecrusher appeared in little digital squares on my screen.

"The online footage looks bad," Nina was saying. "Roof torn off and a whole corner of the building smashed. Early reports say no one was inside."

One good thing about the rink's business being on the lighter side meant no one had been there to evacuate. The rink wasn't open every day and sometimes closed earlier than their posted hours.

"The owner did say she'd been meaning to sell." Barb appeared to stir something in a large stock pot on her stove. "I've known her family for years. I sure hope they can get some good insurance money."

"I'm glad they're safe," Lyah said in a rush. "Except now we're *screwed*."

"We'll be okay," Nina said in a gentle tone I realized I'd heard her use with Lyah before.

"Do you know how many strikes we have against us?" Lyah went on, clearly not having absorbed the *we'll be okay* part. "We were set up to win this season, finally, and then the team imploded. When we finally scraped together a new team and found our own space, we're at square one all over again. I freaking *hate* this."

Barb and Nina murmured encouraging words to Lyah.

Laughter disrupted their soothing. "The Tornadoes got wrecked by a tornado. How funny is that?" Bonecrusher laughed louder. "Now that we know nobody was hurt," she added.

I un-muted myself in the chat. "It *is* rather poetic."

Lyah's mouth hung open. "This isn't a *joke*. I'm the one who has to figure out where we're going to go."

If only I could rewind and delete my comment. There had to be another option. "What about the skate park?" Shoot. If we practiced there, where would I meet with Rob?

Lyah loudly sighed. "That's a *public park*. It won't work *at all*. No more bad ideas, okay?"

She said this at the same time Mary Kiss Kill and Queen Bacon joined the video chat. The group silenced themselves.

"Put yourself on mute, Lyah," Nina said. "I'm sending you a private chat message."

Both of their videos blinked off, leaving two dark squares where their faces had been.

To my dismay, tears formed and threatened to spill. I was in over my head. A stupid kid trying to advise real, grown adults.

Maybe this team wasn't for me. I'd joined it on a whim to belong somewhere when nothing else seemed to fit. Besides, now I was actively withholding information from my parents, and for what? A team who barely knew me who thought I had bad ideas.

"Hey," Barb said as she stirred her pot. "Lyah shouldn't have snapped at you. Nina's handling it, I'm sure. Your idea is good. I forgot all about the skate park. My kids avoid the outdoors. They're into e-sports."

Lyah and Nina appeared again.

"Chelsea, I'm sorry for being harsh," Lyah said. "It's not you. The pressure of leading the team gets to me sometimes, but it's not an excuse. I'm sorry."

My throat grew tight. Thankfully, at home in my room, I could turn off my video any time I wanted.

But I didn't.

"I'll put her down next time I see her, Devil Mae," Bonecrusher said. "As payback. You're gettin' the rack, Lyah."

"I said I was sorry—"

"That's where I pick her up and throw her weak body behind my shoulders and slam her to the mats," Bonecrusher continued. "It's a wrestling move. I'll do it on grass where it's softer."

I was speechless.

Barb began to giggle and Nina reminded Bonecrusher we needed as few crushed bones on our team as possible if we were to make it to Detroit for our first competitive bout.

The last part hooked into me. *If* we were to make it. The destroyed rink set the team back big-time. Lyah taking out her frustration on me wasn't okay, but I could at least understand where her frustration came from. If I was team captain and derby meant as much to me as it did to her, I'd be fired up too.

I'd never been fired up about anything like that before.

"The Brawlers don't have exclusive rights to Ginsburg's rink," Queen Bacon said from her corner of the video grid. "We only left because it was easier to find another location and not have to deal with avoiding them."

"We're *not* practicing there," Lyah stated.

Barb sampled her cooking from a long wooden spoon. "We might not have a choice. Creative scheduling could help."

Mary Kiss Kill unmuted herself. "I'm not practicing at six a.m."

"It'd be more like four a.m," Barb said. "I have to be home at six-thirty for my kids."

Queen Bacon held up a hand. "We're going to eventually see the Brawlers anyway."

The women all talked at once until Nina clapped her hands and threatened to group mute. "I'll find out the Brawlers' schedule from the Ginsburg rink. I'll see what's available. We'll start there. Meanwhile, Barb side-chatted me with an idea for a fundraiser for the old rink to help offset their costs. Maybe we do a Roller Dreams performance and an online campaign. Well, only Roller Dreams if we train two new skaters."

"No Roller Dreams," Lyah said.

Barb, queen of multi-tasking, had already added links to the group chat for a fundraiser site. "When we take the focus off ourselves, ideas tend to emerge. We'll figure this out."

I hoped she was right. Despite all that happened, I wanted to stick around. I wasn't willing to give up yet either.

The next day, I met with Barb in downtown Ginsburg to do recon at the Ginsburg roller rink. She'd sent me her own side-chat before the video call had ended with her phone number and an invitation to meet.

I wasn't totally clued into why Barb needed to go on this mission, given the team used to practice here before the big split. She already knew the lay of the rink. But I didn't have to work until noon, so I agreed.

Also, the real estate woman was scheduled to come to our house, which gave me reason enough to leave. The less I heard about the move, the less guilt for avoiding it.

I parked and approached the rink wearing my Wild Adventure staff shirt since I was headed there after this. The Ginsburg rink was old, but the building was painted in a color from this century and the landscaping looked current and neat. Plus, being part of the lively downtown, the rink stayed busy.

Barb emerged from a slick mini-van with her blowout curls and giant sunglasses. She carried two iced coffee drinks in clear plastic cups with straws and handed one to me.

"You shouldn't have." I took the drink and sipped. Nothing beat a free fancy coffee drink. Better than warm socks fresh from the dryer.

"It's decaf—I warned you." Barb nodded toward the roller rink. "Thanks for meeting. Lyah shouldn't have taken her stuff out on you in the call. Please know we will keep her accountable. I sure wouldn't want her bad behavior to prevent you from fully investing in the team."

Lyah had really popped off, but it wasn't as if I'd been *devastated*.

Okay, I'd almost cried. And considered quitting, briefly. Truth—I appreciated the extra effort and sort of wondered if mending bridges was the reason Barb wanted me to come. Checking out the rink was a convenient excuse.

"My youngest is at day camp—an indoor, air-conditioned one—and my oldest two are visiting friends. I figured I'd show you the rink myself." She headed toward the door.

"That's sweet of you. I've been here before. It's standard for any Ginsburg kid to go to at least one roller rink birthday party."

She held the door open for me. "Not my kids. They like those bounce town places. I make my husband take them. Too noisy."

Inside, two tall windows and actual functioning lighting gave the entryway a much brighter atmosphere than the other rink. No gross industrial carpet. A modern arcade area with a couple skee-ball lanes appeared ahead of us and a rink with bright lighting and a slick, glossy floor.

Barb waved to no fewer than three people as we walked through the rink.

A group of elementary school-aged kids took over the skating area with several adults in green shirts mixed throughout.

"Summer day camps," Barb said. "School's out, so they book daytime hours like this for scheduled groups. Evenings, they aim to keep as much open rink time as they can for the public."

"What did Nina find out about our schedule?"

"They have daytime slots available. Problem is, most of the team work nine-to-five jobs. Night practices are best for us with everyone's schedule."

"Do we have to practice in a roller rink? Could we skate in a gym?"

"When the team first split, we considered skating outside in a vacant parking lot, but the surface is rough on the wheels. Add to that, pavement hurts more than a rink floor. Even with padding, you know what those falls feel like. It can work in a pinch, but not for regular practice." She sighed. "A few local gyms told us they didn't want us scuffing up their floors. Here at this rink is where we need to practice. At night. And we have one option for the summer."

The look on Barb's face told me this option was a non-starter. "It's during the Brawlers practice time, isn't it?"

She took a long draw of her coffee drink. "Yup."

Figured. "What can I do to help?"

"Now you're the one being sweet. I don't know."

We approached a support pole with a poster affixed to one side. The Great Lakes Brawlers derby team. Fake-grimacing women looked back from the photo, dressed in their derby gear.

"They must have updated their photos." Barb traced her finger along the poster. "I love this team in ways I can't always put into words. I feel strong when I skate and my kids think it's a hoot. They don't need me hanging around all the time anymore, and I need that some days. Even if I do treat some of these grown women like they're my own girls."

"The team split must have been hard."

"Yeah."

"I'm guessing you tried to keep them together?"

"I sure did try. There's a lot of unresolved anger. You've seen it yourself. Lyah is nearly bursting with it. Nina's angry too, but for different reasons. I'm wondering if there's a bright side to this tornado business. Returning to our home rink is our best option. And maybe a way the teams can mend."

I had to believe she was right. Sooner or later, the rival captains would figure out they needed to move on from their disagreement or whatever. Maybe I could help with their healing. After all, I'd learned a similar lesson thoroughly the past year. Hanging onto old hurts only hurt yourself in the end.

This team might need me beyond filling the roster. I could really help them.

What would it look like to be a united derby team in one practice space? No tense moments or blow-ups.

"I support you," I told Barb. "If you're the one to break it to Lyah we need to practice with the Brawlers, I've got your back. Anything I can do to help, let me know."

She gave me a warm smile. "I swear, I did not bring you here to butter you up to my side. I wanted to make sure you know we want you on the team. Your ideas are always welcome. Lyah may be captain, but we're a team and we all matter."

"Thanks."

Barb perked up, looking beyond me. "Oh, there's Alma. She owns the rink and runs the schedule. I'll introduce you."

Barb did the introductions to Alma, a petite Latina woman dressed in casual sporty attire as if on her way to a golf course or a power-walking session. "Barb." She smiled at the sight of her.

The two women hugged and talked kids and school district stuff—they worked on a parent committee together—and finally got to the derby schedule.

"Is it true, you're coming back? The teams joining up again?" Alma looked between us.

"We need the practice space, but we're still two teams," Barb explained. "I'd hoped Nina got that across. Things have been...tense."

Alma raised a brow in response and Barb flashed her a look I couldn't decipher.

"We can keep the rink open another hour and cut the Brawlers' time a little. I think it can work. Some overlap, but not the full time."

They discussed details as my attention drifted. It landed on a figure, lean and male. And familiar.

"Chelsea?" Rob, in a Great Lakes Brawlers T-shirt, stopped in front of me. A lanyard with the Ginsburg Roller Rink logo hung from his neck.

Unbelievable. "You *work* here?"

Chapter Ten

♥

Now I'd created my own awkward moment with all-knowing Barb and her roller rink buddy Alma connecting that I knew Rob.

It was only a matter of time before that knowledge spread through the team.

I told my body to act casual and hoped my face took the hint. Barb returned to talking to Alma but I kept my voice low. "What are you *doing* here?"

"It's a new development." Rob refocused his gaze after seeming to hit a snag on my face. "What are *you* doing here? Don't tell me you're angling to get practice time at our rink?"

Irritation raced through me that he referred to Ginsburg's rink as theirs. "The other rink was destroyed. Did you hear?"

He winced. "My parents saw it on the news and told me. I checked out the damage online."

I noted he hadn't texted me an update last night even though we'd been chatting during the worst of the storm. He'd probably wanted to avoid that conversation.

"Well, we don't have much choice, so the Tornadoes will probably end up here," I told him. "After all, it's a public rink."

"It is, but you know it's not that simple."

"Come on, don't you think it's time to patch this all up? Two teams in town is ridiculous enough. Two teams fighting over the same practice space on the same days—the writing is on the wall, Rob. Besides, not everyone has been cool with how the captains are acting. They're sick of the division. It actually seems pretty selfish the captains have kept the teams apart."

Rob watched me, suspiciously quiet.

"Or not..." I trailed off.

"No, you're right, but you're completely misjudging the severity of the team split. My sister and Lyah need to sort through their issues, but a patch?" He made a clicking sound with his teeth. "No patch can fix this. Not gonna happen."

"Okay, more than a patch. Maybe a minor medical procedure."

He pursed his lips.

"Major surgery?"

"More like an intervention."

"Isn't that a self-fulfilling thing?" I jogged my brain to remember the right phrasing. "A self-fulfilling prophecy. You tell yourself it won't work, so then it doesn't."

"You don't know my sister."

If she was anything like Lyah, then she was a grudge-holder prone to angry outbursts. My shoulders slumped. "Well, I guess we won't have to keep our knowing each other a secret anymore."

"Are you kidding? We have to even more now if the two teams' practices overlap. Thanks to the community initiative, "Go Ginsburg!," this rink is booked solid through the summer. The only way your team will fit is the rink stays open longer and we cut the Brawler's practice short."

"That's exactly what Alma suggested."

He winced. "Meg's gonna be *lit*."

Frustration boiled over. "We need to stop walking on eggshells around these captains. They're grown adults. They're acting spoiled making everyone accommodate them."

He looked as if he was going to speak, then thought better of it.

I needed to think better of this. I kept forgetting my place. Back row, part of the chorus, faded into the woodwork. Who was I kidding with this save the team stuff? I was brand new and knew nothing.

"Look." Rob sighed. "This thing with my sister is annoying, but she's my sister. She got me this job here. She's not going to be okay with the two of us hanging out. Please don't say anything. Or act like we're chummy when we cross paths around the teams. I swear, if we meet anywhere else but here, it's fine."

"So, still a secret."

"Secrets can be fun, right?"

I had too many secrets right now. "It feels like lying. I don't want to lie to my new friends. Besides, Barb can see us talking right now."

"She doesn't know we're spending time together outside the rink. Plus, I know Barb. She won't say anything." He let out a small breath. "I know it's not ideal. Right now, things are…too raw."

I needed to keep my expectations reasonable. A secret friendship-to-possibly-more with Rob was offered. Being okay with that was the rational way to think about us.

Except I wanted to be worth him not keeping me a secret. I wanted him to believe a relationship with me was worth mending the anger that broke up the team in the first place.

But what did I know? Other than Elena, I had a string of broken friendships and failed relationships and no clear direction in my life. Here was Rob yet again saying we couldn't be more.

I resisted the pull of disappointment. What did I expect? A brand-new person in my life would betray his own sister to hang out with me? Of course not. People didn't do stuff like that. Not for me, at least.

If I was honest right now, I'd admit all of this was one big fat distraction. What I really needed was to discover my passion, as dorky as it sounded. Mom was right. I needed time to explore.

Only my time was limited.

Right now, it was specifically limited. "I've got to head out."

I left Rob and waved goodbye to Barb.

At least at Wild Adventure, I knew what to expect. I knew my place, as one small part of a larger system, doing one simple part and nothing else. Now, I needed to cast the net wider. Look for more opportunities where I might fit. Where I might belong.

Work was totally annoying. First, it was the hottest day of the summer so far. The humidity expanded my hair exponentially. Hot big hair did not help my mood.

Elena was off today at a camping trip with Jonah and his friends from East Ginsburg. No fun visits to her zone to chat.

I was glad she was having fun with Jonah and all, but this was our last summer together. She'd said as much at graduation—we had all summer. But all summer didn't mean every day and not even every work day.

No one else seemed to be in a good mood either. We were all hot and cranky. Why had I hoped working would encourage me? I was so short-sighted sometimes. Nothing was thrilling about dirty pool towels. I sweated so much I fantasized about wringing out my bra.

I checked my phone at lunch, finding a text thread from the Tornadoes with nearly one hundred messages.

It was like its own part-time job keeping up with derby. The messages all related to the new practice schedule at Ginsburg's rink. Starting tomorrow. I wanted to be excited for practice, but I'd have to somehow avoid Rob. The Rob who not only coached the team but worked at the rink. It would be impossible to avoid him even if I tried.

After my break, I returned to the wave pool. A group of women in tankinis and heavily styled hair lounged by the pool not daring to get wet. As I cleaned off beach chairs and collected abandoned towels, snippets of their conversation carried over.

One was an executive at a tech company. Another a guidance counselor at a school. Another spoke of leaving work to raise her family and lived off investments, whatever that meant. They had busy lives where a day at the pool was a break from it all.

I envisioned myself as one of their group. Older, wiser, employed somewhere other than a water park.

Would I have lip fillers by then? Hopefully by then lip filler technology wouldn't make lips look like little skin-wrapped life preservers.

Ugh. I couldn't think seriously about my future without my thoughts derailing.

My attention landed on Patty, of Lil Adventurer Zone, who was headed my way.

"Chelsea. I need you in my zone if you're free. I left Zoe back there so I didn't abandon my post."

The number one rule at Wild Adventure was never to leave your zone unstaffed. Since I wasn't one of the two lifeguards on duty, my presence wasn't essential at the pool. Part of my role was to float between the pool and the kid's zone since I'd worked both. "Sure, what's up?"

"These kids are running me ragged. I need a little dip into the A/C. Then I'll be good."

I looked closer at Patty. Her face flushed with heat and the area beneath her eyes swelled and creased. One thing I knew, you never told another woman they had bags under their eyes. You didn't look too close at those bags either, lest she see you noticing them. I also knew to never tell a woman she looked tired, even when it was more obvious than a skunk on fire, which sounded truly terrible.

But truth? Patty didn't look well.

I laid the back of my hand against her forehead. Cool and clammy. "Drink plenty of water and take as long as you need." Dehydration was a serious concern we'd been educated on now that Wild Adventure took safety more seriously.

"You're a good kid." Patty flung a limp hand at me which I guessed was supposed to be a pat of reassurance. "Speaking of," she nearly slurred. "Get out of here as soon as you can."

"Sorry, what?" I hated to extend her time in the heat, but she was moving pretty slow already. "I'm filling your post, right?"

"I mean this park. This...life. *Work outside*, they said. *Get some sun*, they said. Less stress than teaching. I'm...so...tired. Too tired to work all the time...still never enough."

I steadied Patty and directed her toward the golf carts parked behind a gate. "Hang on." I physically placed her hand on the gate for support as I unlocked it. I got into a cart and reversed out, then helped her into the passenger seat.

"I'm only going over there." She pointed to Log Jam, the opposite direction of the employee break room.

"Detour. We're going on a longer trip." I left off saying, *to medical*, because knowing Patty, she'd attempt a tuck and roll to bug out as I drove. "We're getting a treat."

"A treat?"

Her eyes, unfocused from heat exhaustion, blinked slowly.

"Yup. A nice cool treat." Water, a cold rag, and a trained nurse.

After dropping off Patty at the emergency medical building at the front of the park, I drove the golf cart to the Lil Adventurer Zone. I grabbed a walkie from a staff station and let the shift team leader in on the latest.

Zoe, a college student who had a fondness for calling everyone she liked her *bae*, covered her mouth in shock when I told her Patty needed time at medical. "She is too old to work here."

"Watch the age discrimination." I'd never felt particularly defensive about Patty, but come on. Barb was probably older than Patty and she dominated roller derby.

I now legitimately had friends decades older than me. It was a weird feeling. Their place in my life was different than my friendship with Elena and Holli and other friends at school, but they had their place.

Zoe lowered her voice, as if worried a toddler might overhear. "But her back and her knees. She's always complaining about her joints. And the bunions."

I cringed. Definitely didn't need to know about bunions.

We each scanned the open play area, keeping watch for calamity or runners making a break for it past the gates.

"You can go on break, Zoe. I've got my eye on stroller parking. I think the redhead over there is aiming to take that Diva Baby Deluxe."

"Chelsea-bae, you're so sharp. I thought she was acting funny. I haven't even seen her with a kid all day. That stroller looks real expensive."

"It's nearly a thousand bucks." I only knew this thanks to working with Patty and her endless stories about what she called bougie parenting.

"You should go for shift leader, like Marcus," Zoe said. "You'd be good at it."

Something low and deep perked up in a corner of my mind, like when I'd once woken up in the middle of the night on a Saturday, convinced I was forgetting something crucial about school on Monday. Only I couldn't figure out what it was, only that it was *something*.

The heat was probably causing my own brain fog. I finished the water bottle I'd refilled when I checked in on the walkie.

"Patty should be a shift leader." I nodded at my own comment. "The position is an upgrade and she won't have to do as much standing in the heat or running after kids." Once Patty wasn't suffering from heat stroke, I'd mention it to her.

"But you're so good at handling things. I let Patty go on break, but you took her to get medical help. I figured she always looked that bad."

Dear God, I hoped Zoe had a filter when Patty was around.

"You're in college, right?" Zoe asked. "Where do you go?"

I trained my focus on the stroller section and the red-haired woman. No stroller theft today, lady. "Your break, Zoe. You should take that now." My words came out tight. "Then I'll go back to the pool."

"Oh, right. Here I am blabbering about school. I'd love to swap stories when I get back."

The something buzzing in my brain climbed forward. It wasn't anything I'd forgotten, but a reminder of what lay ahead for me based on the path I was laying out.

A path paved with heatstroke and endless summers watching other people take vacation. A path going nowhere, slowly.

Chapter Eleven

♥

I walked into derby practice with my mood hovering between defeated and combative. Work hadn't been the escape I'd hoped for. My mind kept playing a hazy vision of my future managing breaks for Wild Adventure staff and fetching towels for vacationers with bigger and fuller lives.

Derby was my chance to do something new. My chance to figure out my life.

I kept telling myself the same thing, but I needed to *feel* it. I needed to leave Chelsea Mae Devlin behind and embrace...Devil Mae Care.

"*Grrr.*" I tested out a grimace in my reflection of the lobby window. Pretty weak-sauce.

The Brawlers had control of the rink while the Tornadoes geared up on the sidelines.

Taylor hopped over to me. "Can you believe they're running a practice match right in front of us? They're probably showing us bad moves hoping we'll copy them."

"Maybe they're actually practicing." I found myself drawn to the rink as the skaters zipped past each other.

A whistle blew from the sidelines. Rob skated along the edge, urging skaters to pass or hang back.

The sight of him nearly knocked me over. He had on a black athletic shirt, more fitted than his usual T-shirts, and shorts grazing his knees. Besides the rainbow-colored sweatband hugging his forehead which made his hair stick up at janky angles, he looked streamlined and put together. He moved with confidence and ease. The hair, though, that was cute.

Okay, the cute hair and the confidence together? That made him hot.

And he liked me. He liked *me*. But only in secret.

Always a catch, right?

Rob fully focused on the team, not seeming to notice the rest of us gathering along the sidelines to watch.

I checked for Taylor's reaction. Did she notice me noticing Rob? Had anyone else? I needed to keep a lid on this crush or I'd make myself totally obvious.

Suddenly, a burst of sound exploded from the locker room. A rap song popular when I was a kid blasted from bad quality speakers.

Lyah carried a hot pink boom box. "Tornadoes, unite! Let's huddle up."

On the rink, two Brawlers craned their necks at the disruption. One of them tripped, taking the other gawker down with her. Behind them, a domino effect cascaded, bringing down skater after skater. A pile of bodies hit the floor.

The boom box continued to blare. Mary, Nina, and Lyah sang along to the song at the top of their voices.

A whistle blared. Mayhem Meg shot like a bullet toward the sidelines. "You made my team crash."

Lyah held the pink radio over her head as the song lyrics played out. "Sorry, can't hear," Lyah shouted.

"I don't think she's sorry," Taylor mumbled beside me.

Barb marched forward into Lyah's space. I couldn't hear what she said over the song, which now hit the chorus. The rest of the team sang along as Lyah scowled in response to Barb. She set the boom box down and lowered the volume.

Across the rink, Rob's gaze connected with mine. His mouth set in a firm line.

My defenses activated. *It wasn't my idea*, I telepathically told him. He didn't seem to get my message, instead glaring at Lyah. Shoot. He was probably mentally tallying the body count for when Meg and Lyah threw down.

"Chelsea," Lyah called over. "Huddle."

I pulled myself together and joined the group. Lyah went through our plan, starting with warming up as soon as the other team vacated the rink.

"We've got to shape up before Detroit. Tonight is strategy. We run plays as soon as the team-that-shall-not-be-named is out of here."

I sensed the other team looking our way. I hated knowing they didn't like us. I didn't even know any of them. Already we'd barreled into their practice space loud and proud. And we'd probably pay for it.

The other team drifted off the rink as we made our way on. Most of the skaters avoided eye contact except for Mayhem Meg who glared at Lyah. The air between them nearly smoked from their hate-stares.

Meg stopped in front of Lyah. "Grow up."

"I will when you do."

"We're cutting our practice short. For *you*."

"Please. As if you'd do anything for me on purpose."

Rob drifted over and laid a gentle hand at his sister's back. "I'll pull up so we can load the bins."

Meg didn't look his way. "Fine. Whatever."

Rob flinched. He looked up, noticing me. "Sorry," he mouthed. His cheeks reddened, maybe even embarrassed at the situation around us.

"*Chelsea*." My name came as a hiss. Suddenly, Lyah's arm hooked through mine and she led me farther into the rink. "Don't talk to them. They're not our friends."

As we practiced, my adrenaline soared. A fifth wind. I funneled my frustration into my skating. I channeled my devilish side. *Oh, I mae care after all.*

With the boom box turned back on, we skated hard. Playing a practice match was a totally different experience than skating laps and drills. Derby was like tag on wheels with a side of touch football. My backyard training would actually come in handy.

Bonecrusher slammed into me. I'd seen her coming up behind me and prepared. I kept my footing, using my elbows as defense. My leg muscles screamed at me, but I stayed upright.

"Nice," Nina called from behind.

We practiced another hour, going through plays and moves. Becky Bruiser stopped early for a sore ankle and Mary Kiss Kill complained over a side cramp. Queen Bacon yawned and checked her watch.

Lyah's tone came clipped with each new play. "Look, Detroit is coming up and we need to be a cohesive team. *Co-hee-sive*. What I'm seeing is sloppy seconds. Our newbies are putting you veterans to shame."

Barb rolled over to her and spoke low in her ear. Lyah sighed and pursed her lips.

"I've got a church thing early tomorrow," Bonecrusher said. "I'm out."

I must have given her an odd look because she nudged me with her elbow. "Biker church. We're doing a ride this weekend."

I felt kind of bad for looking disbelieving enough it led her to explain. Anybody could go to church. To any type of church.

"You wanna come?" she asked. "Free lessons. Helmet required, just like on the rink."

I grinned. "Thanks, but probably not." My parents would freak. Okay, *I* would freak. Me on a motorcycle?

Then again, I'd never tried being a biker. Maybe I'd find a passion for it. Maybe I could join the biker church and they'd take me in as their own. I'd give up one family for another. Did I own any leather?

"Listen up," Lyah called out. "Here's the updated schedule for the next month. I printed it out and it's on our online forum. This weekend is the skate park event where we booked a vendor table. We still need volunteers."

Nina handed out flyers. "The local skate park has a competition this Saturday. The community center is hosting it and they've brought in sponsors and vendors. It's mostly aimed at skateboarders, but there's a division for in-line skaters. We're going to promote derby to bring in fans and sell some merch."

I shot my hand in the air. "I'll help."

Nina beamed. "Awesome. I'll be there and so will Barb."

"We need every volunteer possible," Lyah said with a sigh. "Anyway. Details on Detroit. We're carpooling in our own cars, so sign up in our chat thread if you can drive and how many you can bring."

As derby business wrapped, the lights lowered. We headed outside, each skater making sure everyone reached their cars in the darkened parking lot. It was almost midnight.

I reached my car and dug in my bag for my keys. No familiar metal rattling. Shoot. My keys must have fallen somewhere inside.

I ran back to the rink, assuring Barb I would be fine and she didn't need to wait for me.

The doors had locked behind us. Shoot part two. I pounded on the door. "Hello? Sorry, I forgot my keys!" Someone had to be inside to lock up for the night.

A figure formed through the window. The door opened and Rob faced me.

"Oh, hey." I stepped aside. "Are you closing up? My keys must have fallen out of my bag." I pointed past him. "Can I go back in?"

He blinked, seeming to have a hard time looking at me. "Sure. I can't leave until everyone is out."

I raced inside, finding my keys on the floor near where I'd stashed my gear bag. I returned to the front where Rob waited.

"How are you?" he asked when I said, "That was really messed up."

His head tilted. "When my sister yelled at Lyah or when Lyah played roller DJ with her ghetto blaster?"

A horrified snort burst from me. "You did not just say that."

He shrugged. "She's obnoxious."

The hairs on my neck stood at attention. "She was trying to rally team spirit." I didn't actually want to defend Lyah, but the response came out anyway. I sighed. "I hate this."

"Yeah, me too." He shifted his weight. "You skated really well. They're lucky to have you."

We stood close now, so much I sensed his body's heat haloing around him. "You were watching me practice?"

"I was on the clock. Alma said I might as well lock up the nights we have practice since I'm here anyway."

Which meant he'd been around throughout the Tornadoes practice time. All while we'd been discussing strategy. And strangely, Rob hadn't been obviously visible. "Did Lyah know you were still in the building?"

His cheeks colored. "I stayed out of sight. There's plenty to do around here that isn't babysitting a derby team."

He sounded defensive. "It's probably not the greatest idea for you to be around when we practice. We talked strategy in the open."

"This is my job."

"Convenient."

"Are you suggesting I'm reporting back?" He looked visibly hurt.

"I don't know, are you?"

"I thought you knew me better than that."

Did I? "Come on. It'd be easy to spy. And you did it before." I felt like a jerk for saying it but didn't let the feeling stop me.

"I seem to remember changing my mind and leaving, then getting doused with soda."

The playful banter of our first meeting was absent.

I'd struck him where it counted and didn't like the feeling. I'd seen how hard our team practiced. I couldn't discount how the team had helped me build confidence already and provided purpose. A rival team member reporting any of our business would be super upsetting to Lyah and the others. If they found out I knew about this, well, that wasn't great either.

The ache in my legs didn't lie—I'd practiced with everything I had. "I wish the teams didn't hate each other so much."

"They don't—" He was going to say they didn't hate each other, I suspected, but the fiery glares between Lyah and Meg showed exactly that. "Someone's waiting for you," Rob said, detached of emotion.

He pushed the door open and a cool wash of air hit my skin.

I expected Barb's minivan and her bouncy big curls looking out for my safety. But it wasn't Barb waiting. It was Lyah.

Chapter Twelve

♥

I headed to my car quickly with my keys ready to go. I shook them in the air. "Hey, Lyah. Forgot my keys is all. Have a good night!"

She met me at my car. "Who's inside? I didn't see Alma tonight."

Crap. I glanced behind me. The door remained closed as Rob hadn't followed me out. He must have seen Lyah himself.

"*Chelsea.*" Her tone came as a warning.

"It was that guy…young guy. Rick or something."

"Rick…I don't know a Rick. Weird." She watched me. "Anyway, I saw you run back and we don't leave anyone behind. For safety."

"Thanks. That's smart."

"So look, I've been thinking. The Brawlers already know our play styles from having been on the same team. What they don't know is you. Or Taylor. You two being new are the key to beating them. If you saw the schedule, you'll see regionals will hit in a few weeks and we may end up facing them. We need to be ready. *You* need to be ready."

I ran my fingers across my chain necklace. "I'm more of a seat filler. A skate filler, or whatever. I'm not the key to anything."

Focus came to her eyes and she settled her focus on me. Having Lyah's undivided attention made me nervous. "You're our secret weapon."

I couldn't have heard her right. "Me? I'm nobody's secret weapon."

"You're a better skater than some of our returning members. You were on fire tonight. You took a jammer down in a second flat. Everyone always wants to be a jammer to lap the competition and score all those points. The true strength of a team is in the defense, and you've got good instincts."

Okay, truth: I was proud of how far I'd come in a few short weeks. She'd noticed my efforts. That felt good. Really good.

She rested both hands on my shoulders. "Don't underestimate yourself. Meg will never expect a rookie to move ahead so quickly."

A dent formed in my little bubble of pride. So, this was about Meg.

I gave Lyah the confident smile she seemed to expect. "I'm sure she'll be super shocked when they see us skate."

Her focus shifted to something I couldn't see, something deep in her mind. "I can't wait to beat them."

·♥·♥·♥·♥·♥·

On Saturday, I showed up at the skate park to meet Nina for the competition. The idea here was to promote the team and spread local awareness about derby.

Nina unloaded bins from her trunk. T-shirts and stickers, their team banner (still on the bed sheet), and paper flyers advertising upcoming derby events.

"It's down to you and me today," she said. "Barb had a thing come up with her kids."

"Oh wow, okay." Good thing I ended up volunteering or Nina would have had to do this all herself.

We stopped at our assigned table along the edge of the parking lot. A grassy area divided our vendor tables and the skate park course.

Waiting on my Devil Mae Care jersey, today I had on a plain tank top and tried to do something cute with my hair. High pigtails, like Lyah had done for the roller dance gig. It wasn't quite as cute as her pink and purple hair, but it made me feel different in a good way.

The crowd at the park was a mix of families and cool kids wearing black or shredded jeans. Kind of like usual, but with more of all of it.

"Has the park done this before?" I asked Nina.

"I think last year was the first competition, but it was smaller." She nodded across the park. "Only one food truck last year. Now there are four."

Had this event existed when I was younger, I wouldn't have given up on skating in middle school. I could have gone competitive. I could have been a roller skating phenomenon!

People were already slow-lurking at our booth.

"What's roller derby?" a girl about aged ten asked.

Nina, wearing her tutu and jersey, seemed to enchant the girl. "Some people call it rugby on roller skates, but, well you're young and also American and probably don't know rugby." Nina shook her head, stammering.

The girl grinned, unfazed by Nina's explanation. "Cool. Are you competing today?"

"Not here, we skate in a rink. Here. Take this and give it to your favorite adult in your life and beg them to take you to derby."

She took the flyer and scampered off.

Nina blew out a loud breath. "I hope you're better at giving a derby sales pitch."

"I wish I'd known about roller derby when I was younger."

Nina snorted. "You graduated like two weeks ago."

Yeah, but I wasn't a *child*. "I'm almost eighteen."

"Hey, when's your birthday? It has to be soon right because it's before Detroit?"

"Tuesday." In a few days, I'd become a legal adult.

Life was moving fast and not fast enough.

"Aw dang, we don't have practice Tuesday. We'll do a cake Wednesday though, right? What's your favorite flavor? Chocolate? Oh—I know. Devil's food cake." She grinned. "Tell me you're doing something fun for your birthday."

"I'm on the schedule at the water park," I admitted. How lame. Maybe I'd switch shifts and work on Elena's side at the go-karts. Except I'd forgotten to check if she was scheduled. All I'd been thinking of lately was skating.

"Do you all ever get to ride the park rides after hours? That sounds fun."

"Sometimes," I said. "My friends run the go-karts and we've done some late night rides. It sort of loses its glamour after a while."

"Like anything."

"Hey, I didn't know you did derby." A tween boy I recognized from seeing around at the skate park stood at our table. "Where's your boyfriend?"

I froze. "Oh, um, you must have me confused with someone else."

"No, it was you and that guy who helped me with my trick last week. I'm Brandon, remember? He called me Brando the Rando. Anyway, roller derby looks cool. I'll see if I can come." He took a flyer and left.

Nina made a show of scooting closer to me. "Soooo...boyfriend, huh? Tell me more."

I fanned my neck. "Nothing to tell. He's a friend. We, uh, met here, and skated a little together."

She thumped a hand against her heart. "That is *so* romantic. You know what I'd give to find love at a skate park? My last boyfriend's idea of a good time was betting on fantasy baseball leagues and yelling at everybody when he lost. He was a real jerk and I was the last to see it." She swallowed. "I hope your guy treats you well."

"He's awesome," I said without thinking. "I mean, for a friend. He's a nice guy."

"Clearly, if he's already got Brandon as a fan." She nodded toward where the kid now stood with a group of skaters. He saw us watching him and gave us a subtle chin nod.

Nina shrieked. "I did not just get the *wus up?* nod from a middle schooler. How is this my life?" Her eyes widened and she spun around. "Oh crap. Don't look."

I immediately looked where Nina told me not to.

She swatted me. "I said don't look!"

Too late. The Brawlers were here. A table with their banner stood at the far end of the vendors. A nice prime spot by the main entry point to the park. Two skaters I recognized from their practice chatted with a group visiting their table.

Nina glared their direction. "They weren't on the vendor list. I bet they found out we'd be here and came to ruin it for us."

"This is a public event—anyone can sign up as a vendor, can't they?"

Nina moved her glare to me but softened her features once our eyes met. "I guess so. At least Meg isn't here." She nodded toward the Brawlers' table. "That's Kim Kar-slash-ian and Bomber Betty. I miss those girls."

A sadness floated in Nina's eyes before she blinked it away.

"On the bright side, getting the word out about roller derby is positive no matter the team, right?" I handed flyers to a group passing by our table, letting them know about the next home rink bout.

The people passed before Nina responded. "It *does* matter to the team. We aren't in some co-op league with them. We split. They stole our sponsors and we have nothing."

Wow, okay. So, spinning this too positive was a mistake. "What's the deal with sponsors?"

"It's not simply money they give us to cover costs, it's a relationship. We did volunteer work with some great community organizations, but those ties are severed. We have to find new ones."

A woman with long black braids stopped in front of us. She held a toddler at her hip. "You're a different roller derby than the team over there?"

"Yup," Nina responded first. "We're a new team with our own completely separate schedule."

"Are your matches kid-friendly?" the woman asked as she scanned the flyer. "My oldest might like to come. The other team has a bunch of free stuff for kids. Do you ever do events with the other team?"

"Never," Nina said as I answered, "We practice at the same rink—"

"We're the superior team," Nina told the woman. "In fact, I wouldn't even bother going to watch them unless you want to side with actual, evil villains."

The woman's expression shifted from curious to *back away slowly*. She left without another word, and without taking a flyer or a free sticker.

"You're coming on strong," I told Nina. If it were me acting that way, I'd want to know. She'd chased away a potential fan.

"Yeah, well, the Brawlers really ruined things for us, so I'm not giving them an inch. Not even a half-inch. Or a quarter. Nothing."

No use arguing, so I didn't. I focused on being friendly to anyone who wandered past.

Thankfully, the skating competition provided distraction from talking about how much the Brawlers had ruined life for the Tornadoes. I was pretty over that conversation.

Plus, it was cool watching the kids, especially the younger ones, perform tricks on the course.

After the first rounds ended, I took a break to get water and snacks from the food vendors. Returning to our table, a tug came at my sleeve.

"Hey." Brandon the tween skater again. "Did you see me skate? I made it to the next round in my age division."

"Nice." I high-fived him as we walked. "I saw. We have a pretty good view on this end."

"Your boyfriend just told me if I get famous, I won't be a rando anymore."

"He's not—never mind. Wait, when did—the guy you're talking about, did he say that last time or—"

"He's over there." Brandon pointed.

Because I was a fool who couldn't not look, I followed his point which landed on Rob. He stood with the Brawlers, naturally. He saw me as I saw him. He acknowledged me with the merest of chin nods.

A flurry of emotion filled me. I hated that I was glad to see him, and hated the stupid little spark igniting in me at his nod. It was one stupid nod! Why was it so hard to play cool? I was not great at this secret thing. My blush alone gave me away.

"How come you two are on different derby teams?" Brandon asked.

I sensed a hot stare from where Nina sat, definitely within earshot.

"We don't know each other all that well," I told Brandon. Nosy kid. "Anyway, good luck on your next round. I'll be cheering for you."

He took off, not seeming to mind I was done talking.

"Why does your kid friend think Rob is your boyfriend?" Nina's question came with softened accusation as if she was trying really hard to control her tone.

I waved a hand in the air. "You know kids, always putting two-and-two together when it's really one and some other one that aren't connected at all."

Her nose scrunched. "Are you dating Rob?"

"No!"

Maybe. I didn't know. I was not a fan of dancing around the topic. I wasn't a fan of dancing in general. Roller, tap, or ballet, at least if I had to be performing.

She crossed her arms. "You're new and I'm seriously not trying to tell you how to live your life, but hanging out with him would be very complicated for our team dynamic. It's why we have the oath."

Ugh, the oath. Which I'd mostly taken. I mean, I sort of mumbled the last part about not crossing derby lines since I'd been confused by it. Maybe the oath hadn't took.

Nina was waiting for an explanation. "We skated here at the same time...a few times before I knew about the rivalry and the oaths and all of that, okay?" I blew out my frustration in a huff. "Anyway, I get it. Team before anything else, right?"

Nina looked thoughtful. "It probably seems over-the-top what we're doing. It's just really, really complicated."

As covertly as possible, I looked back to Rob, but his attention was consumed by children mobbing their table for free stuff.

Music blasted from speakers at the Brawlers' booth, catching everyone's attention in our row. Party lights strobed in jagged directions.

"They hired a DJ?" Nina flew to her feet, aiming her phone at the Brawlers. She snapped a picture. "Lyah's going to be furious."

The DJ, a woman with maraschino cherry red hair and big headphones, jammed to the soundtrack behind a makeshift sound booth.

Rob was occupied handing out colorful balloons to kids. The balloons appeared to have the Brawlers' logo on them.

"We should pack up and call it a day," Nina said. "Free stickers can't compete with a DJ and all their stupid merch."

I wanted to say it didn't have to be a competition, but I doubted she'd hear me anyway.

"Aw, poor Tornadoes," a voice said.

Mayhem Meg stood on the other side of our table.

She didn't look very pitying. More like gloating. "The whole Brawlers team is coming out for the event today. We're doing a derby demo at the next break. Are you going before or after us?" She squinted, looking around, as if trying to locate the rest of our team.

I knew that she knew we didn't have anyone else coming to the event today. And we weren't scheduled for any skating demos.

The air around Nina darkened as rage colored her face. "Shut your big dumb mouth, Meg."

"Oh, Nina. Your bark is weak when you're a sidekick without your little Lyah leader."

"I'm my own person," Nina shot back.

"Sure you are." Meg stared at Nina with focused intensity. "Lyah says jump, you don't jump. Lyah says we'll start a new team, you don't follow. Lyah says cut off the friends who helped you through your break-up, you don't cut them off. The very people who held your hair as you cried after your boyfriend hurt you. Over and over and over. Oh, wait. You do *all those things*. Just like Lyah wants you to."

If it were possible for a person to physically shrink in front of your eyes, that's what Nina did. As if someone pressed a dehydrate button on her body and reduced her to half-sized.

Meg, for all her attitude, was slight in build and stature. All that attitude coming from someone without much meat on her bones. Now that I knew what I was capable of on the rink, I wasn't afraid of her. Especially with her rude self coming here specifically to insult us.

The Tornadoes' oath was team first. We stuck beside one another.

"I need to ask you to leave," I said.

Meg blinked, the shock obvious on her face. "Excuse me, who are you?"

I straightened but didn't bother standing up. "I'm Devil Mae Care, rookie Tornado skater. You're being rude and you made it personal. You're aggressive and it's uncalled for. Leave."

She stepped back, putting her hands up in mock defense, sneering past me at Nina. "Shielding yourself with the new blood?" She made a *tsk*ing sound through her teeth. "Sad. Just...*sad*, Nina."

"Meg." Suddenly, Rob was there, looking between his sister and our table. "Leave them alone."

He shot me an apologetic look.

"Oopsie, I'm in *twouble*." Meg stuck out her lower lip in a pout to follow her whiny non-apology. "Little brother has more of a bleeding heart than I do. I prefer the bleeding part." She winked at us, following that with a cruel laugh.

"Let's go." Rob's request was edged with steel. He lowered his voice, leaning closer to her. "You're embarrassing yourself."

"Believe me, I was already going." Meg shrugged him off and marched back to the Brawlers.

Rob pulled his gaze from mine and followed.

He was loyal to her. Of course he was loyal—she was his sister. What did I expect?

I turned to Nina, my heart blasting its own beat to match the DJ. "Are you okay?"

Nina smoothed her palms against her thighs. "You shouldn't have to fight my battles. I froze up. I didn't know what to say."

"She meant to hurt you."

"You said what I couldn't. She makes me so...*angry*."

I felt no remorse for saying what I'd said, even though I was mildly terrified as it happened. "Meg shouldn't attack you personally. There's no excuse."

The rivalry and the oaths, I could understand where it all came from after seeing the nastiness play out right in front of me.

I hugged Nina because she looked like she needed it. She hugged me back.

Nina wiped at her eye and sniffled. "Sorry."

"It's okay."

She'd been open about having a rough break-up. For Meg to use that against her was so gross and ugly. And to think, Rob had to be related to her.

"Let's go." Nina shoved the unsold T-shirts into their plastic bin. "No. We'll go when they're done performing. I don't want them to see us leave and say we left because of their performance."

After the next round of competitors left the course, the Brawlers burst out with DJ Redhead providing the soundtrack. Rob skated ahead of the team and called out their derby names one-by-one through a rainbow-colored megaphone.

He was their cheerleader, their ringleader. The enthusiasm I'd seen from him practicing on this very course and witnessed him cheer on other skaters was on display for everyone to see. He didn't look the least bit conflicted, like when he'd had to drag Meg away from us mid-insult. No, Rob was in his element, and loving every moment.

It hit me. Rob was the glue holding the Brawlers together. He wrangled his sister, he coached them after they'd been ditched, and he cheered for them now. He'd taken that job at the rink because of his sister. He was committed to her, to *them*.

The Tornadoes were doing their best to build up a new team. I had the time and the drive to do something about it. We'd make this team great. We'd have a team kids could look up to, without needing to shame other people.

I could feel the sense of purpose melding into place. I'd come across them by chance, but for a reason.

Rob zig-zagged between the Brawlers, performing his own moves. "See us next Saturday right here in downtown Ginsburg at The Rink!"

Quietly, Nina and I slipped out of the park.

Chapter Thirteen

♥

A text message waited for me after I returned home from the skating park.

Rob: *You okay? You left before I could talk to you.*

I couldn't imagine what Rob thought he'd talk to me about in front of his sister and every one of the Brawlers. Instead of answering, I took a shower and changed into comfy clothes.

More messages had accumulated when I checked my phone again.

Rob: *I'm sorry for what Meg said. I wish I'd stopped her in time.*

Collapsing on my bed, I texted back.

Me: *You shouldn't have to apologize for your sister.*

Me: *And she was rude. Very personally insulting to Nina.*

I started to type *Your sister needs help*, but who was I to tell anybody what kind of help they needed? Still, she was a grown woman acting like how I'd already learned to grow out of acting.

Rob: *Can we talk?*

Me: *We're talking now.*

Rob: *I mean a real conversation. In person.*

I sat up. I really didn't want to deal with this right now. The skin on my nose stretched tight because I hadn't used my usual SPF sunblock. I was headed for a burn.

Me: *Too tired to go anywhere else today.*

Rob: *Can I call you?*

Did we really need to do this? Rob had chosen his side. His side wasn't mine. Rob was a distraction and I needed fewer of those right now.

My phone rang in my hand. "Eek!" I dropped the phone like it was on fire. "Shoot." The phone bounced off my bed and tumbled to the floor. Thankfully, carpeted. Thankfully, phone was in a case. I scooped it up and my finger hit the answer key. "Dangit."

"Chelsea?"

I could hang up. Instead, I said, "Hey."

"You sound out of breath. Are you okay?"

"I'm *fine*. What?" My question came clipped.

"I'm sorry." His voice was soft and very *close*. We'd never talked on the phone before and it felt weirdly personal. Being here in my safe space with his voice into my ear, he felt closer than ever.

I thought of Rob telling Brandon he was headed toward fame as a skater. No more Brando Rando. That was sweet. It probably wasn't fair to write him off when he'd at least attempted to rein in his sister. I'd at least give him that. "Okay."

"I asked Meg what—"

"You know what?" I interrupted. "Can we not talk about your sister? I just can't. I told her what I thought and now she knows."

He was quiet a beat while he took that in. "I wish you hadn't had to do that."

"Yeah, same."

"Look, I wanted to also say sorry it was a surprise to see us there. We weren't on the official vendor list because Meg—"

"Remember when I said I didn't want to talk about your sister?"

He laughed. "Wow. Here I am with a pretty girl's attention and all I can do is talk about my sister."

My face instantly ignited. *He called me pretty.* I wanted to fight it, to not give in to feeling special that he'd said it. I wasn't sure I'd win that fight. "What did you want to talk about? Unless it's about what I already said I didn't want to talk about."

I winced at my own bluntness. But if he thought I'd melt at his feet because he called me pretty? Well, okay, I might melt a little. Puddly toes, if anything.

"I called to explain some things, but you're right. I don't think the details really matter." A pause had me hearing my own heartbeat. "I'd like to see you again."

A warm feeling pulsed through me. "Even after all the drama today?"

"Especially after today."

"Oh. Um..." The cold solid truth was, I wanted to see Rob too. Really wanted to. Despite the drama and despite the team oath. "Only if we don't talk about skating."

"I guess practicing is out then. Does that mean you want to see me for me?"

My heart strummed a little louder. "Are you tricking me into asking you out?"

"I wish I was that crafty. How about I make it clear: Chelsea, I'd like to go out with you. Some place that doesn't involve roller skates."

I liked this idea. "It seems like a bad idea."

"Neither team would be a fan, that's for sure."

"Aren't you worried what they'll think?"

"If they don't know, then what's to worry about?"

I stood from my bed and paced my room, the nervous energy needing a release. "I get free dessert at three different places for my birthday. We could go on a freebie binge."

"Whoa whoa whoa. Hold right up. It's your *birthday*?"

"In two days."

"This changes *everything*. A birthday means this has to be special. Eighteen?"

"Yep."

"Good age. *The gateways shall be opened*." He said that in a British accent, like a fantasy actor voice or something.

I laughed. "Gateways to lotto tickets and military enlistment."

"Hey, both are valid. And since you have a handle on falling and blocking, that could help in basic training."

"I can't imagine myself in boot camp. I'd die."

"I think you'd be okay. My dad told me I wouldn't survive boot. I believe him."

"Why? You're in decent shape. You've got good agility based on what I've seen. Endurance, intelligence..." I bit my lip before I ended up describing his forearms in detail.

"That's a flattering list. But it's not because of the physical training part. Dad said I wouldn't be able to stop myself from smirking if a drill sergeant yelled at me half an inch from my face."

That sounded terrifying. "You'd laugh at that?"

"Absolutely. Then the rest of the guys would face punishment with push-ups or worse because of me. The guilt alone would be miserable."

"Was your dad in the military?"

"Yeah, Army. For the four year thing and then he was done. He's never pressured me to join or anything. Probably my track record being bad at sports clued him in. If I was going to impress him, it was through roller derby."

"Really?"

He laughed. "No. He's fine with derby, but more for Meg, not me. He doesn't get why, as he says, I'm *hanging around the team.*"

"But you're coaching. That's not hanging around."

"He thinks it's a distraction. After I got into U of M, my folks got really into the idea of making me into the ultimate Wolverine. They went all-in on the school merch. They were annoyed when I drove home on weekends for derby stuff. Anyway, we were talking about your birthday."

Right. My birthday. There was so much I didn't know about Rob, but I supposed we had time to fill in those gaps. "If we go somewhere, we should go outside of Ginsburg. I just thought of that. What if people see us? Like, from the team? This date will need to be a secret."

The line went quiet. Why did I do this? Why couldn't I ride the no-drama wave we'd found for two whole minutes? I couldn't help question things.

"I suppose that would be easiest," he said finally.

Knowing how hurt Nina had been today by Meg, I definitely did not want her to know I was intentionally planning time with Meg's brother. Especially for such a special day as my birthday.

Seeing Rob had to be a secret. That was best for the team, and for us.

"Agreed. We'll keep a low profile." I wasn't entirely sure what keeping a low profile meant—literal crouching?—but it sounded like something people with a secret relationship might say.

And I possibly felt a little bad about admitting it, but the idea of a secret boy in my life seemed kind of cool. I rarely felt cool, so I'd take a slice of it when offered.

"One more question," Rob said. "Do you like surprises?"

When I'd told Rob I liked surprises, it hadn't been a total lie. I liked *some* surprises. But I preferred to know the circumstances of a situation before diving in. Maybe that was a control thing. Either way, I'd told him yes to liking surprises and proceeded to beg over texts the next day asking him about the surprise.

Me: *Please give me a hint!*

Rob: *No*

Me: *Just a tiny hint. Surprises make me crazy.*

Rob: *You should have considered that when you agreed to be surprised*

Me: *I signed nothing!*

Rob: *Here's a hint. It's not where you work.*

Okay, so he wasn't taking me to Wild Adventure. That hint gave me nothing.

Me: *Mini-golf?*

Rob: *I can do better than mini-golf. Give me some credit.*

Me: *I like mini-golf. Is it the corn festival?*

Rob: *Do you want it to be the corn festival?*

I really did not want my surprise to be the corn festival.

Me: *Trick question. The corn festival is in August.*

Rob: *You're trying to trick me when you want hints?*

I didn't mind the drawn-out surprise if it kept us texting.

On my big day, I worked a morning-to-early-day shift at Wild Adventure. Marcus brought in store-bought cupcakes for me and my zone crew, waiting for me in the break room. Standard fare for Wild Adventure birthdays, but frosted cupcakes still made the day a little special.

My phone flooded with birthday wishes from Elena, friends from school, my parents, and grandparents. As busy as my folks had been prepping the house, they'd propped up a card on the kitchen counter by a cereal bowl and spoon laid out for me. One of those puffy, expensive greeting cards with a little slot for cash on the inner flap.

I'd already told them no parties. I'd declared myself done with birthday parties when I was thirteen after a mega-sleepover with thirteen guests and thirteen different snacks. After that, I was cool with a shopping trip with Mom to spend birthday money.

And as much as I loved their birthday messages, I wanted to see a happy birthday text from Rob. After our flurry of messages the previous day, not seeing one from him felt like an intentional missing piece.

He'd told me to text him once I was finished with work. He was making me wait. The nerve!

When my shift ended, I clocked out and headed out of the park with my phone in hand, ready to text once I got to my car.

I stopped short at the park gates.

"What are you doing here?"

Rob waved a small flag. It read *Surprise!* with confetti pieces decorating the space around it.

Okay, cute. Really too cute.

"It was either this or a giant balloon and I figured you might like less fuss."

Weird he'd sensed that about me. "Birthdays have always been a mix for me. I like to celebrate, but I also don't like a ton of attention. So, accurate. Are you...my surprise?"

His mouth formed several shapes before words came out. "Not exactly, but wow, you know how to flatter a guy." He grinned. "I'm taking you to a second location."

"Dangerous, if you're a spy."

"Good thing I'm not. Unless you're into spies." He handed me a second thing. A single daisy with a long stem, which he must have been holding behind his back. "Here's a hint."

I took the flower and sniffed. It didn't really smell like much, but it looked pretty. "A farm?"

"Where every girl wants to go on her eighteenth birthday—a farm." He shook his head. "Wrong, but nice try. I'm parked over here. Come on."

I had on my Wild Adventure staff shirt. "I look kind of grubby."

He blinked as if only now realizing I wore work clothes. "You look great. Would you like to change or something? We can stop by your house."

"I've got extra clothes in my car. I'll meet you at yours—give me two minutes."

I detoured to my car and returned to him none the wiser after my quick-change method—new shirt over old shirt, old shirt tugged over my head beneath the new shirt. All from the relative privacy of my backseat where I'd perfected my method over time.

Bonus, I'd picked up a new maxi skirt and chunky bead necklace the other day and forgot to bring in the bag from my trunk. The skirt went well with my tank top in tiny flower print. A quick sweep through my hair with a brush and some lip gloss from my purse and I was good to go.

Rob looked up when I approached, his gaze sweeping my body and landing at my face. "You look, wow. You had all that in your car?"

"I like to be prepared."

His usual confident grin came a little unsteady, and I liked how he looked a little shook.

We rode together toward Ginsburg proper, as Midwest Wild Adventure was on the outskirts of town. He turned toward the highway, but instead of taking the on-ramp, drove past it going south, out of town again.

My poor heart didn't know whether to be excited or worried. It beat hard either way.

"Here we go."

He slowed at the entrance to the botanical gardens. I'd never been here, but my grandparents came here for whatever botanical gardens offered.

He slowed through the parking lot, craning his neck to see where greenery and lavish gardens waited beyond us. "There's a butterfly exhibit in the glass dome over there."

A light gasp escaped my lips. "Butterflies."

What girl wasn't enchanted by butterflies? This girl was definitely enchanted by butterflies.

"Is it corny?" he asked.

"Not corny."

It was incredibly romantic. Like, incredibly.

"You have that necklace." Rob rubbed a mindless hand over his own chest, where a necklace might lay. "Not the one you have on now, but the one you were wearing the first day we met. The one with the butterfly charm."

I swallowed. He'd noticed and remembered. For some reason, a spoken response couldn't find its way out. I nodded and smiled.

"Maybe it's not anything particularly meaningful—"

"Thank you," I said.

He'd noticed such a small detail and turned into this. A surprise date that was very...*romantic*.

The whole date part hit me on a new level. I would have been happy with a movie and popcorn. Rob picking me up from work with a plan made my day already.

Then again, I hadn't ever experienced a guy doing something like this before. I'd only casually dated, mostly hangouts in a group and a few times to movies with guys. My last boyfriend, Craig, one of his ideas for a date involved going to an arcade to watch *him* play video games. When he found me racking up tickets on the *Jurassic Park* shooter, he was at first annoyed I'd ditched him, then impressed by my score. The guy needed a real nudge out of the clueless zone.

Rob parked and we headed toward the entrance gates.

He held up his phone at a ticket window showing digital tickets purchased ahead of time.

I didn't know what made gardens botanical, but so far, the grounds looked nicely landscaped with lots of flowers and bushes and plants, with winding paved walkways between them.

A long building stretched in front of us with a sparkling glass dome visible at the top. Inside the lobby area, a group of people waited. A guide explained about the butterfly house and would lead us through it on a short tour.

Another set of doors led inside to the butterfly room. The guide ensured we'd closed the outer door from the lobby before opening the next. Plants and flowers unfolded in every direction exploding in bursts of color. Butterflies perched on branches and softly fluttered above us.

It was downright magical.

I felt six-years-old again, when something as simple as watching butterflies could make me smile all day.

When I was younger, I convinced my parents I'd be a veterinarian. After all, we always had animals in the house. After years of cleaning litter boxes and picking up after the dog, working with animals as a job became less appealing. I loved our fuzzy critters, but the dream of studying animals faded.

I never replaced the dream with anything else.

It always gave me an unsettled sensation when somebody asked what I wanted to be when I grew up. Why did I have to know? What if I liked different things? What if I changed my mind?

My parents always quickly remedied that stress. I had plenty of time to figure it out.

And I'd believed them.

Only now, age eighteen stared me square in the face. I was an *adult*. New things were legal for me. Now to determine what I'd do for the next eighty-odd years of my existence.

No pressure.

Rob watched me. "Just taking it in?"

Tears threatened and I willed them back. *Not now.* I let my eyes fall shut and breathed.

When I opened my eyes, I found myself alone. Rob had wandered off to talk with the guide.

I felt it then. *Space.*

Peace and a moment of solitude. I didn't need to be anywhere or do anything right this second. I was here, in a butterfly dome, and that was it.

In front of me, a blue and black-winged butterfly sat on a leaf. I wanted to touch it, but found myself holding my breath instead, waiting for it to move. Its wings twittered, but the insect remained. Rather than taking off, it waited.

What was it waiting for? All of its butterfly buddies were buzzing around.

But little Blue-and-Black appeared content sitting on the leaf. Well, as much as a butterfly could appear in any sort of mood.

"Come on, fly," I whispered to it. "Go be with the other butterflies."

It continued to sit, contemplating life.

Great. Now I needed to wait until the butterfly took off. Don't ask me why, but I couldn't leave this spot until the thing flew away.

But as I studied the depths of the cobalt blue shade in the wings, my impatience waned. So what if this butterfly wanted to hang out on a leaf? Maybe it spent all day flying and needed a break. Maybe it wanted to do something different than everyone else. Maybe it didn't know what that different thing was yet.

I looked back to see Rob talking with a larger group from the tour. An older couple and a guy in a leather jacket with a kid.

When I turned back to my butterfly, it was gone.

Chapter Fourteen

♥

After finishing the guided tour in the butterfly dome, Rob and I exited to the outside gardens and walked the grounds. We read signs about the plants every few feet. It was startlingly clear I knew zilch about botanic life.

Rob stopped in front of a flowering bush. "We can go. I can't let you be bored on your birthday."

"No, it's nice. This is the first place I've been in a long time where nothing is expected of me." I watched my own feet as I spoke. "My thoughts are kind of a mess. I feel like they might be starting to untangle when there isn't a lot of noise to distract me. Being here—it's *untangling.*"

"That's a good sign."

"How come you haven't asked where I'm going to school in the fall?"

"Do you want to me to know?"

"You barely know anything about me, and here we are on this...date, in a picture-perfect garden and a butterfly sanctuary. Doesn't it seem weird you don't know what I'll be doing in two months?" Never mind I didn't know what I'd be doing in two months.

"I know you're a hard worker." Rob had an easy-going smile that forced a dimple on his left cheek. Hands in his pockets, he walked with a confident gait that wasn't rushed but had a purpose. "You're stubborn. You're loyal. You like butterflies, and you stick up for your friends."

"I didn't enroll anywhere," I told him. "I got scared. I don't want to live in a dorm with a stranger and I don't want to sign up for random community college classes without a plan. My job will end for the season in September. October, if I stretch it to work the harvest adventure weekends. I don't have a plan. I don't have any idea what to do with the rest of my life. I don't even know what I *like* to do, other than right now, I like roller derby."

"Ah. I see."

We both looked at the flowering bush. All it had to do was flower and we were impressed. Why couldn't I be a flowering bush?

"No advice?" I asked him.

"Do you want advice?"

"No."

He wiped his forehead. "Whew, that was a close one. Good thing I didn't suggest giving yourself time to figure out what you want."

"Now you're *sneaking in* advice."

"I'm a spy, remember?"

I walked a few paces. "I don't like this figuring out part. I wish I just *knew*."

Rob joined me, a gentle presence at my side. "I haven't declared a major. I'm not very excited about fall semester. I'm glad I'm near enough I can drive back to do derby this season."

"Too bad derby coaching isn't a major. Do colleges have roller derby?"

"No, not yet, at least. Derby is grassroots. That's what makes it so cool. The independent, do-it-yourself feel. I like the sense we're doing things on our own terms."

I could understand the sentiment, but it seemed like his sister called the shots. The team ran on her terms. "I like not having to think about college or my future when I'm on the rink. It's simply skating. Just me, and the team."

"I love that feeling—even with coaching. It's kind of less fun with the stuff going on. I'm starting to wonder if I can ever get back the feeling we used to have on the team. Sorry—I know you don't want to talk skating."

"It's okay. This is sort of a different side of skating. You feel like you lost something when the teams split. Is it affecting what you want to do with your future?"

He shrugged. "When I was kid, I wanted to be a firefighter. Or a construction worker. Then a jet pilot. And then, sort of, nothing. I focused on my grades and applying to good schools. *Go to school and you'll figure it out,* is what my parents said. They're decent advice-givers. I'm giving it a shot."

I couldn't even get that far. "I want to press pause so everything stays the same for, I don't know, a year? Two? Then it can change again."

"I'd rather rewind to last summer."

"Back to when you were eighteen, like me."

"Yeah. It was my favorite summer last year."

"Really? Why?"

"High school was done. Meg started derby when I was in high school and me and my friends would go watch. I started helping out the team. At first, they gave me heavy stuff to lift. But by last summer, I was a real part of the team. The coaching, the skating around in costume with a megaphone—I loved it."

Loved, past tense.

For him, derby was the lost thing he wished he could get back. For me it was less clear. It was more like all of high school. Or a snapshot of the past year I could live in every day. I only wanted to stay a little longer and then I could move on.

Time, stupidly, did not work that way.

"Leaving home and then coming back to my parents for the summer is pretty weird," he said. "I feel it every day, wishing I was out on my own again. Even if on my own is a dorm. That they pay for. It's still my own space. It's a chance to make my own mistakes without them hovering. I came home yesterday to a list of chores. One of those was to remember to floss."

A weak laugh escaped. "That's definitely hovering."

"Like, do they think I'm dentally challenged? I brush every day. Floss...sometimes."

"Flossing when you remember is probably more normal than they realize."

"I am fully aware any cavities I form in adulthood will be mine to deal with. Well, once I'm off my parents' insurance. I've got a few years. See? One step at a time. Floss regularly, move out on my own, get my own insurance."

His grin softened the rough edges of my thoughts. Mostly. "I left something out. My parents are moving to Traverse City. Our house is going up for sale. They think I'm moving with them."

"Are they wrong?"

"I think so."

I waited for him to keep questioning, but he didn't. He watched me, listening.

"They don't know I don't want to go with them," I said. "And I don't know how to tell them. If I move with them, I'm putting off deciding on a plan for my life. I know they love me no matter what, but it's like they feel sorry for me for not having any direction or purpose. And I hate that feeling. If I go with them, it's the easy thing to do, but maybe not the right thing."

Rob's expression shifted. He swallowed and removed his gaze from mine. "You feel like they're arranging you to fit into their life. Like you're an accessory to what they want, even if it's not what's best for you."

"I..." Hmm. "Not quite." I watched him. "Is that what *you* feel? Is this about your sister?"

He nodded slowly. "I hadn't thought about it that way until I heard what you said. The job at the rink was Meg's idea. My dad's not happy about it. He wanted me to do an internship and Meg told him she needed me for derby. And it's true. She does. And, you know, I like it."

The way he said *I like it* sounded as convincing as me knowing anything about cone-bearing seed plants.

"You sound a little unsure," I said. "You're great at the coaching and the cheering-on aspect."

"Thanks. Now with working at the rink, it's like she decided for me. My life feels, I don't know, less mine."

"I know we're not supposed to talk about skating, but since we are again anyway, thanks for noticing your sister needed a bouncer at the event." She needed to be kicked out of low-key running brother's life, but who would be there to enforce it? The only person I could think of was Barb, but her momming wouldn't be welcome as a rival.

"Hey, the not talking about skating is your rule." His attention circled past me, then landed again as a small smile crept in place. "I don't have life all figured out either. But this conversation is giving me an idea."

"A good one?"

"You tell me. What is it you need to feel like you have a plan to impress your folks?"

"If I can get them past the shock I don't want to move with them, they'll want to know I have a job lined up and a place to live."

"That's what you think *they* want. But what do *you* need to take the next step? Just one next step? Maybe I can help. After all, I did assist you with an afternoon of untangling thoughts courtesy of a butterfly exhibit."

What was the next thing I needed to come clean to my parents about the move? A clear vision of what to pursue. "Maybe I should make a list of things I like and want to learn more about. I like butterflies but didn't know much about them until today. And being here in nature, it's calming."

He stroked his chin in thought. "Yes. And the list has to be actionable. So not something we just look up on the internet, but a concept we can research in person. Do a thing. *Invite inspiration to strike!*"

He used his fake British accent again. "What's with that? Is it an impression or something?"

"It's Sir Patrick Stewart. *Star Trek*? Don't I sound like him when I do the voice?"

I shrugged. "Never seen the show. Or the movies."

"My buddies say I do his voice really good. I'll play you a clip later. Anyway, back to you. Ideas list. Actionable. Let's do it."

It seemed like I'd been edging closer to this idea but not quite landing on it. "I think this is what I've been trying with roller derby. I liked skating but never knew derby existed. I want to help the team, but I'm not sure how it leads me into a plan my parents will be impressed with." My shoulders sank. "I don't know. Maybe this is all too much."

"Naw. You've got this. Make your list and we'll figure it out together."

"When are we going to do all these activities? We both have jobs, plus the team." Separate teams.

"What are you talking about? We've got all summer." An excited glint gleamed in his eye.

"If my parents don't sell our house before then."

"It takes forever for the after sale stuff. We moved when I was a kid. It took months." The late afternoon sun broke from the clouds, bathing us with heat. "We've got some time. Come on." He took my hand. "Let's finish this garden thing and get ice cream."

The warmth from his hand sent a thrill through me, up my arm and into my body. Without another word, we held hands through a beautiful garden walk on a nearly perfect summer day.

·♥·♥·♥·♥·♥·

The rest of my time with Rob involved ice cream and tacos from a food truck at an art festival held in a park in downtown Ginsburg.

Everything felt perfectly imperfect for my birthday. I'd been up since seven to get ready for work. My feet were killing me. Walking at the gardens and here at the art festival made my feet throb. Still, we browsed expensive paintings, jewelry and other crafts neither of us planned on buying. It provided good conversation.

"Your thoughts on sculptures—go." Rob pointed at me.

We stood in front of a tented booth featuring iron-work designs, some abstract, some shaped like the outlines of people. "I'm curious how someone makes an iron sculpture. Like, how do you bend the metal?"

Rob nodded toward a bearded guy in a tie-dyed shirt and soft brown leather vest who lingered by a large metal piece under the tent. "I think that's the sculptor. Let's ask him."

I swatted Rob. "I'm not going to ask how he bends metal."

"Fine. I will." He walked to the man, introduced himself, and they shook hands.

The man's face lit at Rob's question. Rob beckoned me over.

The sculptor described his workshop and the torches he used to heat metal so he could manipulate shapes and forms. Neat stuff.

After we thanked him and walked away, Rob held up a hand. "I know you're probably thinking, *Okay Rob, I haven't even written my list yet so why would you think I'd want to explore metal craft?* And you'd be right. Sorry. I think *I* wanted to learn about metal crafting."

I laughed. "It's fine. After all, you haven't picked a major yet. If you're into exploring arts and crafts, you could join me at pottery with the elderly this fall."

"And you told me you had nothing planned."

"It's not a real plan. My mom probably already canceled the class because she thinks I'll be up north." I clapped a hand over my mouth. "She's probably signed me up for a new class up north."

By coincidence, we passed a booth filled with vases and other containers. I slowed to look them over.

"Do you feel inspired by pottery?"

"No. But those are lovely," I said that last part loud in case the booth owner overheard. Their pottery was great. I didn't care to do it myself. "I'm not really artistic."

"Me neither. I shouldn't be trusted with a crayon."

As the sun dipped lower, the festival added live music on a stage in the park. It was stuff my parents would be into, a bluegrass country kind of mix, but added to a summer night, felt fitting.

"Play any instruments?" Rob asked me.

I shook my head.

"We're making progress already. You can count out what you don't want to do and that might narrow down to what interests you."

Rob continued chattering about ideas and art and life, inviting me to answer all sorts of random questions. Some of them made me laugh. Others pressed me into deeper thought.

I imagined a snapshot of tonight. An image of us, talking, laughing, and speculating on what life could offer. I needed to hold onto this as time stole the moment and moved on. For some reason, the pressure eased about my future. Throwing out wild ideas was fun. And it wasn't real. The possibilities really did seem endless, and rather exciting.

I could be anything—almost anything. Clearly, having no musical background, I wouldn't be headed to a music education program. We'd covered I wasn't bound for art school. But I'd already known specialty schools weren't for me. The issue was enrolling for a general education type degree when I didn't have any direction.

Yet, here was Rob, already a year in at a good college with no declared major or much of an idea what he wanted. Maybe lots of people drifted through their first year of college and were okay with it. I could probably apply for second semester somewhere and stop obsessing over knowing what I wanted to do before I even started a single class.

Only that didn't feel right either. I *wanted* to find my passion. My path. If I did what most other people did, wasn't I taking the easy way?

So what if it was easy? Ugh, what was wrong with me?

Rob looked me over. "You look like warring factions are taking up arms in your face."

"Why can't I be okay with an easy answer? Go to community college for a year and transfer the next."

"Sounds like a reasonable enough plan. Is it reasonable for you?"

"Reasonable, sure."

I was beginning to understand I didn't want easy. Which was probably very stupid on my part. Why make life hard for myself?

No, it wasn't not wanting easy. It was that I wouldn't be satisfied with easy.

A piece clicked into place. I wanted to be *satisfied* with my choice. So far, nothing about signing up for random classes or going to a state school near home felt satisfying.

And moving with my parents because I couldn't think of what else to do wouldn't satisfy me either.

"Hey, Chelsea."

I turned at my name. "Holli!" Holli Hayes and her boyfriend, Will, waved and came over to us. Holli, lean from years of distance running, had on a cute gingham print sundress with faded pink Chuck Taylors. Will, wearing his usual hefty amount of black, wore matching pink Chucks. "Your shoes. They're the same!"

She tilted her head toward Will. "His idea. How's your summer?" She shot a glance to Rob beside me, grinned, and flicked her eyes back to me.

"Um, great, actually. This is Rob. We know each other from...roller derby, which I joined."

Holli gasped. "Chelsea, that's so cool. I've heard about roller derby. When are you skating next?" She grabbed Will's arm. "Have you been to roller derby? It seems like something you and your friends would be into."

"Never been," Will said. "Sounds cool."

Well, this was new, being able to say I was involved with something cool. It beat fumbling for an explanation about which colleges I hadn't applied to.

"We're in Detroit Saturday," I told her. "It will be my first bout—that's what the match-up is called. Then we're here in Ginsburg the following week. I'll text you the schedule if you want."

Holli already had her phone out. "The Ginsburg Brawlers, is that you?" She held up the team's basic but functioning website.

The Tornadoes didn't have a website. We had a Facebook page where mine and Taylor's photos hadn't yet been added.

"She's with the Tornadoes," Rob said for me, since I'd apparently stalled out. "There are two derby teams here."

"Do you skate?" Will asked Rob. "I thought roller derby was all chicks—er, women."

"I coach," Rob answered.

"He's your coach?" Holli said to me, lower so it wasn't super obvious, but loud enough I was sure Rob heard.

"He coaches the Brawlers," I said. "I'm with the Tornadoes."

"It's not like, forbidden for you to be together?" She laughed, but her smile faded when we didn't join with her.

I cleared my throat. Festival-goers milled around us, seeming thicker and more crowded by the minute. Skaters on either team could be here and see us together. We'd already run into my friends—who was to say we wouldn't see someone we were actively trying to avoid? We'd sort of forgotten that part.

And I was shocked I hadn't run into my parents. They lived for these festivals.

"Uh, sorry if—" Holli started.

"It's fine," I said quickly. "It's a little tense between the teams is all, but we're fine. Everything's great."

"It's Chelsea's birthday," Rob blurted.

Holli's face lit up. "I forgot to text you! Happy birthday." She hugged me.

"Thanks. Just another birthday, I guess."

"You turned *eighteen*," she said. "It's special. Your birthday is so close to mine. I can't believe I forgot. I'm blaming my phone. I had to add my contacts to my new phone and I know I'm missing a bunch of birthdays in my calendar."

"It's fine, Holli, really."

Her shoulders slumped. "I don't want to forget the birthdays I used to remember without thinking."

My heart softened at her words. "I keep wishing I can hang onto how things are, but they've already changed. I know it's dumb to think life won't move on, but I don't want it to."

"Change isn't all bad," Will said. "I used to be *insufferable*. You should ask Holli about when we first met. I was going to therapy and thought I knew everything."

Holli gave him a sympathetic smile. "You were coming off a hard year. But yes, you were...a bit much to be around sometimes."

"I was so annoying you broke up with me."

"It didn't happen *exactly* that way..."

He kissed her forehead and I nearly melted at the care in his gentle touch. And the matching shoes. *My heart.*

Beside me Rob's presence pulsed like strobe. I wanted to both look away from and turn toward him. We were in a messy, awkward space I didn't know what to make of.

I wanted what Will and Holli had, but their relationship was two years in the making, with a lot of ups and downs for them, from what I knew. Plus the part Will said about being insufferable.

There was so much I didn't know about Rob, despite spending half the day with him.

There was a lot I didn't know about myself too. My future was like a Monet, with those dabs of paint somehow connecting into a scene when you stood back and looked at all the dabs together. But not a Monet hanging in a museum. I was like a cast-off practice sketch that never made it onto canvas. That was my life right now.

"We're heading out," Holli said. "It was good to see you. Call me soon, okay?"

I promised I would and waved goodbye.

Rob slid his hand into mine. "Is this okay?"

I liked that he asked. "Yes." I felt warm all over, despite the night growing cooler.

We walked to the edge of the park where he slowed before crossing the street to the parking garage. "It probably sucks feeling you don't have your next steps figured out, but you're not alone. A lot of us are working on what to do next."

"Yeah, I'm getting that."

"It's a step in the right direction. To understand you're not in this by yourself."

I spun to face him and moved in closer before I lost my nerve. One last thing would make this birthday special.

The best part with Rob was I didn't have to say anything. He read my cues and did the exact thing I hoped.

Moving his hand up the back of my arm, he leaned in and pressed soft lips to mine. I kissed him back.

The moment sealed between us. His breath with mine, my hand with his.

He pulled back. "Happy birthday, Chelsea."

Chapter Fifteen

♥

That Saturday, seven of us crammed into Barb's minivan for the drive to Detroit. Today, we'd face off with the Detroit Hawt Rodders. Bonecrusher claimed shotgun with Barb, while Queen Bacon and Mary Kiss Kill filled the middle two seats, and Taylor, Becky Bruiser, and I took the back row.

We talked the whole ride. Not even about derby, but about the latest Taylor Swift album (that would be Taylor's main topic), Barb's kids' latest shenanigans, and dating drama.

I kept quiet on the dating front, and thankfully none of them pressured me to dish deets. For now, Rob was still my secret. Our kiss, between us. I held onto that secret, rolling it through my mind.

In fact, they were all so consumed by their own chatter, I blended in, right where I was comfortable.

I hadn't been as successful at blending earlier in the week at team practice. They'd all known it was my birthday, and as Nina indicated, brought me a cake—devil's food flavor—and my new team jersey.

And then we skated, and I pushed all other thoughts aside. I was getting better at that—the not caring about anything other than improving my derby skills.

As the conversation happened around me, I pulled up the list of things I liked and wanted to learn about saved in a notes app.

So far I'd written:

- *Animals—but I don't want to be a vet or work in a zoo or be a dog walker or groomer*
- *Cake decorating—I like eating cake, how about making it for a living?*
- *Detective—I helped uncover clues with Elena that one time so...*

I hadn't gotten far. Other than visiting a bakery for the cake decorating idea, I wasn't sure how to take action on the others. Rob might have ideas.

I texted Rob my current list. Then, I tucked my phone away.

Arriving at the Detroit rink, it was instantly obvious the venue was larger than Ginsburg's. This rink included a large arcade with modern games and a full restaurant.

We'd been advised ahead that the rink didn't have a locker room like Ginsburg, only public bathrooms, so we'd come dressed in our gear and team shirts.

An energetic buzz filled the rink. The crowd looked older and a little edgier than back in Ginsburg. Younger kids and a few families dotted the area, but more teenagers and twenty-somethings filled out the crowd.

Taylor hooked her arm through mine. "Stop for a sec." She held up her phone and snapped a picture. She tapped the screen to check the image. "You look fierce. The make-up was a good choice."

Queen Bacon and Taylor encouraged me to dig into their make-up stash in the van. I rarely wore lipstick, preferring gloss, and usually did a soft pastel eye shadow and maybe some mascara if I wanted to be fancy.

Thanks to Taylor's steady hand, I had on black eyeliner, gold glitter shadow, a cheek highlighter, and a bold shade of red lips, in matte. I barely recognized myself in the pocket mirror in the van, and definitely did a double-take in the mirrored wall by the rink. Taking in my full body with neon pink tights, leg warmers, and wrist bands, I struck a mix of colorful and fun.

I nudged Taylor with my elbow. "*We* look fierce."

Her eyes were shaded in deep blue and purple hues. She wore pale pink lip gloss and glittering highlighter striped against her cheeks.

This rink had actual stands set up along one side of the skating area, a small section of bleachers which were filled. A decent-sized crowd.

Lyah and Nina came in moments later, quickly pulling us into a tight group in our designated team area.

"Alright, listen up," said Lyah. "This is our first official bout as the Tornadoes. Our first with Taylor and Devil. But as a team we have years of derby in us. We're not new. We're refined. We're sharp. We have renewed purpose."

I found myself nodding along as the inspiration sank in. Purpose, yes, as a team.

She reviewed our game plan. Her no-nonsense directions reminded me why she was captain.

An announcement overhead came on. "Attention. Please clear the rink to prepare for tonight's event: Roller derby!"

Whoops and clanging cowbells sounded from the crowd.

The rink filled with referees. At least five, each wearing official black and white striped shirts, black pants, padding, and skates. They zipped in tight circles, stretching their legs.

The Detroit Hawt Rodders flooded in for warm-up. A sea of black shirts with pops of red and orange to match the flame images on their T-shirts.

Nina clapped twice. "That's us too—come on, ladies."

I'd worn my butterfly necklace again, hoping it might bring luck and a dash of courage. I smoothed my fingers along the edges of the wings.

I adjusted my helmet and skated onto the rink. I ventured a closer look at the Detroit skaters.

One skater wore jewelry that looked like bike chains. Another had biceps any gym rat would kill for. A lean skater wore colorful band-aids crisscrossed on her cheeks and along her arms in a pattern. Her name: Mayor Pain.

"What are the odds of a fair election for Mayor Pain, eh?" Barb asked, skating up beside me.

"Vote early, vote often?"

"I don't like that you had that answer so quickly." She gave me an assessing look. "Don't let the other team psyche you out. Me, I look for the oldest broad in the bunch and make her my target."

I mentally reviewed our practice strategy and what I'd learned skating with Rob. Now it was time to apply what I'd learned.

Music boomed overhead and the crowd sang along as we lapped the rink.

After the song ended, the host announcer, a woman with purple hair and black framed glasses, introduced our team. The crowd broke into applause. They were clapping for us!

It felt pretty cool. Being part of this team satisfied me in a way school activities hadn't. None of the team knew me before this. It was a brand-new slate where I sketched out who I wanted to be.

We gathered as a group, a cohesive team. *We were the Tornadoes.*

Then the Hawt Rodders were called out. The small but loud crowd exploded in cheers.

"Home team advantage," Bonecrusher said. She cracked her knuckles. "And we ain't in Kansas."

I was pretty sure that was a *Wizard of Oz* reference, but all my focus centered on the skaters in their hometown glory. I looked for the youngest appearing person on the team as my target, like Barb suggested. It was hard to tell ages, but one skater, slighter in build, looked least likely to pulverize me. Her shirt name: Hot Lunch.

Lyah pulled us in. "We're starting Bonecrusher as pivot, with Mary, Bacon, and Becky as blockers. Nina's our jammer. The rest of you, stay ready."

A small breath of relief came knowing I wouldn't have to start.

But as soon as the first jam began with a crack, I found myself antsy to get in on the action.

The Tornadoes' blockers formed a human wall to prevent the Hawt Rodders' jammer from breaking through for an initial pass.

"You can do it," I shouted to my teammates. "Block! Block!"

The two jammers, Nina and the Hawt Rodders' pick, started behind us at a different line. Their goal was to skate hard through or around the pack. Each jammer had the chance to score points after breaking through and passing other skaters while lapping the rink.

The opposing team's jammer wiggled through the pack, completely bypassing Bonecrusher like she was invisible. Becky Bruiser blocked but went down. She was back up in a blink, but the jammer had already passed, escaping the hip-checks of Queen Bacon and Mary Kiss Kill.

Nina, angling against the Hawt Rodders' blockers, couldn't manage a break.

The rival team's jammer scored as she lapped the other skaters.

The next round, or jam, Nina moved to the outside while the blockers tried to slow her roll. She hopped over a downed skater. Yes—she was lead jammer!

The Hawt Rodders' jammer broke through behind Nina.

After ten minutes in and down in points, Lyah called a time out.

We regrouped and reset. Cowbells clanged from the audience and they shouted strategic plays at the team. This was a highly-informed crowd.

The next jam, the refs called a penalty against Mary Kiss Kill.

"What for?" I threw up my hands.

"Elbow," Barb said beside me. "It happens."

The other team racked up their own penalty. I'd watched a fair amount of hockey on TV and had to note, the derby skaters didn't fume or throw fits the way hockey players did when they were penalized.

Lyah subbed in for Nina, and Taylor went in for Mary after the next jam. We scored again. Lyah was on fire.

This was amazing. We could do this. We could win this bout.

It was a bloodbath, and not in our favor.

Okay, no actual blood spilled, thankfully, because *gross* and hello, biohazard, but any progress the Tornadoes made, the Hawt Rodders scored double. Triple.

The Tornadoes lost and we lost bad.

The competition was a solid team. I could see their strategy now. They saved their best skaters for the last half, including Hot Lunch. Lesson learned not to underestimate any slight-of-build skaters. She was the jammer who scored the most points for their team.

Lyah was our strongest jammer and she went out in the later half too, but she'd also placed me and Taylor in the second half when we'd never done a competition before. I'd fallen more times than I could count, blocked successfully a few times, and fell some more.

The bright spot was I got back up again. Time after time.

And it felt great.

Losing didn't feel great, but working together, skating hard, and the thought of winning had propelled us forward. That I could see returning to.

This team thing was addictive.

After the bout, the Hawt Rodders invited us for pizza in the restaurant connected to the rink.

"Is this normal?" I asked Barb, because I seemed to ask Barb everything now. "Eating with the rival team?"

She'd changed into a fresh shirt and her hair magically bounced with curls again. "It's what's great about derby. Most of the teams are more than happy to be friends outside of the rink."

"Detroit's always been good to us," said Queen Bacon—or Kam if I could ever remember to call her by her real name. "What's not *normal* is having straight-up enemies in derby, but you didn't hear that from me."

Kam shot a sharp look at Lyah and Nina, now headed our way, before catching up with a blocker from the other team.

"Nice job tonight, Devil," Lyah told me as she corralled us toward the tables in the back corner. "I'm wondering if you'd like to help find new sponsors for us."

Yes! This was exactly what I needed. A purpose and a mission. "Absolutely. I'll do it."

She scanned her phone and then slid it into her pocket. "I'll text you a couple leads. The team needs all the help we can get. Barb or Kam can help you get started. It will really take a load off my back." She gave me her brightest Lyah smile. The one she didn't give often enough, but reminded me why this team worked.

At that, she moved to the other side of the table to talk with our new friends.

Contacting sponsors sounded like a good, purposeful task. A behind-the-scenes move to build the very foundation of the team. And I was singled out to do it.

Innocent bread baskets waiting at the table were instantly devoured. The team put in orders quickly. Once the food arrived, I couldn't eat fast enough. I'd pay later for too many slices of heavy pizza, but for now, this cheesy goodness hit the spot.

"Heard your team has had quite a year," the Hawt Rodders' team captain, an East Asian woman affectionately named Destroyer spelled DSTRYR, said to Lyah, who sat across from me.

Lyah's smile froze in place. "Something like that. We're strong. We'll come back from this loss."

"You know, we had a team rift a few years back and what helped—"

"*We* are our own team," Lyah interrupted Destroyer. She pointed at Taylor who was lifting another pizza slice onto her plate. "Did you see Taylor Fist? She was *amazing* tonight as a rookie. Devil—you did alright tonight, too. Better than alright. You fought off those jammers like a champ."

My heart warmed at the compliment, but I caught Nina's eye when Lyah changed the subject. The concern in Nina's eyes couldn't be ignored.

"Yeah, it was really fun being out there in a real game," I said. "Er, bout."

My little slip of terms caused a few laughs and broke the tension, as I hoped it would. Nothing like playing up the rookie status to shift the mood.

"There are four derby teams in Metro-Detroit now," Destroyer said, taking the hint to move on. "We're a network with connected sponsors. We support each other. It's helped us stay strong to have wider support."

Barb reached a hand across the table to Destroyer. "I love it. We could learn a thing or seven from y'all."

Lyah tilted her chin up with a defiant look in her eyes. She said nothing, staring through us.

The Hawt Rodders' captain suggested we all switch seats and meet someone new. I landed next to Hot Lunch, the top-scoring jammer tonight.

"I can't believe this was your first bout, I'm Cammie." Her cheeks flushed with excitement. "My first time, I immediately fell and then mentally blacked out. I remember nothing after, but I wasn't passed out or anything. I just don't remember."

"I was worried that might happen to me," I admitted. "But I've been practicing with a...friend outside of team practice. It's helped. A lot."

"Awesome. So, you're a student? You look young."

"I graduated a few weeks ago. From high school."

He eyes opened wider. "Wow. You *are* young. I wish I'd started derby sooner. I'm already feeling creaks in my knees. I'm twenty-one, but bad knees run in the family. So, where are you going this fall?"

Having heard this question so many times by now, it finally began to sting less. "I'm taking a year off."

"Good for you. More people should take time off after high school. Proud of you."

Proud? That was a first. "It's not much to be proud of. I don't exactly have a plan."

"That's what the year off is for. You use the year to make a plan."

"I wish it was so simple." Now to sit back and see what magical plan surfaced. Dental school?

"My brother, for example, is somebody who would have greatly benefitted from a year off before going to college. He applied to schools because that's what everyone else he knew did. You know what happened? He switched colleges twice, changed majors three times, and never finished. He turned out okay. He's running his own tech start-up at twenty-five."

I doubted running a company after dropping out was my fate. I just wished I knew what that fate was.

"My point is," Cammie said, "college isn't for everyone and the four-year plan doesn't fit every person either. Taking a pause should be encouraged, if you ask me. Take some time to like, *be*. Okay, enough of me trying to dispense wisdom."

I set aside my drink. "No, I appreciate it. It's actually helpful to hear somebody say that who isn't my family."

"If your family is into the year off, even better. Hey." She took out her phone and showed me the screen. "Here's my Insta. Let's follow each other and stay in touch."

I pulled out my phone to follow her and noticed I had messages. As Cammie turned to another skater, I flipped through the texts.

Rob: *How was the bout?*

Rob: *P.S. You're no longer a newb!*

My fingers flew over the keys.

Me: *We lost. Bad.*

Me: *But it feels okay.*

Rob: *Sorry to hear. Not about the feeling okay, but the not winning part.*

Rob: *Obviously.*

Laughter carried over from down the table. I'd actually forgotten about our loss until I'd typed it to Rob. The teams joining together fused a different feeling onto tonight's loss.

Sometimes winning wasn't everything.

Chapter Sixteen

♥

Rob sent messages the entire way home from Detroit. I tried not to ignore my teammates too obviously, but most of them were thoroughly wiped and not talking a mile a minute like on the way here.

Barb and Kam were deep in a conversation about family members involved in a hoarding situation to put the fear into Marie Kondo, so I gave them their space. It sounded like someone else in their life needed space too—actual, floor space.

Rob: *So, your list. It needs some padding.*

Me: *Like my knees?*

Rob: *Okay not padding. Just more ideas. Though I have a bakery in mind to visit. Would that be okay?*

Me: *Who wouldn't want to visit a bakery? YUM.*

Me: *Another idea. I'm going to help the Tornadoes find new team sponsors. Maybe that could be helpful? Look for sponsors and explore my interests at the same time?*

Rob: *One of our sponsors is a pizza place. We could do a double feature bakery and pizza tour!*

Me: *Now I'm hungry again*

Rob: *I don't know if I should actively help with sponsors though...*

My eyes fell shut. Of course he couldn't help me with sponsors for the Tornadoes. He was our rival. Derp on me for suggesting it.

Rob: *I want to help you, but I don't want to be a conflict for you and the team.*

It always came back to that, didn't it? What was a conflict for the team. The team I wanted so much to prove myself to.

I slept in the next morning to recover from Detroit. When I checked my phone, Rob had already sent a time and meeting place. The address was outside of Ginsburg. A bakery in another town.

With no work this afternoon, I dragged myself out of bed and drove out to meet Rob.

The meeting location was a freestanding store off a two-lane road with pale yellow siding and a plain sign reading *VanHooten's Bakery*.

Ah, VanHooten's. Their cakes were awesome. Elena's family bought one for her graduation party. Out of all the open houses I'd attended and all the cakes eaten, Elena's had tasted the best.

Moments later, Rob sprang out of his car. Today he had on a short sleeved button-down shirt and dark gray pants. Not dressy exactly, but not what he wore skating or working at the rink. He looked nice.

"Am I underdressed?" I surveyed my plain tank top and shorts.

He took my hand. "You look perfect. This isn't a job interview, but I did call ahead to ask what time might be slow business-wise so we could ask questions."

My nerves bubbled up, similar to when we'd been at the art festival and we'd questioned the metal-bender artist. Part of me felt silly for even suggesting a bakery as a career. I'd said I liked cake. I liked to *eat* cake.

I stalled at the door. "I don't know about this. This is pretty corny. Who needs to ask questions at a bakery?"

"Hey. Don't look so worried." He punctuated his request with a kiss.

I drew him closer to extend the moment. Kissing was a pretty great stall tactic.

He pulled back. "I'm guessing you like this bakery idea. And who cares if it's corny. Would you rather explore a possible interest or sit around worrying you don't have a life plan?"

"It's annoying when you're right, you know."

"I know." He squeezed my hand.

The same cheerful yellow covered the walls inside. An L-shaped counter was positioned along two walls with glass cases filled with delectable treats. Only one other customer stood at the counter talking with bakery staff.

A different staff person came over to us. A White woman with dark curly hair piled into a messy bun, her cheeks were flushed probably from oven heat in the back. "Can I help you?"

"I called ahead to ask questions on bakery operations," Rob said.

The woman snapped her fingers. "That's right. I took the call. School project?"

"Not for school, though we are students. We're looking at career options."

Rob said this so professionally and matter-of-factly. I liked how he'd said *we* so I wasn't completely thrown to the wolves. Well, a nice-looking baker wolf.

The woman nodded, as if this made total sense. My nerves eased. Maybe it was Rob's more professional look adding some legitimacy to our visit. He was taking this seriously. He was taking *me* seriously.

"I'm Rosie," she said. "I'm not a VanHooten, but I've worked here ten years and run the shop when they're not on shift. The early donut rush is over, so come on back. I've got hairnets and gloves I'll need you to put on."

She let us around the main counter to the back workings of the bakery.

"I can't believe they're just letting us in," I told Rob in a near whisper.

"When you're with me, you get VIP access anywhere." He made a show of sliding sunglasses on.

I elbowed him. "You're *so* cool."

Rosie graciously gave us a tour of the kitchen as two other staff worked on projects. One decorated cookies and the other cleaned the stainless-steel countertops and sinks.

"This is a family run place, so they work hard to keep local business," Rosie was saying. "VanHooten's has a stellar reputation. We do weddings, bar mitzvahs, desserts for every holiday. We're real solid with the church crowd for donut orders. What makes you interested in working in a bakery?"

This time, Rob didn't come in with a smooth answer. This was all me. My list had said I liked cake. I felt like an idiot for not having a better reason for checking out a bakery, but honestly, the idea had come to mind and felt like a fitting direction to explore.

I took a second to gather my thoughts. "I don't think I'm cut out for a traditional four-year college. I'd like to work somewhere I can learn a skill."

Unlike the water park, where checking access wristbands and scooping up pool noodles didn't exactly translate into usable skills anywhere else.

"Trade jobs are great for that," Rosie said. "I had my daughter young and the VanHooten's are long-time family friends who offered me part-time hours. When my kid moved into kindergarten, I shifted to managing orders and supervising staff. I like the business side of the bakery. I'm taking business classes so I can one day open my own bakery."

Pride beamed from her face. She'd carved out her own career path, something I could totally respect.

"I'll be looking for bakers." She winked at me. "Probably not anytime soon, but it's a goal."

She had a goal and was taking steps toward it. That was encouraging.

Rosie let us peek into the back office, which was cluttered but not messy.

A staff person called to her from the front.

"Let me walk you out." Rosie escorted us back up front into the customer area of the bakery. "Don't take off yet. I'll send you with a few almond buns."

True to her word, she gave us each a small box of sticky rolls along with a business card.

"This was really great," I told her. "Thank you."

Rosie smiled. "Not too many young folks think through their career plans the way you're doing. I sure didn't when I was your age. Good luck and call us if you're looking for part-time work. I can't promise anything at the moment, but we're losing a high schooler once fall hits."

A potential job lead. Promising. "Thank you."

Back outside, I looked at Rob. "Now what? I don't have to work today. Do you?"

"Not until later. There's a mall not far from here. We probably won't run into anyone we know since it's not in Ginsburg."

Right. A place to hang out, secretly. I wanted more time with Rob, and if we needed to watch our backs, a mall in another town might do the trick.

We headed over in our separate cars. Once there, we took our time walking by the shops. Every so often, Rob would pull me closer and kiss my cheek, or run his fingers along my palm, sending a shockwave of welcome chills.

A stop for pretzels was essential, and we carried on from there. Rob bit into his half of a soft pretzel. My fingers laced into his free hand as we strolled a long corridor toward a now-shuttered department store. Shops filled most of the smaller storefronts, but the hall now ended in a large indoor children's play area.

"You could work at the mall," he said. "It's got A/C. Free pretzels if you make friends with Aunt Annie."

I kissed his cheek. "My guess is Aunt Annie promotes from within the family. Probably a dead end, that one."

"Could be. Besides, if you wanted to find any old job, every place here is hiring."

I could secure a part-time job or two and make enough for rent if I shared a place with somebody. My plan wasn't hopeless. I didn't want any old job. What would be better would be to learn a skill. To work somewhere that excited me.

"What do your folks think about you working at the rink?" I asked him.

"Oh they *love* that." He chucked his pretzel wrapper and napkin in a nearby trash bin. "My dad had a lead on a summer job with an accountant, but I told him no."

"Sounds boring. I don't blame you."

"I actually like accounting. I'm considering it as a career."

I waited for him to say he was joking, but he didn't. "Oh, you're serious. I figured you wanted to be a teacher."

"Because I coach derby?"

"Because you're *good* at coaching derby. And you're good with kids."

"Huh." He ran his hand up the back of his neck. "I never really thought about going to school for teaching. Anyway, like I said, I haven't declared a major and I'd prefer to save any intern work for later. This year, it works better for me doing what I'm doing. Alma needed the help at the rink, and I could give it."

And his sister pressed him toward it, as he'd admitted to me. "Will you keep working there after school starts?"

"No. Only winter and spring break, if they need me. My parents put their foot down. Once the semester starts, they don't want me unfocused, as they say. It was struggle enough for them to get that I'm sticking with derby."

We slowed at the play area and circled back toward the stores.

"So, I know working with you on sponsors is off-limits, but can I ask you something about it?"

"Of course."

"I was looking at the list of the Brawlers' sponsors and saw a few non-profits listed. Don't they need the money themselves?" I didn't quite get how giving money to roller derby helped them.

And admittedly, it had felt wrong to cross the digital derby line by poking around on the Brawlers' website for the sponsor list, as if watchdog Lyah lurked in my search engine. But I'd done it so I could compile a list of who not to contact if a group already worked with the Brawlers. Necessary to our end goal.

Unlike the rather unnecessary line I'd crossed sneaking around with Rob, but I didn't need to dwell on that now or ever.

"It's more of an underwriting aspect for smaller non-profit organizations," he said. "It's almost the same thing as sponsorship, but less flashy than a big donor sponsor. It's more like a partnership. The non-profits get advertising when we show off their support. Banners at events, program ads, stuff on our website. We've done service work for community charity events and some fun promotions with local restaurants. Lyah hasn't told you any of this? It's usually a selling point of derby, the community involvement."

"I haven't been at this long. I probably missed that part."

Lyah had said they needed volunteers for everything. But Nina and I had been the only ones to show up at the skate park event. It wouldn't help our image of a struggling team to admit we'd been purely focused on having enough members for the bouts and getting our team to be cohesive.

"It's a lot of work to run a team," Rob responded to my unspoken thoughts. "I'm sure the Tornadoes are busy enough getting off the ground."

"It seems like the sponsors could have split with the two teams, to make it fair."

Rob stopped walking. "Fair to who? The sponsors, or to Lyah?"

"Fair for the rest of us trying to build a team. Not everything is about her."

"The sponsors contracted with the Brawlers. They had no obligation to specific skaters. It's just business."

We were treading into territory that ruined the nice kissing vibe we'd had earlier. "No more skating talk."

"You're right, we didn't come here to talk about skating." He slid his hand into my hair at the back of my neck. The look he settled over me turned my knee joints to foam. He kissed me, sweet and deliberate and taking his time.

"Oh, look at that young couple," a woman said from behind us.

I pulled back from Rob, my cheeks instantly heating as I spied the gray-haired woman.

"I remember when I couldn't keep my hands off my man," her friend quipped, knowing we could hear her.

I covered my mouth with my hand. That could have been my own grandma watching me make out.

"She's worth it," he called over to the women.

They loved that and collapsed into giggles.

After the ladies moved on, I ran my hand along Rob's forearm up to his shoulder. "You're *very* charming."

"To the over-sixty crowd? Yes. Yes, I am."

"To me, too. Though, I'm thinking we should find a less public place to, you know." I was tired of walking past the same stores and didn't feel like shopping. "But like, not to do anything seedy."

He caught me wincing at my own comment. "No seeds, got it. Obviously, my house is out."

Because of Meg. "Does your sister live at home with you and your parents?"

"No, she has her own place. My parents, they'll put it together you're on the other team—"

I put my hand up to stop him. "Understood." Being a secret meant keeping us from his family too. A layer I hadn't given much thought to. More like any thought. "My house is open, but my mom is probably home. Which is fine, but she likes to ask questions and she'll have several dozen if you walk in the door."

He held up a hand, mirroring my earlier gesture. "Let's keep parents out of the mix for now. There are plenty of back alleys where we can make out."

"I said nothing seedy."

"How about a well-lit alley, then." His eyes glinted in amusement.

I gave him a quick peck on the nose. Our only audience at the moment were unseeing eyes from stuffed animals in a gift shop window.

"I like the idea of connecting with the community. Maybe looking for sponsors will spark more ideas. We should put together more places to visit."

"And we'll make out there?"

I shoved him.

"I see we've moved on from the kissing part of the conversation."

I tried another shove, but let myself get held in his embrace when he caught me. "I was thinking about ways to be together that don't involve skating or our families that could also benefit my search for purpose in my life, was all."

"A simple task."

"Is anything worthwhile simple?"

He thought on that and kissed me on my forehead. "Some things are."

Chapter Seventeen

♥

At derby practice that week, our two teams passed like ships in the night, with no acknowledgment we knew each other. Rob wasn't on shift for our practice, but he was of course at the rink with Brawlers to coach them.

Seeing him sent an immediate thrill through me. No one here knew we'd spent time together outside these walls. Our contact was...forbidden.

There was something dangerous and exciting about our secret. Right now, the secret felt welcome. It was fully my own, and something I'd built up apart from the team.

I hadn't heard anyone mention seeing Rob working at the rink. Other than Barb, they must not have known. I couldn't think about that too hard. It wasn't like it was my job to tell everybody who the roller rink employed.

Sometimes my brain created problems that didn't need solving.

After wrapping up practice, Lyah gathered us together for final words. The clock inched toward midnight and a yawn escaped several of us. These late nights were no joke after a full day working.

"Anything new with team sponsors?" Lyah asked.

It took longer than it should have to realize she was directing this question at me. I scanned my teammates' faces, all of whom were now looking at me along with Lyah. "Oh, uh, not yet."

I'd gotten as far as making a list of who not to contact—the Brawlers' sponsors—and...that was it. I'd actually been proud I'd started, though I hadn't made it any further. The rest of the week I'd been working or skating with Rob. And kissing Rob.

Barb fluttered a hand in the air. "I was supposed to help you with that, wasn't I? That's on me. We'll connect, Devil Mae. I'll call you this week."

Barb to the rescue.

I couldn't help feeling like I let Lyah and the team down. I'd offered to help and had sort of forgotten the part where I needed to contact the businesses.

Our next bout was on home turf and not for another two weeks. Plenty of time to get going on the other team activities.

After being dismissed for the night, I caught up with Barb. "Thanks for saving me back there. I totally forgot to get going on the sponsors."

She slowed and pulled me aside as the rest of the team fanned out to their cars in the lot. She waited until we were out of earshot to speak. "I'm sorry you were tasked with something that should be reserved for a senior member of the team. Please do not apologize. The sponsor work was dumped on you unfairly."

"No, I volunteered. I told Lyah I would help. I guess I don't know where to start."

"All of which you should not have had to do. Chelsea Mae, you do not need to bend over sideways to be part of this team."

"I'm not bending—I offered. I want to do this."

She glanced past me and took a measured breath. "Typically, we do an in-person visit with our press kit. We don't have any new ones for the Tornadoes. The team is broke, so I'll cover the cost of copies and folders. It's not much, but it's work. I'd love a helper."

My skin bristled at her use of helper. I was eighteen, not one of her elementary school-aged kids. "I appreciate your assistance, but I want to do this. I'd like your help, but as an equal. Not a helper."

Barb's mouth formed a small O, and then she shut it. A smile formed. "I apologize. I didn't want you taking on more than you felt was fair, especially if you were doing this to impress Lyah."

I *did* think it would impress Lyah and didn't mind doing so. I also wanted some responsibility to take on. "What day are you free?"

She dug into her purse. "Honey, right now I'm nearly sleepwalking. I'll have to raincheck you on a day and time. I'll text you in the morning."

Knowing Barb, her text would come while I was still asleep.

"Oh, and before I forget," she said. "I know you're dating Rob."

My chest tightened. My secret, my forbidden little personal thing I had just for myself, wasn't so secret after all. I should have known Barb would sniff us out after having seen us talking at the rink together. Not to mention Nina already had suspicions after the skate park event. "Are you going to tell her?"

We both knew who I meant.

"I'm sorry. I didn't mean to sound threatening. No, I'm not telling. I don't judge who anybody spends their time with. I'm so tired, I'm rambling. I wanted you to know that I know, but I'm not fixin' to blab it."

"I don't like lying about us being together, but we agreed it was best not to say anything. For now."

A small smile appeared. "He's a sweet guy. I like him for you."

Barb had to know he worked at the rink. "Does Lyah know he works here?"

She pursed her lips. "Probably not. She's a big girl and can find out herself."

Lyah would uncover that Rob worked at the rink sooner rather than later. I was surprised she hadn't seen him working there already. The longer she didn't know, the more sinister it seemed.

And us? Well, that was a secret I'd need to work a little harder at keeping.

Sure enough, the next morning Barb messaged about working on the sponsors. Only she wasn't available to meet for a couple days.

I had the day off and itched to get started. We only had two weeks before the home event. It would be great to bring a few businesses on our side to get momentum going. I could make initial contacts and maybe follow up when Barb was available later in the week.

She texted she was off to an appointment for the morning.

I had questions, so I texted Rob.

Me: *Do you prepare an elevator pitch for the sponsors?*

Rob: *What's this about elevators? It's not even eight in the morning*

Me: *You responded so...*

Rob: *I heard my phone buzz and it woke me up*

Me: *Lies. I sleep through text notifications all the time. You're up and ready to roll.*

Rob: *Okay fine, I'm not asleep. But not ready to roll. What's an elevator pitch?*

Me: *I looked up how to do a sales pitch. A website said practice a pitch that takes as long as an elevator ride.*

Rob: *In a four-story building or the Empire State Building?*

Rob: *You've got a lot more time in an elevator if you're in a skyscraper.*

Why did I text him? Useless.

I began a list of potential sponsors by bookmarking different vendors' website contact forms. I looked up the Detroit Hawt Rodders' derby site and noted their sponsors, looking for more ideas of similar businesses we could reach out to.

My phone buzzed.

Rob: *I have coffee now. Do you need help making contacts?*

Me: *But it's a conflict of interest for you to help us.*

Rob: *Hey, you contacted me. Also, I don't care?*

Me: *You ended that with a question mark. Do you care?*

Rob: *I care about you. I care about the teams. Both teams.*

Something I couldn't put my finger on finally broke free. Rob did care. It was super obvious. Yet he bent over backward to protect his sister—protecting the division of the teams.

The way we danced around our captains and kept certain information from them, that protected the division too. It kept the two teams apart. *We* kept the teams apart.

Me: *I care about the team too. We only need sponsors because we're on our own. We don't even have a website up and running. What do I show the sponsors?*

Rob: *We can do this. Let me come over.*

Me: *To my house?*

I tugged my blanket to my chin, as if he'd walk through my bedroom door any second.

Rob: *We could meet on the street if you prefer.*

Me: *No, it's fine.*

His family was the true conflict. They couldn't see me, but my parents, they knew nothing. Which kind of made me sad. I didn't like keeping my life from them. I wasn't ashamed of what I was doing. Roller derby gave me a sense of belonging and purpose and I was actively working on job and career ideas. I had a guy who cared about me and supported me.

Not telling them about my life had felt reasonable at first. I was only trying to protect them from having a strong reaction to my decision not to move with them. My excuse wouldn't last much longer.

I needed to face them and face the changes I was making.

Rob planned to meet here in an hour. I showered, dressed, and toasted English muffins—one spread with peanut butter, the other with jam.

I peeked into Dad's office off the family room. Empty. He must have gone into the company office today. Mom gone too.

No one home meant our secret was safe another day. So what if that made me relax a little? It wouldn't be a secret forever.

The doorbell rang. Chucky B went nuts barking.

I opened the front door. I held the dog back from jumping at him. "I keep telling my parents to put tape over the doorbell. The cats run away and Chucky B can't handle it. Most people know to knock." I shook my head at myself. "Sorry, come in."

"Next time, would you prefer the derby megaphone?"

I rolled my eyes, but internally laughed at the visual. I quickly scanned behind him to check for lookie-loos in the neighborhood who might report back to the parentals. No one spotted. I nudged him inside and shut the door.

He shifted uneasily in the entryway. "Why are you looking at me like that?"

"Like what?" I was nervous. About having him here, about...a lot of things.

"Can I kiss you?"

Now that would make things a whole lot better.

My nerves instantly eased as I closed the distance between us. His lips were welcoming, unlike how I'd been to him just now. I deepened the pressure and flicked my tongue against his.

He responded with a small groan and kissed me more deeply.

Chucky B barked. A nip came at my leg.

I herded the dog back with my leg, slowly pushing him away from us as we kept kissing.

Rob pulled back, a little breathless. He looked at the dog. "See? She likes me. No need to yell."

Chucky B chuffed and sniffed Rob's pants.

"So, you're here to help me with the sponsor list," I said in an attempt to clear my head from the emotional rush of kissing him. "I'll get my laptop."

"Hold up." He ran his hand along the underside of my arm, sending shivers through me. "I think we should hit the road. Pound the pavement. See folks in person."

"What if people see us together?"

"I assume you mean people from the team. We can say we ran into each other."

"Seems suspicious."

"Well, that's not our problem if they're following us now, is it? Come on—there's not telling my sister and Lyah and there's not going anywhere in public out of fear we'll be found out. Different."

Then there was the little matter of the oath I'd taken.

Then again, Rob was offering assistance to help the team. Looking for sponsors placed the team as a priority. What was the real problem here?

After a last peck on his cheek, I opened the front door. "Let's do this."

We took off in his car and brainstormed as he drove. "My mom volunteers a million places, so I can ask her for some potential leads tonight. At dinner." That was it. I would throw a dinner for the family like they'd done for me and tell them all about roller derby and my in-progress plans. "I saw one of the other teams has a physical therapy clinic as a sponsor. There's one of those in a strip mall by the Costco."

"Would this be a double duty visit? Are you interested in helping people therapeutically by physically being...um, what does a physical therapist do?"

"They handle sports injuries."

"Oh. Sure. I thought it was called sports medicine."

"Maybe it's the same thing?" I shrugged as he turned on the road where the big box stores lived. Surely, a bounty of potential sponsors. "I thought you'd know about sports therapy and stuff being a coach."

"I'm not a real coach. You know that, right?"

I twisted in the seat to look at him full-on. "What do you mean? You're coaching the team."

"I'm a college sophomore whose sister is the team captain. I'm available and I like roller derby. Those are my qualifications." His knuckles tightened against the wheel.

"Did something happen? You seem agitated."

He blew out a breath. "My folks are on me about job stuff. They want me to quit working at the rink. My dad thinks it's a joke."

"I thought they were supportive of derby."

"For my sister, but because it's a hobby. She doesn't live with us so they don't see how she's obsessing over the team. They think I'm the one who is obsessed. As Dad said, the Brawlers don't even allow guys on the team. He thinks I'm wasting my time."

"It's good experience if you want to coach for schools when you become a teacher."

A thin smile appeared. "You're really on this teacher thing, aren't you?" His smile was short-lived.

"You'd be good at it."

He grew quiet again. I let the silence sit since he did that for me sometimes. He gave me room to think.

"I sort of got in a fight with my dad." He shrugged up one shoulder. "He implied I needed my own life and friends and not to mooch off my sister. He was totally out of line. It's like he can't even appreciate I did exactly what they asked by going to U of M like he and Mom did. I never cause trouble for them. They still manage to find something wrong to fix."

He turned into the lot for the physical therapy offices and shut off the car. "Sorry to unload."

"I asked. And I'm sorry they're putting pressure on you. If you're happy doing derby, you should keep doing it."

"Thanks."

We walked together toward the offices. I stopped short. "What do we say? Barb said the team used to have folders and materials. We don't have any of that. They have a Facebook page."

Rob removed a flyer from a folder he carried which I hadn't noticed. "I found a handful of Tornadoes' flyers on our table at the skate park event. Probably some people dropped them on our table."

Yeah, when they'd seen all their free stuff and shiny merch. And the DJ. I should have thought to bring our extra flyers. Rob had me all flustered back at the house so I hadn't been thinking straight. "We'll give it a shot."

"I'll play like I'm coaching your team and you can follow my lead. Any contact information you give them for follow-up should be yours."

With a game plan set, we headed inside.

Ten minutes later, we left the office. "That wasn't so bad," I said to Rob, now back in his car.

We'd waited by the front desk until a manager came to talk with us. She'd been interested in the idea of roller derby, having gone to a Brawler's bout a few years back. What she hadn't known was that Ginsburg had two teams. We had a lot of work to do promoting the new team. This was a start and the offices had interest in sponsoring an upcoming event. She said she'd talk to her management team and get back to me.

Score!

My other ideas were an auto body shop where one of Elena's Go Zone coworkers worked, and the family-owned sports equipment place where I'd picked up my derby gear. We hit up both places, leaving our remaining two flyers, and then stopped at a fast food Greek-style restaurant for lunch.

"I've got to head to the rink," Rob said after finishing our lunch. "Good doing business with you. Shall I take you home?"

His formal way of asking made me smile. "Thanks for doing this with me today. I know it's awkward because of the team split."

He gave me a look tinged with guilt. "That fight with my dad really got to me. Helping you feels like I'm doing something worthwhile. I kind of felt like I needed to prove to myself—and to him too—this matters. I know you'll take what we did today and run with it. Just like you're doing with derby. I can teach you and then, well, then you won't really need me."

He opened the passenger door and waited for me to get in. I paused, holding the door frame. "I like having your help. I do need you right now."

"For now. But you won't for long."

He didn't say this in an oh-pity-me kind of way. He said it as a fact. "When I don't need you for derby stuff, maybe I'll need you for other things. Or just want you around."

Like a boyfriend.

We hadn't made anything official and it felt like time. "Will you be my boyfriend, Rob?"

He stood back as his face cycled through expressions. "I am so glad you asked. Yes. Yes, I will be your boyfriend."

I found his hand and pulled him in. "I suddenly find I'm in *desperate* need of a kiss."

His breath came quick and he searched my face, looking deeply into my eyes. "Happy to deliver."

Chapter Eighteen

♥

Rob dropped me off at home. I felt light on my feet as I sailed through the house. I had a *boyfriend*.

And I'd asked him myself. I loved the feeling. Deciding something felt so good and well, decisive.

Like how I'd decided I wasn't moving with my parents. And how I'd decided it was finally time to break the news to them tonight.

I was ready now. It finally clicked. I didn't need to know every single step in the path of my future. I had the workings of a plan to go out on my own. I had a team who counted on me, and now a boyfriend. Potential career options in the works. Even if those were sketchy, I could at least find a job.

Piece of cake. In fact, maybe I'd even be *baking* cake in a real bakery.

On to dinner. We didn't have lasagna noodles in the pantry, but been there, done that. I rummaged through the freezer until I came up with frozen chicken I could air fry and a package of deluxe mixed vegetables. Leftover rice in the fridge could serve as a second side. And a lone box of brownie mix for dessert. Perfect.

I texted Mom and Dad in our group chat I was making dinner and it would be ready whenever they thought they'd be home.

I couldn't help notice parts of the kitchen had been packed up. The usual row of cookbooks on the open shelf near the stove had been replaced by a simple stack of white dishes. The counters had been cleared of everything except for white ceramic canisters we usually kept in the pantry. The toaster was shuttered away, the air fryer stowed in a lower cabinet. No dish drying rack.

House showings would happen soon. My parents were only waiting on a repair to broken tile in the guest bathroom before listing the house, from what I last remembered.

Mom excitedly texted back she'd love to have a family dinner. Dad said the office might keep him late because he was wrapping up work before his move to the Traverse City office. I'd been so focused on my own stuff, I hadn't kept the days straight. This was his last week working in Ginsburg.

Me: *Call it a celebratory dinner, in your honor.*

Dad: *Well, then, I better get moving!*

After all, this was Dad's big move. He just didn't know I wouldn't be part of it.

Based on my parents' ETA, I got to cooking. I was almost successful at having dinner ready when they walked through the door. The chicken wasn't done and the vegetables and rice had to go back into the microwave since I'd put them in too early and now they were cold.

Tonight's meal was great practice, since I'd be doing this most nights on my own. I'd have to learn to cook or I'd be living that frozen box pizza life. Hopefully, I could convince my folks to offload their air fryer as a parting gift.

Dad came in through the garage. "Hey, kid. Let me do one quick thing in my office, and then I'll be fully present for dinner."

Mom followed shortly after. "What a wonderful, sweet idea, Chels." She set down her purse and hugged me. "Thank you for thinking of us and getting dinner ready. It's been so hectic prepping the house for showings tomorrow."

"Tomorrow?" Eek, that was news. "I thought the bathroom tile needed fixing."

"The tile was done on Tuesday. See? We've truly outgrown this house if you haven't had time to look at the guest bath."

I hadn't been home much. And I hadn't packed a single thing.

"Speaking of the showings, I straightened up your room, but I really want you to pack up your desk and move those plastic bins by your bed. At least stow them in the closet."

I vaguely recalled her asking me to do those things, but I'd sort of had a light ear toward any home selling-related conversations. It had been easier to avoid that discussion entirely.

Which, okay, not ideal or great. But tonight was my night to set it all straight.

I'd assumed the dining room and dining table would still be loaded with boxes, but a quick peek showed it nearly sparkling. Only the table, chairs, and a furniture piece holding decorative dishware remained. Had I bothered to check, I'd have known the house showings were even closer than I'd realized.

"Did I miss that the house is listed for sale?" No for sale sign yet in front of the house.

"This is a pre-showing tomorrow," Mom answered. "Our agent is bringing in select clients first. The listing will go up shortly after. We may get lucky and have a buyer right away."

My throat dried up at the thought of strangers in our house. I couldn't wrap my brain around people with their own furniture and food having their dinner in this spot where we sat. Only it wouldn't be our home anymore.

"I told you this already, don't you remember?" Mom was saying.

I sat down and waved Dad over, who was now puttering around in the family room.

"Sorry, I'm looking for the wireless mouse I bought." He flashed me a grin as he looked over the food. "What a treat. Thanks for feeding us."

It was pretty simple food, but they were genuinely grateful, which made me smile. The truth was, I'd been ignoring my parents the past few weeks because it'd been more convenient. They'd been busy, and I'd taken advantage of that.

"This chicken is delicious, Chels." Mom made an exaggerated *mmm* sound, which was probably overkill for what I'd made.

As they ate, they chattered about their day, instantly filling any silence.

I couldn't take a single bite.

I folded my hands and placed them on the table. Awkward. I slid my hands to my sides and then sat on them. Nothing felt right. "So," I started. "We've all been busy the past few weeks."

"Can you believe the dryer had the nerve to go on the fritz?" Mom said to Dad across the small table. "I think the vent cleaning cleared the issue, but I'm concerned."

I tried a new angle. "I've been working a lot and making plans."

Dad pulled out his phone. "Deb is texting from the Traverse office. Let me respond to this one thing."

I really needed to get this out. Dad finished his text and set his phone facedown on the table. "How's the water park going?"

"It's fine. But what I'm really excited about is—" I took a breath and gathered my courage. "I joined roller derby. The Tornadoes. I've been skating with the team and we had our first competition last weekend."

"The roller thing in the corn town?" Dad squinted as he worked through his thoughts. "Didn't that rink get hit in the storm?"

"It did. We're at the Ginsburg rink now."

"Did you say the Tornadoes? The Tornadoes' rink got hit by a tornado?"

Dad was weeks late on the joke. "Yes. There are two roller derby teams in Ginsburg. The teams split and I joined the team who needed an extra skater. Both practice in Ginsburg, so I've been skating on off days from work."

Mom hovered her fork above her plate. "So, the skaters needed a fill-in for a few weeks? They know you're moving, don't they?"

I swallowed. "About that. I...I'd like to stay here. In Ginsburg."

My ears rang from the hollow silence.

"Chels..." Mom trailed off.

"We'll have a great room set up for you, kid," said Dad. "It's a big change, we understand, but we're moving as a family."

He said this as if to assure me. To soothe me. Like he always had when I'd expressed doubts. But these weren't doubts. I had to do this. I had to or I was a failure.

"You can take the time you need and if it suits you, enroll in community college in Traverse," Mom explained in her calming tone. "It's beautiful up there. And so many young people in the summer who work the tourist season. Then winter is ski season. You're going to love it."

I clenched my hands on the chair seat. "I decided I'd like to stay here. I'm going to find another job after the Wild Adventure season ends. I'll probably get a roommate. I'm sure rent will be easier when I split it with someone."

My parents shot panicked looks to each other.

"That's a nice, forward-thinking offer, honey," Dad said. "But you don't have to do any of that. You're not a burden on us."

"I need to do this."

Mom's expression was equal parts shocked and pitying. "But it's you, Chels. You're not ready. You told us yourself you weren't prepared to move out."

"What I said was I didn't want to go to college." I spoke in measured beats. "And I'm still not ready to go. I want to live and work here. In Ginsburg."

"No, Chels, you're not ready." Mom shook her head. "I'd ask Aunt Kate to take you in, but the boys are already a handful."

"I can do this," I said, with more force. "I'm already looking into what I want to do long term. I visited a bakery—I could work there. I'd learn baking skills and business skills—"

"A bakery?" Mom blinked. "Other than raiding the pantry for snacks, I've never seen you take an interest in the kitchen. You always escape outside with your cousins when we're cooking with the family."

Ugh, she wasn't seeing the bigger picture. "It's just an example. It doesn't have to literally be the bakery. Just something where I learn a skill and work toward a career. The point is, I want to make a go of it here. I have the derby team now, and they're counting on me."

Mom sniffed the air. "Is something burning?"

Crap. I flew up, nearly knocking over my chair. I whipped open the oven. The brownies blackened at the edges. "The timer didn't go off."

I set the pan on the stovetop and shut off the oven. The brownies were salvageable. They sure didn't make my case for a baking career.

I returned to the table without making eye contact with my parents. To their credit, they said nothing of the semi-burnt brownies.

"You can't have been on this team for more than a few weeks," Dad said. "You'll need to break it to them you have other commitments."

"But I don't have other commitments." They weren't nearly as receptive to my plans as I'd expected. "I need to start somewhere with being on my own. If I don't, I'll fall into the same pattern of letting you both take care of me. I'll never move forward."

Mom moved a gentle hand toward me. "There's no rush—"

I jerked back. "Yes, there is. The house could sell this week. Even if it takes longer for the deal to go through, it's *going to happen*. And soon. You're the ones who rushed this." My breathing came quickly now. I was losing control. Losing my confidence.

"This is exactly what we mean." Dad, with both elbows on the table, was total focus right now. Total focus on me. "You're not thinking through what it takes to live on your own. How will you furnish your apartment? Who will be your roommate? Will you have first and last month's rent? Renter's insurance?"

This was what I'd been dreading. I hadn't prepared nearly enough. "I will figure it out. I promise."

Now Mom and Dad exchanged concerned, telepathic communication.

"We just don't think—"

"I have a boyfriend," I blurted, cutting Mom off.

Dad's face shifted from mildly ruddy to ripened tomato. "You will *not* live with a boyfriend."

"No—that's not what I meant. He's in college and going back in the fall."

"*You have a boyfriend and he's in college?*" Mom enunciated each word with critical emphasis. "And just how long has this boyfriend been around and where does he go to college?"

I refrained from letting my head fall into my hands. "He's an incoming second year student at University of Michigan. He lives in a dorm. I don't have plans to live with him. We've only been dating since around the time I joined derby. He does derby too."

"There are roller guys?" Dad asked.

"He coaches— Look, I get this is a lot to take in, but it's important for me to make my own decisions. I don't want to be swept away with you and let you decide everything for me."

"We're doing this to help you." Mom's voice caught on the last word. Hurt had clearly crept in.

"I know. And I appreciate it so much. When you told me Dad passed up a job opportunity to not disrupt my senior year, I realized what you sacrificed for me. I want to repay you. You should live your life and not worry about making decisions for me."

Mom pushed food around on her plate.

Dad, on the other hand, still had the tomato effect going on with his face. "We're making decisions for you because we're your parents. It's our job to help you grow into an adult."

"So let me. Let me grow."

Dad shook his head. "You couldn't answer my simple questions about the apartment. So far everything you've shown us this year proves you're not ready."

A rival team's jammer couldn't have knocked the wind out of me like what Dad said. He saw me as not simply his child, but *a* child. I was a kid who wasn't capable of becoming an adult without heavy doses of handholding. They were going to hold my hand all the way across the state.

"I'm eighteen," I said with barely any fight left.

Mom looked up from her plate. "It's only a number, Chels. It doesn't mean you're ready."

I hadn't eaten a single thing and knew I couldn't stomach the dinner I'd made. Any confidence I'd had was shredded. My parents weren't simply upset by my decision, they didn't believe in me. I couldn't remember a time when they didn't have my back.

For the first time, I was truly on my own.

Chapter Nineteen

♥

I closed my bedroom door, having abandoned my dinner and excusing myself to what I'd hoped was the comfort of my room. For once in my life, my bedroom didn't offer the solace I needed. All I could see were belongings to pack. Mere steps away downstairs, my parents didn't believe I could make it on my own.

The tears came. One by one, I removed school awards and participation trophies from my desk shelf. Folders from classes long finished went into a box, along with Funko Pop figurines. Photos of me and my friends in cute frames. Everything that fit into the first available box, I packed away. I slid the low box beneath my bed. Out of sight, just like that.

Digger the cat crawled out from under the bed. He blinked at me, back fur ruffled, seemingly perturbed I'd invaded his space.

"I hear ya, buddy."

I filled the next box and the next until any personality from my room had been removed. Only books remained on the bookshelves and a framed art print of Paris above my bed.

I waited for the anger to surface. My parents didn't believe in me.

But how could I be angry when Dad completely called me out for being unprepared? He was right. Who cared about a potential career at a bakery if I couldn't even manage a brownie mix without burning it. I hadn't had a clue about renters needing special insurance. How much did that even cost?

Maybe it was useless to fight them. It might not be so bad living there. I'd figure something out.

My phone vibrated on my desk. I grabbed it, finding a photo on the screen of Elena and Jonah sitting on a log at a campsite. One of her legs was swung over Jonah's and her wide smile nearly split her face in half. Happy and goofy in love.

Elena: *Postcards from the great wilderness! I have a minute if you're free to talk.*

It was as if she knew I needed her. I pressed the green call button, but the line rang and rang with no answer. It didn't click over to voice mail. I tried again and immediately got her voice mail.

Instead of leaving a message, I texted. *Looks like you're having fun. Are you still free?*

No response. Probably her cell phone reception was bad in the woods, wherever she was.

More tears came. Elena looked so happy. Like how I'd felt hours ago, with my brand-new boyfriend and what I'd thought was a life plan.

Was this what life would be like in the fall? I'd be here in Ginsburg, but Elena had college and a boyfriend as her focus. Sure seemed like this was what life would look like. Missed messages and bad connections.

The derby team promised to be there for us when we needed. My finger hesitated over my contacts list. Taylor, Nina, Barb...they were all older with their own busy lives. None of them lived with their parents. Barb *was* a parent. Would any of them understand what I was feeling right now?

I scrolled through my texts to Rob's name—no longer listed as Skater1 in my contacts.

I texted him.

Me: *I told my parents I wasn't moving with them. Did not go well.*

His response came right away.

Rob: *Oh no. What did they say?*

My face crumbled as the crying started up again. I couldn't get myself out of this funk to even explain it in a text.

Me: *I need to see you.*

Rob answered my text within a minute.

Rob: *Can you get to the rink? I can take a break.*

I left without a word to my parents. Okay, I caved and sent a text before I left the driveway. I told them I was going to see a friend at the skating rink. But I didn't wait for their reply. *I'll show you independent.*

I drove downtown and parked at the rink. Before I could get out of the car, Rob headed toward me across the parking lot.

The mere sight of him sent relief pulses through my veins.

He slid into the passenger seat, his cheeks flushed, employee name badge askew. His presence filled my small car like an unfurled blanket. For a second, I forgot what drove me here. Well, *I'd* driven here, but the *reason* I'd driven here. For a second, it was just us, together, away from my stresses.

"Are you okay?" His question came nearly out of breath.

My lip trembled. "It's good to see you."

He took my hand. "Good to see you too."

I choked out my sad story. I felt like the biggest bummer who'd ever bummed. My words came out waterlogged with emotion. So many conflicting feelings were stuffed inside me I didn't know how to let them free.

"I'm sorry," he said.

None of it was his fault, but he meant he was sorry for what I felt. The confusion and blocked-up sensation I couldn't quite get past.

"I feel so...dumb," I admitted.

He squeezed my hand. The silence in the car grew louder.

I glanced at him. "Aren't you going to convince me I'm not dumb?"

"We both know you're not dumb. Besides, you said you *feel* dumb. That's totally different. You're allowed to feel dumb."

I picked at the leather steering wheel. "But I hate it."

"How about this. Think of a time you felt even dumber and see if this is worse."

"Like when I wore the clown wig and roller danced?"

"See? That has to be a dumber feeling than now. There's a reason for that to feel dumb. What's your reason for feeling it now?"

"I guess because my parents are moving on and I can't. I tried to come up with a plan, but my plans are more like half-baked ideas. No pun intended on the baked part. Because it did not go over well telling them I might want to work in a bakery." Reluctantly, I mentioned the burned brownies.

"You expected this. It's why you stalled on telling them. It's why you wanted to research first. You were right they would doubt you."

Only I hadn't wanted to believe it. "I've never had them not be on my side. About anything. Even failing to apply to colleges, they understood. They didn't like the lying about it part."

Should have seen that coming. Secrets never led to anything good.

I continued. "Even though I knew they wouldn't like the idea of me staying, to hear them tell me they know me better than I know myself, and I can't do it, it makes me feel like such a loser."

"I'm sure they don't think that."

I wasn't sure what they thought, other than they didn't trust me to live here on my own.

"There was a time when my parents separated." Rob ran a finger along his name badge and traced the plastic edge back and forth. "I was eleven. I didn't understand what was happening. My dad moved out. It was probably only for a few months, but it felt like a year. I was so...mad but couldn't put the feeling into words. I remember I'd stomp around the house. I'd slam doors and throw things because it felt good. I'd get yelled at, but I stopped caring. Meg, she barely talked to me."

"We ended up in family counseling," he went on. "I hated it but only at first. Our counselor was a guy, and he was funny. He was the first adult to talk to me like a real person, not like I was a little kid. I guess I connected with him somehow in a way I didn't expect. I saw him a few times where it was only the two of us. The other times were with my parents and sister. It was weird and uncomfortable, but you know what? Dad moved back in. Things were different after once we got through it all—a good kind of different. There were ways our family functioned I hadn't realized were a problem until everything blew up and we had to put ourselves back together."

"Wow, I'm sorry you went through so much. I can't imagine what it's like to have your family hurting like that."

He touched my face along my chin. "I'm only telling you this because the helpless feeling, it's happened to me before. When your family isn't stable, it affects everything."

He trailed his hand from my face to my neck, resting it there, sending warm waves through my shoulder.

"The thing is," I said, "my dad is jazzed about his new job. He's been kind of miserable the past few years. He only stuck around at his current job because of me."

"The move is good for him. For them. But not necessarily for you."

"I don't fit with their plans." My breath came shallow at my own words. That was what I couldn't find the shape of in my thoughts. "I'm an afterthought. I'm the daughter who can't leave the nest. They expect me to move with them because they don't believe I can find my way on my own."

He squeezed my hand again.

"I think I was riding a fake-out high because of us—er, you," I said. "The boyfriend stuff. Because you're awesome." I was a blubbery mess of emotion right now. Me trying to be sweet and failing did not improve my mood.

"Always glad to be awesome. Look, you'll figure this out. A more solid plan for the apartment might help since your dad was complaining about that. You could ask around at work if anyone is looking for a roommate. Hit up any friends you know who are staying local and ask them. Not everybody goes off to college. A few guys I graduated with rented a big old house together in downtown Ginsburg. Two of them commuted to classes and the other guy worked a construction job. They throw parties during all the college breaks so it was like a little reunion when we all came home. You've barely scratched the surface."

His hope drove my sadness deeper. Finding a roommate and researching apartment leases should excite me. All of it sounded so freaking *difficult*. There was so much I didn't know. I couldn't wrap my head around where to start.

And if I couldn't even start, well, that spelled it out loud and clear: FAILURE.

"I forgot to mention," I told him. "There's an early house showing tomorrow, so I need to be gone."

"What time?"

"No idea. Probably early."

"Up for a morning skate?"

I smiled, picturing us arriving to the skate park at sunrise. "That doesn't sound half bad."

"I'll ignore the half part and call it a win. Let's plan for tomorrow at as early as you're willing to get there, as long as it's not before seven."

"Okay. Eight in the morning should be good."

"Eight o'clock it is." He punctuated his statement with a kiss. "And Chelsea?"

My skin tingled hearing him say my name. "Yeah?"

"I believe in you."

Chapter Twenty

♥

The week stuttered by. I avoided being home as much as possible. Mom kept me updated with the house showing schedule, making it easy to avoid being there. Strangers tromping through our house was reason enough to stay away. I refreshed my bag of extra clothes in my car and threw in my make-up bag and a toothbrush and toothpaste just in case.

Work, skating, Rob, and avoiding my folks. My new normal.

The team became my driving purpose. I called a few new potential sponsors to get another round going. I'd follow up with the others over email next week.

By the time Saturday rolled around, I was eager for our home bout against Lansing's Capitol Rollers. My first home event was a move in the right direction toward putting down deeper roots.

Walking into the rink felt like a comforting hug. Ahead of me, Barb, Nina, and Taylor chatted together in a tight group, like a less intense tri-formation. Seeing them decked out in their derby gear made me smile.

I'd almost invited my parents to come tonight. Force of habit. They always came to my stuff—school play, school assembly, my very short-lived career in a youth soccer league. If these moving shenanigans hadn't been our reality, they'd be here and decked out in team T-shirts.

A pang of hurt hit knowing they wouldn't be here because I hadn't bothered to invite them. Then again, had I invited them, would they have come? They didn't understand why I was doing derby or why I wanted to stay.

I could have showed them. But my head was too messy this week to think straight.

I found myself scanning the crowd looking for them before I shook sense into myself. My gaze landed on Meg. What was she doing here?

Shoot. Lyah better not see her or she'd go nuclear. Where was Lyah?

Taylor approached and hooked her arm into mine. "Hey, Miss Devil. You ready to rumble?"

I turned back to where Meg had been standing, but she was gone.

"Um, yeah." I needed to get out of this funk. It wasn't my job to worry over Lyah and Meg. I was here to skate.

Lyah arrived and rounded up the team. I checked her expression for any hint of awareness she knew her sworn mortal enemy lurked about in this very rink.

"This is going to be real fun," Lyah told us. "The Rollers are a young team—they've only been at this a couple years, so this is an even match-up for us. We've *got* this."

She reviewed pre-game strategies and my excitement for tonight returned.

As Lyah wrapped up her pep talk, the refs skated onto the rink. Music overhead cued up, signaling to the crowd we were getting started.

"Ladies and gentlemen and everyone who's a little of both or none of each, welcome to tonight's derby!"

I spun around at the familiar, amplified voice. *Rob?*

Concrete filled my limbs. Rob. My boyfriend—secret boyfriend—was here. Announcing *our* home bout.

And he hadn't told me.

He glided around the rink wearing a headset microphone. A black bow tie circled his neck above a plain black T-shirt and athletic pants.

Lyah's entire body shot forward at attention. "Who approved *him* to announce?"

"Probably Alma, she runs the place," Barb answered casually. "Now, who's ready to get rollin'?"

"This is a *big deal*," Lyah fired back to Barb. "It's unacceptable. He coaches the other team!"

"The team who isn't playing tonight," Barb reminded.

Lyah scowled. "This isn't happening. I'm pulling him off the rink."

Barb stepped in front of Lyah and placed a cautionary hand at her shoulder. Barb was not a small woman. With her gear on and show curls cascading from her helmet, she stood as a solid block to Lyah's path. "You are our captain. Act like it."

Lyah stiffened, appearing to brace herself for impact. "That's right. I'm the captain. What I say goes. And I say *he can't be here.*"

Lyah pushed past her. Barb tipped her chin up and urged the rest of us toward the rink to warm up. "Come on, folks. The Capitol Rollers have a head start on us."

The other team was already lapping the rink. I moved forward and my eyes landed on Meg again, now sitting with...a bunch of the Brawlers.

Like, a bunch of them. Like, their whole team.

This was not good. This was—

"What are *they* doing here?"

Ah, so Lyah had seen who I'd seen.

"Team captains," a referee called out and gestured for them to skate over.

"Get it together, Lyah," Nina was saying to her.

"I will not. They can't *watch us*."

"Usually, we're begging people to watch us," Queen Bacon grumbled as she squeezed past me.

"Scoot your boot, young recruit." Bonecrusher nudged me at the shoulder to get moving. "We're skating no matter who's watching."

She and Kam were right. I needed to put Lyah's concerns out of my mind or I'd be a mess on the rink.

I now understood an article I'd read on Serena Williams where she talked about the mental game being as crucial as physical training. Even the G.O.A.T. of tennis found mental focus a challenge. Then again, that was Serena Williams on the world stage of tennis, and this was me spazzing out over small-town roller derby.

But Rob—he hadn't told me he was going to be here tonight. We'd talked all week. We'd talked earlier *today*.

I caught Rob's eye as I rounded the rink. *What gives?* I mouthed to him.

He half-shrugged, his expression apologetic.

Think fast. Rob worked here. His boss probably told him he had to do this tonight as a last-minute thing. It wasn't as if a slew of roller derby announcers were just kicking it in Ginsburg waiting for a call.

Still, why hadn't he warned me?

In the center of the rink, Lyah gestured wildly at the refs and pointed at Rob. I couldn't hear what she said, but I could fill in the blanks.

Rob threw up his hands and skated backward to put distance between them. If Lyah hadn't known Rob worked at the rink, she knew now.

A ref blew her whistle. At Lyah.

Laughter carried over from the Brawlers. Just great. We were giving them a show, and the wrong kind of show.

"You want the penalty box before the bout begins?" the ref said to Lyah, loud enough for those of us skating past to hear.

Lyah folded her arms. "It's not right and it's not fair."

The ref responded in an even tone. "He's what we've got. The other guy called off. He's got a sick kid."

Nina skated to Lyah and spoke to her, too quiet for me to hear.

"Mama's real mad," Bonecrusher said to me. "She gets so fired up. Let's see if she can channel her anger in the jam."

At least Bonecrusher had the bright side of things in mind. From the looks of it, Rob was in, and Lyah lost her quest to get him kicked off the rink. She stormed out with Nina trailing behind her.

The rest of us warmed up. Half the team murmured to each other, probably about the spectacle our team captain displayed. A bright but forced smile was affixed to Barb's face. Bonecrusher bobbed her head to the overhead music, and Taylor waved to friends in the crowd.

An unsettled sensation formed in my gut. The team was all over the place tonight. Our captain was furious, my secret boyfriend was part of the bout and hadn't told me, and our rivals filled the seats to watch every move.

I forced my racing thoughts to calm as Rob and the refs got the bout started and we readied for the first jam.

Lyah put me in as a blocker. I focused my energy on forming a solid block with Bonecrusher and Queen Bacon while Lyah went in as our jammer. Lyah cut through the Rollers' pack and lapped the other team.

Applause erupted from the crowd as the Tornadoes scored.

Lyah lapped again and scored more points. She was on fire. Bonecrusher had it right—if she channeled her frustration on the rink, we might be in good shape after all.

Lyah came around again, this time stopped by the Capitol Rollers' blockers. She hit hard and their blocking took her down. Cheering came from another part of the crowd.

Lyah hoisted herself up. I watched her connect who was cheering for her take-down. Meg and the Brawlers.

"Roll-ers! Roll-ers!" They chanted and clapped as the Capitol Rollers' jammer lapped and scored.

They were actively rooting for the other team.

"Well, that's rotten," Queen Bacon said from beside me in our block formation.

I grimaced. "Not great team spirit, that's for sure."

Bonecrusher steadied herself next to me, readying for the next jam. "They're not our team anymore. They made their choice."

The momentum the Tornadoes had started with faded fast. The Capitol Rollers rolled right past us, jam after jam, scoring points.

And the Brawlers cheered them on. Loudly.

Lyah grew angrier with each jam. She vented her anger at us during a time-out. Barb fought back, telling her to calm down or get out of the rink.

Standing in our huddle on the sidelines, the team grew quiet as Barb and Lyah faced off. The tension made my stomach hurt.

"You're telling *me* to walk out?" Lyah seethed. "This is *my* team."

"This is *our* team," Barb said with steely calm. "You've forgotten our oath. This team is all of us. You are the one out of control tonight. If you were one of my kids, I'd ground you and lock away your electronic devices."

Lyah's eyes narrowed. "Well, good thing I'm not your kid. Stop trying to parent me." She looked at the rest of us. "Are we gonna win this thing? Or are you going to let the Brawlers intimidate you?"

"Us," Nina said quietly. "You're part of this team and you're letting the Brawlers intimidate you."

Lyah pressed her hand to her forehead. "I don't mean to take out my frustration on all of you. I'm sorry. But tonight, what we're dealing with? It's ridiculous. Boy

Wonder as the announcer and Meg and her brood here to gang up on us? It's too much."

I flinched when she mentioned Rob. Barb made eye contact with me and her expression softened. She shot a stormy look back to Lyah. This wasn't over.

A ref blew their whistle and we reported back to the rink without a plan. Our whole time out hadn't involved any strategizing.

And it cost us. We managed to score a few more times, but in the end, we lost to the Capitol Rollers. I guess it was a good thing my parents hadn't shown up to witness our unfocused skating.

Rob made a hasty exit off the rink. He headed straight to the Brawlers.

What was he doing? He had to know how bad it looked. They'd come here to heckle us, and now he was hanging out with them? Had he even bothered to consider how I'd feel after our loss?

Everyone separated into cliques. Nina and Lyah argued. Barb and Kam spoke with intensity and neither smiled. Bonecrusher, Mary Kiss Kill, and Becky Bruiser huddled together and looked over their shoulders as they spoke. Taylor joined her non-skater friends.

I stood, alone. This did not feel like a team.

Glancing back to the Brawlers, I caught Rob skating toward a door marked Employees Only.

I followed him.

"What was that?" I asked once we were enclosed in the safety of the back room. A heavy rubbery smell assaulted me, along with a crisp note of cleaning supplies. Racks of rental skates took up one wall with storage bins lining the other.

He whipped around. "Chelsea, I'm sorry. I was asked to announce tonight at the last second. The other guy had a family emergency."

"I heard. I mean afterward. You walked right over to them."

He paused to consider my question. "You mean to the Brawlers? They're my team."

It stung to hear it, even though this was the obvious answer and had been the reality the entire time we'd known each other. "They laughed when Lyah fell. They were cheering for the other team."

Rob snapped the bow tie off his neck. "Yeah, I noticed."

"It hurt when they showed up together and cheered against us. How can you be part of that?"

"I wasn't. I was *working*."

"You are a part of it. You're on their team." This was always going to be a problem. I just hadn't wanted to believe it. "I finally felt like I belonged with the Tornadoes. I was beginning to think I had a reason to stay here. And now...I don't know."

Hurt flashed across his face. "The team is your only reason for staying?"

My breath caught. I had to be honest here. "I'm staying because leaving doesn't feel like the right choice."

If he wanted me to admit I would stay for him, well, it was complicated. I couldn't totally separate him from my reasons, but he was loyal to his sister and the Brawlers. As evidence proved tonight.

"Your captain had a very public meltdown on the rink," Rob said. "*She* is the embarrassment."

"She was provoked."

He let out an exasperated huff. "You should reconsider who you're committing to. A team who can't handle any criticism, with a captain who tantrums like a toddler? Scratch that. That's an insult to toddlers. You can do better."

I couldn't dull the shock from his accusation. "What am I supposed to do? Join your team? I couldn't turn on the Tornadoes. It would be a betrayal."

"You've already betrayed them by being with me."

I swallowed. He was right. My allegiance wasn't exactly pledge-worthy.

I'd reasoned with myself that the team shouldn't have a say in who I spent my non-skating time with. Their problems were not my problems. But I also wanted the support the team provided, which required following their rules.

I wanted competing things that didn't work together. Now what?

"I don't know what to do," I admitted.

He moved toward me. "I'm sorry for what happened tonight. It must have been confusing to see me working when I hadn't told you."

A sliver of my tension fell away. "This all sucks, you know? I like what we had."

"We can still have it." He reached for me, tentatively.

I rolled closer—on skates—and took his other hand. I searched his face. Rob had always been truthful with me. He'd only kept things from his family and the team, to protect me. To protect us.

He bent to press his lips against mine. Slow and a little hesitant, but with purpose once I met him with my own lips. His kiss gave me comfort. We could find a way through this.

Rob pulled back as the door swung open behind me with a noisy creak.

"What is this?"

Lyah. As if I needed another complication.

Resigned, I turned to her. "Lyah, please—"

"You're *seeing* him?" She looked between us and scoffed. "You're new so I've given you slack. You said you knew him but not—how long has this been going on?"

A sickly panic welled up. Rob and I had gotten sloppy. We'd been discovered right here at the rink.

She held up a hand. "Never mind—it doesn't matter how long. This ends tonight. No crossing derby lines, so just end it here. You have no idea what his family did to me."

"You mean my sister," Rob cut in. "She's your problem."

"She's definitely a problem."

Rob shook his head. "I've tried and tried to get you two to talk. You've thrown away a friendship and a team. I won't stand by and let you bring Chelsea down. She deserves better than your embarrassing behavior and your nasty grudge against my family."

Rob looked at me. "Don't let Lyah call the shots in your life. You don't owe her anything."

Lyah crossed her arms. "She took an oath."

Okay, I really did not like her talking about me like I wasn't standing right here. Still in my skates fresh off the rink. "Look, I understand the team has been through a lot. I wasn't there to see it all go down, so sure, I'm missing the emotion of it. But Rob is right. You can't tell me who I can be friends with—"

"You kiss your friends like that?"

Okay, fair. "So, maybe we're more than friends. It doesn't have anything to do with the team."

"It has *everything* to do with the team." She moved her hands in the air like she wasn't sure what to do with them. "Our derby oath is about trust. We have each other's backs. They had my back when I was betrayed. When Meg used everything she had against me, they were by my side. We're only strong when we stick together and keep our word. So yes, it definitely matters that you're one of us and dating her brother."

The truth was, I wanted Lyah to like me. To accept me. It was becoming clear she didn't.

"You have to choose," she said. "Him or us."

It came like a punch to the gut.

Rob or derby? The choice wasn't fair. Rob had been there for me when I needed him. The team gave me confidence, new friends, and purpose. "I...I can't."

Rob scowled. "Lyah, this is absurd. You can't control what people do outside the team."

She stood firm, directing her cold glare at me. "You can't have both."

"I don't want to leave the team," I said. "But I'm not breaking up with Rob because you said to."

Her icy stare fragmented. She gathered herself. "Fine. Your indecision is the decision. You're off the team, Chelsea."

Chapter Twenty-One

♥

Kicked off the team. I'd never been kicked out of anything before.

Except for my own house, because my family put it up for sale. But that was different. Sort of.

And here I'd been hanging my hopes on roller derby as my reason not to move with my parents.

Lyah stormed out of the rink's back room in a fury, leaving Rob and I alone together. He held my hand. "I'm sorry."

I had Rob. He'd stood beside me when it mattered. I couldn't believe I'd hesitated to name him as a reason to stay. He'd been a big part of shaping my summer and my plans going forward.

My breath came short looking at the door. "I don't trust her."

"Well, duh."

I yanked Rob's arm to lead him out of the storage room. "I mean I don't trust her *right now*."

Back out in the rink, the Brawlers grouped together on one end, chatting away. The Tornadoes on the other.

They'd chosen their sides with an empty skating floor between the group.

Lyah's back faced us as she talked to the remaining Tornadoes. She turned our way as we approached. I held Rob's hand and stopped in front of them.

"Ah, look. They're here," Lyah announced. "Chelsea has chosen to betray us by hooking up with the enemy. The one major rule we have on this team, she broke. She defied our oath, and because of that, she's off the team."

I faced the Tornadoes with Rob at my side. Their expressions ranged from surprised to confused to hurt.

Nina's lower lip trembled. "You lied to me. At the skate park event. You lied about knowing him. He was your boyfriend this whole time?"

"No doubt she told him all our team business," Lyah said in a grumble.

My defenses instantly activated. "I didn't tell him team business. Nina, I'm sorry about keeping the truth from you. I never meant to hurt you. It was hard to know what to say at the time."

"How about not lying? Did you try that?" Lyah's smug grin indicated she'd recovered from the betrayal part.

I had lied. I knew it hadn't been right. "I'm sorry."

"And guess who messaged our Facebook page today?" Lyah asked, looking around at the group for emphasis. "A physical therapy office following up on the cute couple who came to talk to them about sponsoring roller derby. A guy and a girl couple. So yeah, Rob was made aware of our team business because Chelsea was using him to get sponsor contacts."

I cringed. That did not look well on us.

"Nope." Barb parted through the crowd. "We are not doing this to Chelsea. Our team put her in an impossible position with this silly no crossing derby lines. She asked for help with the sponsors and I was busy with family obligations. A job no new member of the team should have been tasked with in the first place."

"Check yourself, Barbie." Lyah circled the team as she spoke. "Chelsea was a full member of this team and offered to find sponsors."

"Because you intimidated her into it," Barb said. "She's a teenager who looks up to you. And you're acting cruel."

"Who knows what she was planning to do with the sponsors when he was involved." Lyah glared our direction. "For all we know, they were planning to undermine us. Chelsea could be a plant from the other team."

Barb faced off with Lyah again, blocking her from moving forward. "This rivalry is tiring. You don't want me to act like your mother—fine. I won't. If Chelsea's off the team, so am I. Note my official resignation."

Kam shot a hand into the air. "I'm resigning too. I'm so over this pettiness. Derby was supposed to be my fun thing outside of grad school. This isn't fun."

Lyah looked across the team, sputtering. "No one is *resigning*. Chelsea is off the team because she violated our oath. The rest of you stay."

"Having trouble with team commitment?" a voice asked behind us.

Meg sauntered over. Her smarm exceeded critical levels.

Lyah spun to face her. "You must love this. Team destruction is your favorite pastime."

Meg tossed her hair over her shoulder. "It was pretty entertaining to see you fail. Tonight and right now."

More of the Brawlers followed behind Meg. "What's going on?" a White woman asked, wearing a T-shirt reading: *I like to party and by party I mean read books.*

"Lyah's little team experiment is self-imploding," Meg answered. "Skaters are resigning left and right. Aren't they pathetic?"

Instead of laughs and jeers, the Brawlers watched with cautious glances. Murmurs surfaced through their small crowd.

"You can have our cast-offs," Lyah said. "Starting with your brother's girlfriend here."

Meg's brow furrowed as her gaze landed on her brother, then followed the line of his hand to mine. Her mouth parted. "Rob? What is she talking about?"

Lyah took an audible intake of breath. "You didn't know. It's perfect. I'm happy to report: your brother is dating our newest cast-off. I caught them kissing in the back room when they thought no one would catch them."

"Rob," Meg kept her voice low. "How could you do this?"

Then I felt it. Rob's hand slipped from mine.

He threw his hands in front of him. "I'm sorry, Meg. I've done everything else you asked for and—"

"I didn't think I had to *ask* you not to date the other team," she spat back.

"Come on, that's not fair. I even took the job at the rink to support the team and make life easier for you and our practice schedule."

Meg moved in, her voice rising. "Is it true you were helping them with sponsors? What on earth were you doing that for? Why are you helping them?"

"It's not like that," Rob said.

The absence of Rob's touch blared louder than the harsh words hurled in front of me. Rob was scrambling to meet Meg's needs.

Of course he would choose her over me. He'd choose his sister, his blood relation, over the girl he met a few weeks ago. Even when I thought I was close to figuring out my life, everything spun out of control.

I'd refused to choose, but Rob had. He'd chosen loud and clear.

"Meg," the woman in the partying for books T-shirt said. "This is making a lot of us uncomfortable. The rivalry has gone too far."

Meg flinched. "What's too far is cavorting around with the other team. They're the ones who split from us."

"Because you tore into me at my mother's funeral," Lyah yelled.

"Stop." Another woman came forward, Black and wearing hot pink lipstick, and stood between Lyah and Meg. "This anger and this rivalry goes against the spirit of roller derby. We haven't been a united team in months. This stops here. No more."

"What do you mean, no more?" Meg asked incredulously. "I'm the captain."

"Maybe you shouldn't be," another Brawlers skater said.

"Both captains are out of line," a voice spoke up. Nina. She looked terrified. She was now holding Barb's hand. "Lyah, I love you—you're my best friend on and off this team. But you're out of line. Bomber Betty is right. None of this anger reflects the team spirit of roller derby. I've gone along with the rivalry because I wanted to support you, but this—I can't support what this has turned into."

"We've been divided too long," Barb stated, holding onto Nina. "The problem isn't us, it's our captains' refusal to address their grudge against each other, and we've all suffered."

"Agreed, not cool," said Bonecrusher.

The remaining Tornadoes exchanged worried glances, not yet willing to say anything. All but Taylor, who wasn't here at all. She'd probably left with her friends. Lucky Taylor.

"Emergency team vote," Bomber Betty from the Brawlers said. "Hold up your hand if you agree to suspend the current team captain and re-evaluate our team goals."

Hands shot up around the Brawlers. Only a few kept their hands at their sides. Hands went up among the Tornadoes too.

"You can't vote with them." Lyah tugged her faded pink and purple hair out of its ponytail, letting the strands go wild. "This is mutiny!"

I raised my hand, unsure if my vote counted, given I'd been dismissed as a team member. Showing solidarity with those who'd been hurt was more important right now.

One hand wasn't raised that should have been, and it told me everything I needed to know. Rob's.

Chapter Twenty-Two

♥

Outside the rink, rain pelted in solid sheets. I had no idea it had started raining, but the unstable weather fit my mood.

I drove through hard rain, crying the whole way, to Elena's. She was back from her camping trip, but we hadn't had time to catch up in person. Thankfully, she was home, confirmed by text as I parked in front of her house.

She met me at her front door. "You're fast. You must have—oh." She drew me into a hug at the sight of me. "What happened?"

Thunder boomed and she closed the door behind us.

"Everything is a mess."

"I can tell. Your mascara took a trip south on your face."

When my lip crumpled again, she drew me into a second hug. "Sorry! I joke when I'm nervous. And when I'm not. I didn't mean to make light of what's going on." She pulled back. "What *is* going on?"

"Sorry it's so late. I just came from the rink. We lost. And, well, I lost pretty big-time."

"Oh no—doesn't sound good. Come on back."

I ditched my shoes in the foyer and followed her down the hall through the kitchen to their back living room area. The TV was on but no one else was around.

"It's only us," Elena said. "My parents drove my brother to soccer camp and made an overnight of it. Sit down and I'll get you some pop to drink. Tell me *everything*."

I sank into a deep chair and told her my scattered thoughts. How I felt like a loser for my parents not believing in me and how I'd just been kicked off the derby team. Oh, and the boyfriend I'd thought would be there for me sided with his sister, the enemy.

I wasn't sure who my enemies were anymore. Barb had my back and had been texting since I'd left the rink, but I needed space from all of them.

Rob might have been texting too, but I didn't let myself look. Everything felt too overwhelming. I was a walking raw nerve and needed BFF time.

Elena listened until I ran out of words. She relaxed back on the couch across from where I sat. "Is it terrible of me to think it's bad-ace you were kicked out of roller derby? That's legit street cred."

I bit the inside of my cheek. "I don't want that kind of cred. I liked being on the team. I was only getting started."

"Well, phooey." She made a face. "Yeah, that word doesn't work for me. I heard Nando at work say phooey and thought I'd try it out but nope. Anyway, wow, those derby chicks have a lot of emotional baggage. It's probably a good thing you don't have to deal with them anymore. And it sounds like the teams both sort of imploded, so maybe there aren't any teams left to even deal with?" She winced, noting my pained expression. "Okay, maybe I'm not being so helpful."

"I don't know what I was thinking believing Rob would stick by my side. He's going back to school in the fall."

"To U of M, right? It's not far. In fact, it's close." She held her can of pop as she gestured. "But it doesn't matter if he let you down. Boo on him. Boo on all of them! I'm so sorry you've had a rough summer, Chels. I haven't been around much to help you through it."

True, she hadn't. I'd been bummed but that was reality. Life would only grow busier for her once she moved on campus and started classes. Plus, with Jonah at a different college, her weekends would book up spending time with him. Just as they already had.

I couldn't hold onto to what we had because it had already shifted. I kept getting reminders of this very thing, but couldn't seem to accept my new reality.

"All the things I thought I had going for me, aren't going for me at all," I admitted. "Rob didn't even come after me when I left the rink."

"After the blow-up with the teams?"

"Yeah. He dropped my hand and focused on his sister. He saw me skate off and did nothing."

"Almost like he knew you needed space."

"Um, no. If he cared about me at all, he would have come after me."

"Remember all the times I tried to talk to you my first summer at Wild Adventure? You literally left me in your dust cloud. Multiple times. It took me those multiple times to see you needed time to get where you were good to talk."

"It really sounds like you're defending him."

"I'm providing context. You tend to walk off—in this scenario, you skated, which was cool, by the way, skating away from this guy and the team who dismissed you. But if he had followed you, would you have listened to him?"

"I don't want to hear anything he says right now." Oh. That sort of proved her point. "I would listen—" No, I probably wouldn't have. "I'd have gotten in my car but maybe..." Hmm. No. I'd have driven off just the same. I'd been too upset to think about hearing his side of why he constantly defended his sister. "The point is, I would have liked to have seen him come after me, even if I didn't give him any attention."

"I'll accept that."

I smiled a little at Elena's assessment.

But my current reality stared me in the face. No team, no boyfriend, and my family's house up for sale. "I don't know what to do. I haven't even been on my own yet and already I failed."

"Failed what?"

"Failed to move on. I can't even get started."

"You haven't failed anything. Stop being a drama mama."

"I'm not a drama mama."

"You're acting like you failed a test. This isn't school, it's life. You get to do things the way you want and if you don't know what you want, you try some stuff and find out. Exactly like what you're doing."

We were both quiet for a few moments.

"So, hear me out," Elena said. "You've been fighting against this move from the jump, but agonizing over what to do seems to be making you miserable. What if you moved with your parents to Traverse City? It wouldn't be the end of the world. It could be temporary. You said they'll have a room for you either way. Moving is not giving up. It's adjusting your plan based on new information."

I hated the idea. I hated it because I'd worked so hard to think of ways to not give into it. "But what would I *do*? I don't know anyone there. It's completely starting over."

"How about you take it slow. Just move, breathe a little, and figure out your plan. You said you don't want your parents' handholding. So don't let them. Don't take a long-term job up there when you don't want to. It really feels like you have the control here."

Her perspective made sense. I didn't have to view moving with them as a failure on my part. "Maybe..." It was hard to shift my thinking. Moving felt like giving up.

"You have more time to think about this without derby." She winced. "I am the worst. Sorry—I'm sure it still stings. You don't have to roller skate anymore. Try some things that don't require oath taking."

"I really thought derby was the key to figuring out who I was. I guess there isn't an easy answer."

She moved from the couch to perch on the oversized armrest of the chair I sat in. "You're going to be okay. Worst case scenario, you move with your parents to a new city, find a cool job there and forget all about me.

Marry a wealthy Dutchman and have a litter of blond babies."

I tried shoving her off the chair, but she was surprisingly resilient. "I'm not going to forget about you and marry a Dutchman."

"There *are* a lot of people with Dutch lineage where you're going," she pointed out. "It's a possibility."

It turned out I did have texts from Rob. And like Elena confirmed, I wasn't ready to listen to his groveling. If what he said even was groveling. It might have been more excuses why he needed to support (actually enable) his sister and devote himself to a broken roller derby team.

Not to say the Tornadoes were in any better shape. I skimmed Barb's texts. The team decided to temporarily suspend Lyah of her captain duties in the same way the Brawlers had with their captain. The Tornadoes called an emergency meeting, in person, for tomorrow.

All of it exhausted me. Since Elena had the house to herself with her parents and brother out of town, she invited me to stay over. I sent a quick message to my parents I was staying overnight, and fetched my duffle bag from my trunk Lucky me, I had my toothbrush.

We filled a big bowl with popcorn and watched a movie until we each fell asleep on the couch.

Both of us were scheduled for work for the next day, making it an easy decision to ride together to Wild Adventure.

The familiarity of the water park let me work on autopilot. Rainclouds hung out overhead, making the pool traffic a little lighter for the day.

Checking my phone at lunch, more texts waited for me.

Barb: *Chelsea, you're right to feel put off by our mess, but you're welcome at the team meeting. Lyah will not be there. We have a separate thing planned with her later. If you can't come, I'll fill you in.*

Barb: *I'm sorry things happened this way.*

Barb: *My kids say my texts are too long. I just wanted to explain everything. It must be hard especially how this all involves Rob.*

I could make the meeting if I went directly after work. I wasn't sure I wanted to.

Mom: *We have an offer on the house! I know that might not be your favorite news, but I wanted to tell you right away. We have plenty of time for the transition.*

Mom: *I miss you. Let's talk soon.*

My heart ached. I'd felt like a ghost walking around my own house. It no longer felt like ours with half our stuff packed away and furniture arranged like a showroom. I couldn't hold on to my present because it had already changed.

I had to decide. Would I change as life moved ahead, or would I keep grasping for what could no longer be held?

That was the issue making me agonize, as Elena pointed out. I'd been resisting so hard against changes already in motion. My own resistance blocked my path to the future. I couldn't see ahead because I hadn't fully admitted my roots had been uprooted. They were already above ground. I couldn't stuff them back.

Replant them? Whatever. I should probably stop trying to think about my life using plant metaphors.

I trekked to the Go Zone for the remainder of my break to hash out my feelings with my bestie. My phone buzzed in my hand.

Rob: *I'm sorry I let you down. I let myself down.*

I hadn't replied to any of my messages yet and I sure wasn't going to reply to his. Not yet. I wasn't ready.

Rob: *I wanted to give you space, but I couldn't stay quiet. I couldn't see it, but I was letting my sister direct my life at the same time I told you not to let Lyah direct yours. I'm sorry. I tried reasoning with her the same way I always had—by trying to please her, even if it hurt other people.*

Rob: *I hurt you, and I'm sorry. This is a lot for a text, but I needed you to know. You deserve better, even if it means someone better than me.*

Well, dang. He *was* groveling. And it was a good grovel. I needed to hear exactly what he said.

Rob's apology came across as sincere and very much him. I knew he'd felt sorry for siding with his sister even as the drama unfolded, but he just couldn't figure out how to pull away. Kind of like how I couldn't figure out myself lately.

He had his own issues to work through and probably needed time like I did.

Instead of responding, I slipped the phone into my back pocket and continued my walk to the next section of the park. As I approached the track, I caught a glimpse of Elena and Jonah standing beneath the open-walled shelter area where staff prepped the karts. I paused, still a ways back.

They stood facing each other, laughing. Jonah, tall and broad shouldered, was a tough nut to crack. But Elena could always make him laugh. Those big shoulders shook as he reacted to what Elena said. Her hands moved a mile a second as she spoke.

They would have to adjust going forward now that they were attending separate colleges. They'd gone to different high schools, but moving out of Ginsburg and building new beginnings at college added new layers. Life was changing for them too.

The idea of leaving had seemed like failing to me. Mainly because it involved moving with my parents and not striking out on my own. But a new city and surroundings might be just what I needed to uncover a fresh perspective on my life. If I hung onto only what I already knew, how would I ever venture out on my own?

Life would be different either way.

I liked having time to think through decisions, and I was getting better at it. The making decisions part, not the taking time part. I wasn't a failure for that. I was...me.

Devil Mae Care. I cared about my future enough that I refused to rush decisions that would cloud my path. I cared about my family, my friends, and now Rob, enough to take the time I needed and make the right call. For me.

Maybe I'd end up back in Ginsburg. Maybe I'd go somewhere else entirely.

The best part was, it was all up to me.

Chapter Twenty-Three

♥

Our house didn't look any different other than the bright red SOLD tag swinging from hooks on the underside of the For Sale sign in the yard. It was the same house I'd seen every day of my life. Only something felt different.

The sensation stayed with me as I walked in through the kitchen. Smaller changes existed inside I hadn't been around to see. The middle chunk of the kitchen table had been removed so it was round instead of oval, making the eating area off the kitchen look larger.

The pet food bowls had been relocated to the laundry room off the garage instead of by the sliding door. Every surface sparkled. The kitchen and connecting rooms looked bright with all the blinds pulled up and curtains tied back.

Almost like this was someone else's house already.

I waited for the pang of loss to hit. It was there, but dull. With so much packed away, the house didn't feel like ours anymore. And it wasn't.

Dad appeared from the hall coming from his downstairs office. "Hey, Chels." He waited a beat to speak as he took me in. Probably assessing whether I'd bolt. "How are you?"

"I'm okay. Thanks for understanding I needed some space."

"Of course. You worked today?"

"Yup. Just got back."

He stuck his hands in his pockets and rocked back on his heels.

Awkward.

"So, I'm no longer on the roller derby team," I said to break up the total weirdness going on. "And the boyfriend's gone too, so… I guess nothing's holding me back from moving now."

"Honey!" Mom swept in from upstairs like a whirlwind with Chucky B and both cats at her heels. "Did I hear you say your boyfriend is gone? Does that mean you broke up? I imagine that was your doing. Who would break up with you? He clearly doesn't have his head on straight."

I rolled my eyes. "Yes, we're done. It's a…long story."

Dad filled a glass with water and set it in front of me. "And no more roller girls? I mean, roller derby?"

"It wasn't going to work out." I looked at the water provided for my comfort. My instinct was to reject it, because my parents were trying to manage me again.

But I was thirsty, so I took the glass and drank. My dad loved me—the water wasn't some trick. The past few weeks had really done a number on me. I didn't trust anyone's motives anymore.

My parents were doing their quiet telepathic communication again.

"You don't have to worry," I told them. "I'm moving with you. It's fine. It will all be...fine."

Mom rubbed the already-spotless counter with a kitchen towel. "We were thinking, since you're so against the move, we could help you find a place to live here."

"You'd be responsible for the rent," Dad added. "But we could drum up a deposit and help you with rental insurance. The couch in the basement could be yours for the low, low price of free."

Mom set the kitchen towel aside. "Violet at the animal shelter has a daughter who will be looking for a roommate in September. She's a little older—twenty-one—but she's very sweet. I met her once. She plays piano and works at the library."

I watched my parents' eager faces. They were trying so hard to be okay with suggestions I knew had pained them to make.

"It's okay, really. I'll move with you."

"But you don't want to," Dad said. "We admittedly had a hard time hearing it, but we've since talked it through. You've grown up, and we should recognize that."

Their compromise should have been exactly what I wanted to hear. Even a week ago, I would have been ecstatic.

They were saying exactly what I wanted.

What I thought I'd wanted.

But like this house looking so similar but different, I was different too. I didn't need to scramble for a life plan to prove to my parents I wasn't a failure. Or to prove it to myself. I could figure out a plan on my own timeline, with their support. I had my parents and I had Elena. I had dozens and dozens of choices to make, but I wouldn't make them alone.

"I'm sort of grown up." I slid onto a barstool seat at the counter. "No offense, Mom, but I don't want to live with your friend's daughter. I'd rather find a roommate myself when I have a better idea where I want to go."

Why limit myself to Ginsburg? I'd only ever lived here, and in this very house. There was a whole big world out there I hadn't explored. Elena reminded me of that. And so had Rob. Both of them had shown me opportunities existed I hadn't even considered. Locking myself down now would be a mistake.

"I'm thinking Traverse City can be a home base while I take some trips and explore jobs." The decision to move felt even more fitting the longer I spoke it out loud. "Maybe I'll even find a Dutch guy to hang out with."

Mom burst out laughing. Before Dad could ask, because he looked concerned, I explained: "It's an Elena thing. Never mind."

Dad picked up a whining cat circling his feet. "We were hard on you about not being ready to live alone. It's tough for us to see you grow up. It happens so fast."

I couldn't say they were completely in the wrong. "I can't help thinking if I'd really been ready to live on my own, I would have looked into apartments and roommates. Instead, I kept focusing on a bigger purpose, like a career, and to belong somewhere. I was sort of all over the place and couldn't focus, except with roller derby. I thought staying here was the best option because I don't know anything else. Now I can see how all of what I'm used to is going away. You guys, my friends, our house..."

Derby, my boyfriend. Even the small things I'd cultivated over the past few weeks were already fading into memories.

Mom wrangled the dog away from the cabinet he'd been pawing where treats were stored. "Are you sure you want move with us? I feel like we pressured you into this. It was our decision to move, not yours."

Weirdly, I did feel sure. I was okay with moving now because it wouldn't be forever. I didn't have to let it be forever.

And I hadn't failed. My life was only just getting started.

"And it's my decision now to go with you. I don't know how long I'll stay, but I don't want to rush into a plan I'm not happy with."

"Sounds reasonable," Dad said. "As long as you're okay with it, we're *thrilled* you're coming."

Finally, he looked more himself again, smiling and probably about to say something corny.

He tapped his phone awake and faced the screen toward me. "Not sure it's relevant given what you just told us, but I found this."

A website showed a posed photo of a group of women in red and white athletic gear.

"Well, look at that," Mom said from over my shoulder. "The Cherry Pickers. I had no idea Traverse City had a roller derby team."

A zillion texts waited for my response. So I responded. I told everyone I needed time. And I'd be disconnecting from social media for a few days.

I noped out of attending any derby come-to-Jesus meetings. While I appreciated hearing from Barb, Kam, Nina, and Taylor (who was very confused about the state of the team since she'd left the rink early), their derby problems felt like their problems to solve.

I read through Rob's grovel texts again, and I thought of how often he'd listened to me. How he'd encouraged me to explore and discover what I wanted out of life.

When he wrote I deserved better, even if it meant better than him, my heart ached. He'd apologized for hurting me, but ultimately, he was letting me go.

Conflicting emotions hit me from every angle. He said what I wanted to hear, what I needed to hear. But he had a lot to work through himself. His relationship with his sister and the decisions with the team.

Besides, I was moving. I'd tell him eventually, but for now I decided to keep my response simple.

Me: *Thanks. It means a lot to hear your apology. And how you understand I need space.*

The space to figure things out part was the truth. I switched shifts with Zoe to give me several days off in a row. Then I spent the next three days doing what I'd been putting off: packing.

I made a checklist and busted out the label maker to mark my boxes. More empty boxes appeared in my room (thanks, Dad), and I filled them.

I liked having a project. To put my things in order and toss out what I no longer needed. Okay, to be fair, my donate pile wasn't so big after all. I liked my stuff.

The business card for the bakery floated down from a pile of papers I kept moving from one place to another. I picked it up, thinking of Rosie and her pride in running the bakery. She was so energized about business school.

The card had her direct business email on it.

I stopped what I was doing and wrote her an email from my phone. I wasn't interested in working at the bakery—I'd need a crash course in brownie mix 101 before I'd even consider applying. I wanted to hear about her business classes.

After sending the email, a notification popped up about a direct message on Instagram. I saw the sender was Cammie from the Detroit Hawt Rodders, and I clicked over to the message.

@HotLunchCammie: *Hey, girl! I thought of you when I heard the Ginsburg teams are fighting again. (The derby grapevine is chatty!) I'm so sorry. That's got to be hard when you're new.*

You didn't ask for my advice, but you were so sweet when we talked in Detroit, so I wanted to reach out. Derby is supposed to be about supporting each other. We've all got our personal troubles, but it shouldn't be a fight to be on the team. I hope you keep your chin up and all, but if it's too much drama, don't feel bad walking away.

I took a moment to think through what she wrote. I *was* walking away. I hadn't thought of it like that—it was too hard to put what was happening into words.

Part of me felt guilty for not staying to fix the team. But Cammie had a point. It shouldn't be a fight. The team wasn't for me to fix. I had to fix myself.

Maybe fix wasn't the right word. I wanted to *find* myself.

@DevlinsInThaDetails: *Actually, my parents are moving up north and I decided to go with them. I'll be leaving the team anyway. I see Traverse City has a derby team. I might check them out.*

@HotLunchCammie: *Fantastic! I've met the team. OMG - you're going to love them. I'll connect you with their captain if you're interested. (No pressure)*

@ DevlinsInThaDetails: *Wow, awesome. And thanks for checking in on me.*

@HotLunchCammie: *I hope your move is an exciting adventure. Derby or no derby. Hugs!*

This summer wouldn't have been the same without roller derby—drama and all. I might not have come to a decision about moving if I hadn't joined. Or I might have stayed mad about the move.

I returned to cleaning. My butterfly necklace lay tangled with another in a shallow dish on my dresser. Carefully, I separated the two thin chains from each other and slipped the necklace on. This reminded me of so many things now. Of Rob, and how he noticed my necklace and set up our date at the butterfly dome. How the charm felt like my personal lucky butterfly.

Okay, maybe not lucky. Empowering, somehow. Something so small reminded me how much I'd changed this summer.

I wasn't afraid anymore. My future was mostly blank, but it wasn't empty. I had friends, family, and so many possibilities.

And I didn't need to fear those possibilities. I could tackle them my way. With a little extra time, and sure, a little parental handholding. Hopefully, less of the handholding. Maybe only a graze of hands.

My room was almost unrecognizable from its state a few weeks ago. I smiled. Life was about to move on.

Chapter Twenty-Four

♥

On my last day off before heading back to work, a text came from Rob.

Rob: *If you can make it to the skate park tonight, I'd love to see you.*

Rob: *I might have a surprise.*

Rob: *Okay, I do have a surprise. I wanted to warn you ahead it's a surprise in case you want to say no.*

Rob: *Which is a great way to ruin the whole idea of a surprise, but well, times are strange right now.*

Rob: *I fully understand you may have shut off your phone or changed your number. In that case, hello to whoever is reading this.*

Me: *This is Blade. I'm a buff bodybuilder. Stop texting me!*

Rob: *...*

Me: *Okay that was a joke.*

Joking aside, I needed to decide. I could push off talking to Rob, or face him.

Me: *Sure, I'll come out to the park.*

Rob: *WHEW. I already ticked off a guy named Dagger. Didn't need to add Blade to the list.*

That evening, I arrived to the skate park not knowing what to expect.

"Hey." Rob waved to me, getting out of his car at the same time I exited mine. "Thanks for meeting me."

He had on the shirt he'd been wearing the first day I'd met him. "Nice shirt. Could use some pop spilled down the front, though."

Rob grinned the wide grin I loved so much and my knees melted at the caps. Why was he so darned charming even when he barely tried? Part of me thought him wearing the shirt was a happy accident, but it could have been intentional. He knew I'd be charmed by it.

"It's been a real week," I said as I laced up my skates.

"You're really going to skate?"

"Um, yeah. You aren't?"

"Let me grab my skates." He returned a minute later. "I wasn't sure if you'd start with, *Rob, you're a selfish jerk and I came here to tell you in person.*"

"I would have texted and saved myself the trip."

His shoulders eased at my comment. Even though the words weren't all that comforting.

The crowd was a little sparse tonight with only a few older kids using the skateboard ramps.

"Honestly, I'm glad you're tolerating my existence right now."

I turned and slowly skated backward as I faced him. "Your apology meant a lot. The worst part of what happened was how you pulled away from me, literally, to defend your sister. Meg and Lyah are so awful to each other. Everyone's been living under this weird spell of their dysfunction. I don't think any of us realized how bad it was until they blew up."

He skated forward facing me as I continued backward. "You knew. You tried to tell me. I kept trying the same things over and over, hoping my sister would stop being so mad if I fixed everything else."

"She's your sister. You owe it to her to keep trying. You do that for family."

Another reason I couldn't stay mad at my parents. They'd been there for me my whole life. It was worth it to work through the hard parts. They would always annoy me at times, and I'd have to set boundaries for sure once we moved. I was eighteen now and not a little kid.

"I was putting aside what I wanted in order to do whatever she told me," he said. "It wasn't healthy. I'm finishing the summer at the rink so I don't put Alma in a bad spot. But as far as derby goes, I'm done. It's the best choice for me and the team."

"Oh, wow. You love derby so much. Is this what you really want?"

He looked past me, in thought. "It is."

Rob seemed pretty distracted as he focused his attention across the park. I turned, and my mouth fell open.

A stream of roller skaters entered the park from the opposite end, coming in through the paved trail. Barb with her bouncy blond curls led the pack, followed by Kam, Mary, Becky, Taylor, and Bonecrusher.

"What is this?" I asked.

The surprise. I'd forgotten the surprise! Rob and his non-pop-stained shirt and knee-weakening smile wiped my memory of the surprise he'd *told* me about.

Behind the Tornadoes, more skaters arrived. I recognized Bomber Betty and faces from the Brawlers. Wrapping up the derby train, Meg skated in.

She cast a tentative wave my direction.

The skaters wound in a figure eight, passing each other at the center point and skating out and around to continue the loop.

They then broke the eight and assembled in a formation facing me. The teams blended together into one larger group.

Barb spread her arms wide. "Introducing..."

"The Brawlers 2.0!" the group finished as one.

A surge of joy filled me at their happy expressions. They were like a new and improved version of the Brawlers. The skaters high-fived, hugged, and slung arms around each other. They looked downright giddy.

"We chose to keep the Brawlers name because we already paid for the merch." Meg skated toward me. "Hi. I'm Meg. I'd like to start over. I'm incredibly sorry I was rude to you when we first met." She glanced to her brother. "I was out of line being upset when I heard about you two together. I wish I could take back everything I said."

This was a lot to absorb. But I didn't have to think too hard on it. "Thanks. I'm good to start over too."

"When you defended Nina and threw my sass right back at me—wow, that stung. It was a memorable sting. It caused me to start reconsidering the team split. It just took some time to get there."

"And a public display of combustion," Bonecrusher added from her spot in the group.

A trickle of laughter cascaded among the skaters.

Barb and Nina rolled over to us. "We're sorry," Barb said at the same time Nina exclaimed, "I can't believe you put up with us as long as you did."

"I'm glad you resolved the team split," I told them. "Even if it means the Tornadoes are done for."

"There were signs," said Nina. "Like, you know, an actual tornado."

"And someone who kept reminding us we needed to support each other." Barb made a point to look at me. "We're here to say we're sorry and we'd love to have you back with us."

Emotion bubbled up inside me to nearly bursting. I threw my arms around Barb. "Thanks for always looking out for me."

She hugged me back. "Of course. You're one of us."

Taylor and Queen Bacon drifted over with a few members of the original Brawlers.

I scanned the group. "Where's Lyah?"

Meg spoke first. "We tried to bring her in, but she wasn't interested. I suppose that's on me. These ladies" —she gestured with her chin toward the others— "sat us all in a room together with an honest-to-goodness licensed therapist."

"A fellow parent from the PTA," Barb said. "Available on short notice by favor."

Meg's cheeks colored pink, reminding me of Rob when his cheeks flushed. "We made progress at the meeting, but not enough to fix everything. Lyah and I left on okay terms. She thought it was best to take time away from derby for now."

It would have been great if they'd been able to re-form the team as it had been before the split, but I supposed everything went through a change sooner or later. Trying to re-create what used to exist was never really the same.

Funny, the Brawlers' journey the past few months felt similar to what I'd gone through with my parents. We'd both thought we wanted something different, but circled back around, only neither of us were unchanged from the experience. We were stronger after weathering the storm.

The Brawlers having faced a literal storm.

"Hi, I'm Jackie," the woman nicknamed Bomber Betty said. "Two of the original Brawlers are taking a break. With you and Taylor in the mix, it really will feel like a new team along with everyone else."

"That is, if you'll join us." Meg smiled with hesitation. "We'd be honored to have you on the Brawlers."

I absorbed their apologies and wrapped their invitation around me like a comforting blanket. I was wanted here. I belonged.

"Thanks," I said finally. "If I can think on it, I'd appreciate some time."

"Of course," Meg filled in instantly.

Nina nodded. "All the time you need."

"Until the next bout," Bonecrusher added. Nina made a sucking sound through her teeth. Bonecrusher threw up her hands. "What? Devil's an excellent blocker. We need her."

Barb hooked an arm through Bonecrusher's and placed her other hand at Nina's back. "We should skate around a little."

They skated off, leaving me with Rob once again. As much as I loved seeing the re-united team, I liked this moment with just the two of us.

My heart clogged up my throat. This conversation was going to be harder than I expected. "What a fun surprise."

Rob looked at me with sadness in his eyes. "You're moving with your parents, aren't you?"

I gasped. "How did you know?" The only person besides my parents who even had an inkling was Elena, and I hadn't shared my final decision with her. I hadn't wanted to blurt it out to the team just yet, but I'd tell them soon.

"It was a guess. I figured you might."

"Because I gave up? And it was too hard to plan my life here without derby and without you?"

He flinched at the sharp edges of my tone. I hadn't meant for it to come out so blunt, but he'd nailed my next move so easily, he clearly assumed I didn't have what it took to live here on my own.

His eyes fell shut. "I never thought that." He looked at me again. "I assumed you'd be invited back to derby and might even consider keeping on if the teams voted the captains out completely and joined the two teams back together. But I don't think you were ever planning to stay here because of roller derby. Or because of me. Your decision wouldn't have been based on those factors at all."

"You *were* a factor. You were definitely part of me thinking I could stay here. But probably more important, you helped me see that staying was too limiting. There's so much I can do, and signing an apartment lease here, right now, would be the easy route, even though it felt hard. Really figuring out what I want and where I want to be is harder. It takes more time."

I nodded for him to follow me to a shadier spot away from the skaters. "I'm finding I take longer to work through things. You noticed I needed time. It's why you let me walk out of the rink the other day and didn't follow me."

"Technically, you skated. But yes."

"It was weird not changing into shoes on the way out, but I didn't want to spend another second in the rink. I grabbed my stuff and got out of there. The parking lot felt pretty rough on my wheels."

"Yeah, not the same as a surface meant for skate wheels."

"Sure isn't."

For a split second, I felt myself looking down at ourselves, talking awkwardly and avoiding what we needed to say. Laugher carried over from the Brawlers skating around the park.

"So, you are moving, then?" Rob asked.

"Yeah. Then I'll consider my options."

He nodded, seemingly in thought. "I know I said you deserved better and I meant it. I see two paths. One: beg your forgiveness and ask if I can be your boyfriend again. Two: let you go so you can do what's best for you."

I watched him, waiting. "And?"

"I'm having a real problem deciding. One path feels selfish. The other feels like the mature route."

"Seems like you've been pretty selfless putting other people ahead of your own needs. What's wrong with doing something for yourself?"

His eyes danced with renewed hope. "I guess I'm scared of what's to come. Pleasing other people is easy for me. Doing what I want and risk hurting someone? That's the tricky part."

I put my hands on my hips. "I like how you're giving me space, but between here and Traverse City is a lot of space."

He searched my face. "Would it be easier if you had another supportive person in your corner? On weekends and school breaks?"

"Or weekdays because I'm an aimless drifter living on my parent's dime."

He grinned again and my untrustworthy knees nearly buckled.

"I don't want to break up," he said in a rush, grabbing my hands. "I don't care about long distance. It's what, a four-hour drive or less? We can each have time to focus on what we need when we need. But I don't want to lose you. I already lost you when I tried to save the team and failed. I don't want to fail with you."

"I don't want to fail with you either." I squeezed his hands. "Maybe our way forward is to try again. This time, we don't have to listen to other people tell us we can't be together. We won't need to avoid being seen. We can do whatever we want. That feels like the mature move. Our rules. Our timeline."

He inched closer. "You want to stay together? I'd like to be your boyfriend again."

"Only if I can be your girlfriend."

Rob slid his hands up my arms, resting them lightly at my shoulders. One hand moved into my hair as he looked over my face until a blush flamed my cheeks. "Deal."

He kissed me with purpose and intensity. A decision that felt wholly good and right.

I pulled back. "How long do we have?"

"The park closes at sundown."

"Not that. How long until school starts?"

"I go back the last weekend in August."

"I'll finish up at Wild Adventure the same weekend. Then, go on my own...wild adventure."

He cringed. "I didn't know if you'd go through with saying it, but you did. Truly awful, Devil."

"Hey, you're not supposed to call me Devil. Besides, I'm off the team."

"They'll have you back anytime. You know, there's a team in Traverse."

"I saw. My dad found their website. I'm not sure I'll be able to commit. I hate to join and flake out. I already did that once."

"You did anything but flake out. I'm sure the Traverse team will let you train with them mid-season since you have experience."

"I'm not making long-term commitments while I'm up north. I could end up anywhere. Like in Ann Arbor at University of Michigan."

His mouth dropped open. "Are you serious? Wait, no. I can't let you move back...are you saying you'd move here for me? That misses the whole point of finding what you want."

I laughed. "I'm kidding. I can't get into U of M unless I audit a class for free. Besides, I don't think I'm going to change my mind about the four-year college thing. When I was packing my room, I found all the college brochures and looked through them again."

"And it doesn't fit?"

"Not really. I wrote to Rosie at the bakery. She told me about her business classes. Then she gave me a list of culinary programs. It's cool how many options there are, and they're all over the state. Some up by where my parents are and some down here. I don't know if any of those are a fit for me, but I'm thinking through it."

Rob trailed a finger down my arm giving me welcome shivers. "I hope you find a something you're excited about." He kissed the edge of my ear. "If not, there's always metalsmithing."

"Or pottery." I nipped at his chin.

He kissed me again. "Or taking the slow route and doing more of this and less of everything else."

I kissed him back. "I like your idea."

"I'm glad you're moving even though I hate the idea of it."

"I'm also glad, even though I hate it too."

As the sun retreated lower in the sky, we joined hands for a lap around the skate park. We wove in and out of the path of the Brawlers.

Like old times, but different now. Different in a definitely good way.

We'd create new memories these last few weeks here, before everything changed all over again.

Crisp fall air cooled my skin while the sun shined bright against a cloudless sky. A perfect fall day. All around me, voices carried over with laughter and cheering.

"If this is what college is like, maybe I'll enroll after all," I told Rob as I grabbed a hot dog off the portable grill.

He handed me a hot dog bun on a paper plate. "In my opinion, tailgating represents the best and worst of college. Best." He nodded toward the growing pile of stacked, grilled hot dogs. "Worst." He cast a look past us to a group of dudes with faces painted in U of M's blue and gold. The guys were bare-chested, wore capes, and each had on a different animal head hat. The guy yelling loudest wore what looked like bear ears around his head with brown fur hanging to his shoulders.

"Those guys look too old to be students."

"Exactly," Rob said. "U of M games are crawling with people who don't even go here."

I gave him a light shove at the comment. I didn't go here, and likely never would, and that was fine by me.

But it was fun to get a glimpse of the college experience, and a welcome change to be back downstate after a month up north.

"Thanks for coming." Rob moved closer and landed a soft kiss on my cheek. "Also, if you put ketchup on your hot dog, I'm going to make fun of you."

"Ketchup is for fries and we don't have fries, we have chips."

Rob patted his gut. "I need a vegetable and preferably not a starch. Not skating while eating the same as I used to means my pants are kinda tight."

Rob pulled at the waist of his jeans, which looked to fit just fine to me. Then again, I was a biased about Rob in general, and wouldn't mind if he gained the notorious Freshman Fifteen so long as he was happy and doing what he wanted.

I grabbed a chip bag. "These are sour cream and onion flavored. Onion is a vegetable."

He rolled his eyes and took a chip. "These are criminally good."

"I can't believe you still don't know how to make a proper S'more." Beside us, Holli Hayes hip-checked her boyfriend Will, scooting him aside from the grill.

Will held a smoldering marshmallow, attached to the stick he used for roasting, out of arm's reach from Holli. "Freedom from excessive S'mores legislation!"

"Hot dogs are ready." I pointed to the plate, using the non-marshmallow food as a distraction. We had more food than people at this point, at least in our little tailgating area outside University of Michigan's football stadium. I supposed we could make new friends with a sign for free hot dogs if no one else ended up showing.

"We're going to be really sick of hot dogs," Rob said, seeming to read my thoughts.

Just as he said the words, it was if we'd sent out a beacon to summon hungry friends.

"Hey, folks!" Grace Hayes, Holli's older sister, arrived with two others I knew from my days at West Ginsburg—Lila and her boyfriend Aiden. They'd all graduated two years ahead of me.

Grace now attended Wayne State in Detroit, while Lila and Aiden both ended up at Michigan State.

"I'm probably supposed to make a Spartans vs. Wolverines joke here," Rob said as Aiden and Lila approached. "But I'm really over the whole team rivalry thing."

"We're not really sports people," Aiden said.

"Unless you count mini-golf or live action role playing," Lila added. "In that case, we are fully committed sport-os."

Lila and Aiden descended on the hot dogs—yay!—while Grace scooped up Holli in a big hug. "My favorite sister is a college freshman!"

Holli shirked away, laughing. "I'm your only sister and you just visited my dorm last week."

"Did you meet my friend?" Grace immediately moved on. A guy had been walking behind her who I hadn't noticed. He looked to be South Asian and wore a Taegeuk Warriors shirt, the national soccer team in South Korea. "This is Kwan."

Holli gasped and rushed to hug him, then held back. "Sorry—I'm a little excited to meet you."

Kwan laughed easily. "It's okay. I'm a hugger."

Grace, Holli, and Kwan formed a huddle, each talking excitedly.

Funny, Elena still hadn't shown. There were thousands of people out here. Maybe she couldn't find us.

Will wandered over, as Holli appeared consumed with her sister. "Hey, Holli tells me you started working with a food bank up in Traverse. That's really cool. The community service group I was in during high school did some work with food pantries."

I nodded. "Yeah. I'm really liking the food bank. It was shocking to me how many people deal with food insecurity, even in areas where you think people all have money."

The position was a volunteer role, but I could already see myself working in a paid position when one opened up. As soon as I'd heard about the opportunity, from my mom who had already signed herself up for a volunteer role, I'd jumped in with both feet. Weirdly, it sort of fit with what I knew about myself. I liked food, but maybe not enough to bake or cook professionally. However, I was finding I believed strongly that every person should have access to food, especially healthy food. I wanted to be part of getting that food to people who needed it.

Belonging to an organization who provided community access to food felt satisfying and empowering. Things I knew I needed in whatever profession I ended up choosing.

It had only been a month since my family relocated our lives to Traverse City, and though it didn't feel like home yet, the change excited me. Dad was happier than ever with a new and slower pace at his job, and Mom decided to fill her time volunteering at a pet shelter and the food bank.

Turned out, she was researching her own passions for her next phase in life, just like me.

"Sorry we're late!" Elena hustled over to us loaded down with plastic bags. Beside her, Jonah carried several foldable camp chairs over one shoulder and pulled a wheeled cooler with the other.

Rob's eyes turned saucer shaped. "This is so much food. After hearing what you told me about food waste, we're going to have to give a lot of this away."

"I also brought containers," Elena announced. "For leftovers. My dorm room has a mini-fridge and our floor has a lounge with a bigger refrigerator."

Another group appeared, all who knew Holli from her short time so far at school. Then a few more trickled in, friends of Rob's. Introductions went around the group. We were still Ginsburg dominant, but our group had grown and extended. The hot dogs disappeared.

Brass anthems from the marching band could be heard from our spot outside the stadium. The air crackled with excitement.

"This is fun," I told Rob. "Are you sure you want to leave all this to visit me in two weeks?"

Rob circled his arms around my shoulders. "I can't wait. That pull-out couch in your dad's home office is the best sleep I've had in years."

He was lying. That mattress bent up in the couch had given him a bruise his first time visiting. Which had been one week after we'd moved.

So much had changed since I'd met Rob. We'd both left roller derby. While I'd made contact with the

Traverse City team and planned to attend their next bout, I hadn't jumped on joining the team. I'd be traveling downstate at least one weekend a month, and well, I was a gal who needed time to think through a thing. Maybe after I saw the team in action my mind would change. After all, I still owned a pair of skates.

Speaking of skates, more familiar faces appeared.

"It took us forever to find y'all!" Barb spread her arms for a big ole Barb hug. She wore a U of M jersey bedazzled with blue and gold rhinestones.

I let her squeeze me a little too hard, then turned to Taylor, Nina, Bonecrusher, and Kam. "You all came! I'm so glad to see you."

"Lyah couldn't be here," Barb explained. "She wanted to specifically tell you she isn't making an excuse. She really did have somewhere to be."

"Hi Rob," Nina said. "I probably said it already, but sorry and thank you."

Rob waved her off. "You don't have to apologize for anything. The Brawlers are one big team again. That's what matters."

"Yeah, but it was a rough road for a bit. I tried to steer Chelsea away from you."

"Because of the *oath*." Bonecrusher rolled her eyes. Half her face was painted blue and gold with the other half in orange and red flames. "We took a vote on the oath. We decided against revising it and instead got rid of the thing. Thus, the Brawlers have retired the oath."

I looked at the other skaters. "I liked the part about being there for each other."

"That part was crafted into a mission statement," Kam said. "Continuing to call it an oath felt icky."

My former teammates caught me up on how Lyah and Meg had been working on reconciling. Rob had already filled me in on some of the details, but he was still protective of his sister. Just knowing they were on the road to working things out made me far less stressed. After all, I was planning to spend Thanksgiving with Rob and his family. We'd been making all kinds of plans.

"We're actually out of hot dogs," I told Rob.

"Because Ben took FOUR." Rob gave his buddy a pointed look.

In response, Ben threw up the *Star Trek* hand greeting and took another bite.

I knew the *Trek* salute, of the Vulcan variety, because Rob and his friends had a mission to convert me to a fan. I was willing to give it a shot.

"Good thing I brought these frozen burgers." Elena cracked open a cardboard box and laid four patties on the small grill. "We've got bean burgers and tofu burgers. A vegetarian's delight."

The skater crowd got to work opening more chips, trays of dips, and someone unearthed a bag of apples.

Rob snatched one. "This might be the closest I get to a whole food today."

I took in the scene. All these people coming together from so many walks of life. We passed into each other's lives for this moment and that might be it. I wanted to remember this time and carry it with me.

Rob reached for my hand. "I wouldn't want to stand outside of a football stadium with anyone else but you."

It was oddly sweet, even if his tone was more teasing. "Same. I like seeing you happy and with your...hungry friends." His other friend was leaning a casual arm against a truck bed while chatting up Taylor.

Rob barely glanced at them. "I'm so glad we met. I know it hasn't been very long, but I can't imagine my life without you."

His words wrapped around me like a warm hug. His gaze connected to mine with solid confidence. He believed I could do anything. I believed it too. I believed in us. "It's so strange, isn't it? How quickly everything can shift."

Ignoring everyone around us, Rob kissed me. I knew my life would shift again, maybe in a few weeks with a paid job at the food bank, or maybe in months with another change. Taylor mentioned she'd need a new roommate next summer. A whole new summer to make plans for.

But right now, I was right where I wanted to be. Life might not stand still, but I knew how to roll with it.

What's Next

Thanks for reading. Reviews help readers find books. Please consider leaving a review on your favorite retailer.

Read on for chapter 1 of **All-Star Love**, a young adult tennis academy romance!

All-Star Love

♥

"Traitor."

The word came out in a cough—one of those not-actually-subtle cover-ups on a remark meant to be heard. I gritted my teeth.

"Chin up," my bestie Nia said beside me, shrugging her gear bag over her shoulder. She nudged me forward. "Let's go."

So much for being a hot-shot senior. Four years ago when I started at Six Lakes Tennis Academy, I'd dreamed of walking into general session as a senior. All the groveling, the extra practices, would pay off. Once I dazzled the college recruiters, I could coast my way through the year, enjoying my senior status before heading off into the sunset.

That was all before. My life was split now: Before Scandal, and After Scandal.

People would pay attention to Maisie Maxwell all right. There's a joke how nobody expects the Spanish Inquisition. Kind of like how nobody expects their school to succumb to financial scandal at the start of one's all-important senior year. Or to expect said financial scandal to involve one's own uncle, Coach Corbin Maxwell, who apparently took the advice to "clear your head and take some time off" too literally by fleeing the country along with tuition funds.

I couldn't imagine anyone expecting that. Even my mom, who said my uncle was a dirt bag from the start, usually countered by Dad's quick defense. Coach Max was his brother after all. Not even Coach Max's string of Grand Slam victories in the 1990s or the fact he co-founded an affordable Midwest tennis school could excuse his running off.

So yeah, my uncle was a criminal. On the run.

I followed Nia through our academy's lobby, an aging sports facility converted for our use. We headed to the academic corridor, ignoring the heat rising on my pale skin as my classmates lasered their scorn at me.

They should have known I was equally disgusted with my uncle for taking off. It wasn't like my family knew where he'd gone. Even an FBI-led search turned up empty. I imagined him on an island south of the equator fanning himself with large bills, periodically tossing tennis balls fresh from the can into the surf. What a tool.

Ahead of me, Nia entered the assembly room. A room that had once seemed so prestigious with its thick, kelly green carpet and mahogany wood-paneled walls. Now the graduating classes framed along the walls stared back at us in horror. *You tarnished our legacy!*

Sorry! I sent back through time and space. *Not all us Maxwells are low-lifes. I swear.*

I stopped in the doorway. Something was weird about the room. Empty rows of seats, that's what. Even with people still hanging out in the lobby, this turnout did not bode well. Our total full-time enrollment usually capped at fifty students—if that. I counted seven sitting down so far. Either everyone was late, or more families pulled their kids after the debacle.

My new reality: After Scandal.

Nia chose a chair in a middle row. I sat beside her and scooched closer. I needed her good vibes. She gathered her long black braids into a loose knot at the base of her brown-skinned neck. "It's not your fault. You know that."

I shrugged off her reminder, even though I appreciated hearing it. "Did you hear Katie Mack dropped?" I picked at a split fingernail. "Allison's gone too."

"We both need to keep focus. We're going to finish strong. Besides, the school has insurance for a reason. We might have a rebuilding year and all, but it's not like the place is folding. The summer camps seemed to do okay."

Except we both knew the bad press still hadn't died down weeks after the story broke. Now, Six Lakes wasn't simply a middle-ranked academy in a less-than-desirable Midwest location (no sunny Florida or California year-round outdoor courts for us here in eastern Michigan). The scandal set us on course to place dead last on the annual ranked list of U.S. tennis academies. Even Bazooka Bill's Buccaneer Training Camp outranked us. They'd just relocated to a new host club with custom clay courts. With Bazooka Bill's face on the clay. We were *worse than Bazooka Bill*.

It killed me to have anybody look at Six Lakes like that. We were already underdogs, even though our academy sat on the grounds of a golf resort in a high-end community surrounded by beautiful recreational lakes.

I wore the underdog label as a badge, firmly affixed at any regional tournament. *Think we're low rent? Get on the court and let's see what happens.*

"Welcome, students." Academy Director Deborah "Debs" Flannery positioned herself at the front podium wearing her trademark wind suit and gold jewelry. With short brassy hair and skin that had seen many summers courtside, she'd ruled tennis in the 1980s and was the type who could fit in a mixed doubles match and close a deal with a sports agent over her lunch break. She was like if one of the *Golden Girls* had been an elite athlete and time-traveled to this decade. "Let's fill in the front seats here." She looked our way and waited. "Nia? Margaret? Please set an example."

Painful silence coated the room while Nia and I rose from our safe middle seats to move to empty chairs in the front row. Plus, Debs just had to call me Margaret when only my birth certificate did (and my mom when she was in a funk). If I could manage to call her Debs, she could manage Maisie.

A sarcastic laugh sprang up from the back. I turned in time to see the students from the lobby trickling in—all ten more of them. A smug-faced Caleb Thompson sneered my way. "Don't need her kind of example."

Debs kept smiling, undeterred. It took a lot to 'terr Debs. "As you all know, we've encountered changes in our coaching staff for this season. The good news is our head coaches Czarniak and Nelson are here to stay. Come on up, coaches."

Czarniak, or Coach Zak, a hefty drill-sergeant type with pinkish-pale skin and a buzz cut, lumbered forward. He was followed by Coach Nelson, a former top-ranking player who trained internationally at an academy in Spain, though she was originally from Boise or someplace like that. We called her Killer Nelson. No pun or play on words. She just made you want to slowly sink into a fresh grave after hours of pre-season training.

"Thank you, coaches," Debs continued. "Our assistant coaches will rotate in when needed. We'll have a smaller full-time class this year across all grades due to...unforeseen circumstances." Debs' smile froze in place and she scanned the room, making sure each of us registered the *things are going to be okay* vibe pulsing behind her eyes. "Meanwhile, we're busy recruiting for our part-time, non-boarding program and camps. We also have plans in store for a bit of a shake-up."

To my horror, Debs held her hands up like she was holding castanets and mimed the shake, jewelry jangling and wind suit...wind-ing? Beside me, Nia made a "nuh-uh" sound only I could hear.

"So," Debs went on. "Given our *unforeseen circumstances*, we at the Academy have been brainstorming how we can, let's say, return to the public's good graces. It turns out, we came across a *wonderful* opportunity." She clicked the remote to the TV at the front of the room.

The screen lit up, and familiar music played. A montage of prestigious-looking buildings and students in prep school uniforms appeared. Oh, right. This was from a reality show I'd seen in binges during recovery with my ankles iced up.

The Academy, the screen displayed in a fancy font. In a flash, a tennis ball graphic swooshed past the title, leaving a wash of yellow-green in its wake, followed by the word: *Served*.

"Oh. My. God." Nia stared straight ahead at the screen.

"What?" I whispered to her. Oh—*Ohhh*.

Debs paused the TV. "If you haven't guessed, we've been in talks with the reality TV series *The Academy* about featuring our very own Six Lakes for their upcoming season. They sent us this title promo just in time for our first General Session."

The boys who'd been slouched in their seats now sat at attention. The younger girls squealed and talked over one another.

"Here?" I said to Nia.

Her eyes lit up. "They've already done a New York prep school and a London academy. Can you imagine? Us on TV?"

For a national tennis match, sure. On a reality show? No, this could not be good. This meant more attention on the scandal. I'd be outed as a Maxwell immediately and probably accused of being an accessory to my uncle's criminality. A reality show?

"Maisie, are you even listening?" Nia swatted my knee. "This is good. Quit thinking about your uncle."

Before I could reply, Debs cleared her throat. "All right, settle down. Nothing has been confirmed yet. Of course, once we sign on, your parents will be notified through personal outreach. Nothing can go forward without their permission, and most importantly, from you. We'd love to know what you think." Her hands clasped together and the room fell silent. "Right now. Let's hear it."

This was where Debs' smile seemed like a cover barely stretched over her cracking composure. That smile pasted over a whole host of *Oh Craps* she'd probably been dealing with this summer. The academy Facebook page had derailed into a constant trash fire of angry comments.

"Isn't this just a last ditch effort to save the place after Coach Maxwell stole our money?" Caleb asked.

I sank lower in my seat.

Nia raised her hand. "I think it's a great idea. I'm guessing the buzz from the show will help our reputation. Maybe dig us out of debt?"

Debs smile remained. "Something like that. And how about your feelings about being on camera. Anyone? Won't it be exciting to see yourselves on screen?"

The younger students shot hands in the air and shouted responses. A returning sophomore asked whether the coverage would boost chances to rank in the junior tournaments. Right. Because the whole tennis tournament system would decide to cater to Z-list celebrities on a cable reality show. Was this show even on streaming?

The only reality TV I watched was the cooking show where the British guy yelled at everybody. He made Killer Nelson seem like Light Stab-wound Nelson.

Debs clapped. "Alright, thank you for your candid responses. The good news is, we are very close to a deal. The producers have already scouted our school and have done *pre-production* work." She said pre-production like she was introducing us to advanced level vocabulary. "It turns out, their planned filming location for the season fell through at the eleventh hour, so they're quite desperate."

And, apparently, so were we.

"I have a question," Gretchen, a returning senior, asked from the second row. "I heard Shane Wagner is enrolling. Is it true?"

Nia gasped beside me.

"What am I missing?" I asked her in a whisper.

"He just ranked number one, Maisie."

The number one junior player? Who in their right mind would transfer to a last-ranked academy thick in the throes of scandal? Unless the TV show was more of a done deal than Debs let on.

I swung my attention back to Debs for her response. "I believe we're in final talks with Shane's coach. If he accepts, he'll be one of our new top talent recruits. Not every tennis academy can boast they have a television series—*pending* television series. Six Lakes can put a future tennis star in front of *millions*."

We might become minor basic cable celebrities, but would it help me score a full-ride to college? That was my reason for being here. This whole reality show sounded like one giant distraction.

Debs and the coaches talked through the weekly schedule. We started with early morning trainings two days a week followed by classroom time, lunch, and a study session. Practice on the courts in the afternoon every day. On Friday nights, the school planned activities for us, unless we had a scheduled tournament. Then there were off-court training times and mandatory rest days.

Debs dismissed us to change clothes and meet the coaches on the courts. Day one was always the best because we skipped classroom time. I had to work harder off the courts than on.

The moment we were let loose, *The Academy* was the only point of discussion. It looked like our enrollment was down by almost half, with maybe twenty-five students in the assembly room. With under ten seniors, we were looking at the smallest graduating class since the school's first two years in business.

Since Nia and I had dressed in practice clothes, we skipped the locker room and headed straight outside. I shouldered the glass doors open leading to the outdoor courts. "A reality show? I mean, how desperate do they think we are?"

Nia flipped down her sunglasses from her head. "This could work out for us. Six Lakes needs money and a better reputation. It might help me go pro."

I let my annoyance show. "You know that's not the kind of fame you want. You need to rank in the Top 100. You need the U.S. Open, and you can only do that by training and winning matches, like you've been doing."

"It's one thing to be the top player at your last-ranked academy and winning Midwest tournaments. It's another to be shown dominating the court on TV. I might get a bigger name coach to take me on."

I shielded my eyes from the glaring sun. "I can't help thinking how Coach Max would hate this. He was focused on the game, not on image."

"Ironic, since he ran off with the school's money."

Nia wasn't wrong. I spent just as much mental energy fighting the truth of the whole situation as I did trying to figure out why he did it. Why he'd been so desperate for cash to resort to stealing from his students.

From us.We each chucked our bags in our familiar zones along the fence beside the benches. A wheeled wire basket full of clean tennis balls waited courtside.

I unsheathed my racket and headed for the ball basket.

Nia was already trotting to the other side of the court. We'd been running drills and working extra hours training together since freshman year. Another reason we came dressed to play so we could get a few minutes on the courts to ourselves.

I fed a ball to Nia, who hit a forehand lob down the middle of the court. I returned with a backhand, my strength, and the ball careened left of her. She circled around and whacked the ball, sending it whizzing past me. I looked back as the ball hit within an inch of boundary.

"You trying to kill me?" I called over to her.

"I'm just getting warmed up over here."

I sent another ball over. Nia delivered it wide. I lunged and made it. The ball soared past her to the baseline, just inside the white stripe of paint.

"Dang it, girl!" Nia turned toward me after watching the ball bounce out of reach.

We played back and forth a few more times before switching sides. Now the sun hit me head-on. I adjusted to the glare and focused on returning every ball Nia hit my way. When my head was in the game, everything else slipped aside. Obsessive thoughts over college scholarships took a seat while front row attention went to each forehand delivery. I was going to nail my forehand this year.

"Hey, Maxwell! Way to skip out early. Can't handle the criticism?"

Stupid Caleb again. I ignored his comment and slammed a backhand return.

Nia returned mine. The jerk taunted with garbage about my uncle. "Son of a—" I put all my strength into my next forehand. The ball torpedoed over the net, not even bothering to bounce within the boundaries. Nope, that sucker was headed for the fences.

"Ahh!"

A figure in the distance went down, knees to the court. A crowd of students suddenly appeared, gasping and rushing over.

"You hit him!" someone shrieked.

I caught a flash of red splattered against the green court.

My breath lodged in my throat. *I'm sorry, I'm sorry, I'm sorry!* I jogged over, terrified to breathe until I knew my accidental victim was okay.

Caleb directed a dirty scowl at me. "You really are the worst, Maxwell."

I angled to see the fallen student. "I'm so sorry!"

"Oh, Maisie," Nia mumbled, now beside me.

"I'm okay," the guy on the ground said, attempting to stand. His sun-bleached brown hair was unkempt and curling over a tanned white forehead. That perfectly shaggy look some guys could get away with. He wasn't a returning student. The face turning toward me could easily belong on a clothing website, the kind with ninety-dollar T-shirts with holes in them for a *distressed* look. Basically, he was very attractive. A swath of blood streaked across that very attractive face.

That part was definitely my fault.

Sorry floated across my tongue, but my lips couldn't form the word under the pressure of so many glaring classmates. Any hope of being an admired senior this year shriveled and burned like a tissue set aflame.

He accepted a clean towel and pressed it to his nose. "I expected I might not be welcome here, but your forehand really confirmed it."

"Way to go, Maxwell," Caleb said with a sneer. "Is this any way to welcome Shane Wagner?"

Oh. Wait, what? "You're ... you're—"

"Shane Wagner," the bloody-faced model boy said through the towel.

Shane Wagner. *The* Shane Wagner. I just nailed the face of the number one-seeded player in junior boys' tennis.

Also by Stephanie J. Scott

♥

Young Adult Books
All Last Summer
Sunset Summer
Big Wild Summer
Free Wheeling Summer
All-Star Love
Alterations
Adult Romance
Falling Into Place
OMG Christmas Tree

www.stephaniejscott.com/books

About the Author

Stephanie J. Scott writes young adult and romance about characters who put their passions first. Her debut ALTERATIONS about a fashion-obsessed loner who reinvents herself was a Romance Writers of America RITA® award finalist. She enjoys dance fitness, everything cats, and has a slight obsession with Instagram. A Midwest girl at heart, she resides outside of Chicago with her tech-of-all-trades husband and fuzzy furbabies. Photo: Leah Lewis Photography